PRAISE FOR
THE SUITORS

"Incantatory. . . . It is into this familiar narrative mold that Ehrenreich pours his fresh magic, sometimes with the charm of Raymond Queneau, sometimes with the grit and verve of Celine—both Americanized. I admire this book, its authority—minus any preening; its daring not to be safe—not to be another well-made boredom turned out from the trade schools. There is not a line of waste in the telling, not a tired verb, not a cliché of sentimentality in this novel tense with romance, not a sorry gap in the story as it drives at a pace at once leisurely and speeding, not one gimmick in its originality. This is truly a ravishing book."

—Frederic Tuten, *Bomb*

"One of the most compelling features of *The Suitors* is its distinctive and provocative use of language. . . . Ehrenreich's novel embarks on a compassionately conceived storytelling expedition into a world where epic struggles from the past and the present converge and converse."

—*Los Angeles CityBeat*

"A richly imagined novel loosely based on Homer's *Odyssey* and inspirited by a dazzling display of verbal gifts. . . . Delicious . . . Ehrenreich's prodigious, Joycean prose establishes him as a writer to watch." —*Booklist*

"*The Suitors* is an immensely clever novel, dense, demandingly allusive and powerful—but it is not in the least intimidating. Ben Ehrenreich is too compelling a narrator and too playful and subversive a writer to provide anything for his readers other than unbroken pleasure."

—Jim Crace, author of *Genesis*

"*The Suitors* is smart and funny, taking swipes at the Bush administration, the Iraq war, and the notion of heroism, in this or any other age." —*Los Angeles Magazine*

"At once anarchic and stirring, Ben Ehrenreich's *The Suitors* has the well-earned confidence of its own crazy music, and of an original vision that sees no contradiction between subversion and compassion."

—Steve Erickson, author of *Our Ecstatic Days*

"With his linguistic acrobatics, caustic wit and mix-and-match structure, Ehrenreich . . . shows the stirrings of an original talent. . . . For those with a lust for American modernist fiction, Ehrenreich's will be a journey they'll gladly take." —*Publishers Weekly*

"Brilliant, and at the same time moving. It's a relief to know that literature exists yet." —Juan Goytisolo, author of *Marks of Identity* and *The Garden of Secrets*

THE SUITORS

THE SUITORS

Ben Ehrenreich

A HARVEST BOOK

HARCOURT, INC.

Orlando Austin New York San Diego Toronto London

www.HarcourtBooks.com

First U.S. edition published by Counterpoint,
a member of the Perseus Books Group, in 2006.

Library of Congress Cataloging-in-Publication Data
Ehrenreich, Ben.
The suitors/Ben Ehrenreich—1st Harvest ed.
p.   cm.
"A Harvest Book"
1. Courtship—Fiction.   I. Homer. Odyssey.   II. Title.
PS3605.H738S85   2007
813'.6—dc22   2007011877
ISBN 978-0-15-603183-7

Text set in Fairfield Light

Printed in the United States of America

First Harvest edition 2007

a c e g i k j h f d b

If you know what love is, make allowances
for whatever follows.
—Louis Aragon,
The Adventures of Telemachus

There is a happy lend—fur, fur away.
—Krazy Kat

1

also known as

18

A Beginning

But First, the End

A Nation's Gloried Baptism:

This Is How Things Start

So much meat. Try if you can to recall them as they were, before this latest transformation. Recall them with blood still flowing through proper channels, concealed and contained, good yet for setting cheeks aflush and hearts aflutter, for throbbing warmly down below. Recall them with their eyes undimmed, blinking still with hunger and lust. Remember them wanting, always wanting—for what else are we but want?—lips open to loose a laugh, hands as always where they shouldn't be. Remember them eating, drinking, grabbing, stroking, fucking, frigging, fighting, sucking, all innocence and need. Remember them moving, not like this. Remember them in blessed, living disarray, not in this frozen order.

So much meat. All these bodies, now just that and nothing more. Did they know, do you think, that they would become such a thing? Flesh unsparked, food for grubs and dirt and buzzards. From eater to ate without a pause. Life begets life and tumbles onward. It's done, irreparable. What moments ago might have attracted—all this skin, its curves and straightaways and subtleties of shadow—can now only repel. This scene might be touching if they could just awaken, wash themselves off and laugh about it later, one more strange debauch beside the battered banquet table. They lie atop one another. They're tangled and intertwined. A hand here caresses a cheek, there sneaks a grope at a breast or a groin. Heads loll on neighbors' shoulders, on bellies and on backs. Some are almost kissing, others holding hands. What a gorgeous tableau this might be, such delicious indolence, easy sensuality—*it's naptime at the palace!* But their repose is not so peaceful, their affection not so free. They're hacked apart. The color scheme is off, too much red meat and yellow sinew. The world is pretty sometimes, but not today.

So much meat. Try not to look. If you look, the faces will stay with you. Take Arthur's there. You'll see it always as it is now, skin ashen, eyes abulge with agony from the wound that tore his gut, expressing neither gratitude nor surprise at the small black aperture in his temple which, in its sudden opening, relieved him of further worry. You'll see his lips poised for a final suckle at the breast of his beloved, a desire that will never be addressed, much less satisfied, for she hangs above him from the rafters, blue-faced, swaying slightly in the thick and breezeless air. Blood drips from her toe. Try not to look. Avert your gaze from Felix's tiny, dirty-fingered hand, which shields his tight-closed eyes forever from the carnage splayed around him. He no longer sees what's left of Joseph clutching beside him what may have once been Sally, or Izzy separated from all that once made Izzy whole. Please don't look. Don't look for Nellie or for Hans or anybody else. Don't search among these twisted dead, some with faces to the floor, others with faces so immutably altered that their identities, if I can use that word, will forever be amiss.

So much meat. Blood puddles and streams on the parquet floor—dining room realized as charnel house, banquet hall revealed as abattoir. Meat on the table, meat on the ground. Some cooked, most raw and bleeding, all rendered equal in the end. Run to the kitchen, please. Tear off a paper towel. Bring the whole roll. Don't let the blood seep from this page into those that follow. Sop it up fast! Else it'll soak through the paper, buckling and bloating each sheet, eating away at the glue, unbinding a chapter here, a chapter there, dissolving from the start a tale already barely sewn together. Clean up this mess. Wipe it from your mind.

So much meat. Forget for now these ruined stares. If only in your remembrance and not here in this too-bright fluorescent hall, close their eyes for them. Allow them that little dignity denied them by pain. If you can afford to, and can bear to touch them at all, before they cool and stiffen place a single copper penny atop each muted eye. It won't cost much. A small pocketful of change. Give them that, one penny before each eye forever, a penny they can keep.

i

2

Starting Over

or

Before the Collapse
of the State

or

Penny and Payne:
Competing Mythic Hypotheses
as to the Origins Thereof

PENNY WAS BORN ON THE SIDEWALK, beautifully. If only you could have seen it, her mother's body splayed at angles oblique to the cracks in the cement, her white dress soaked red and writhing, red with blood and the reflected light of the neon tubes sketching the word "open," the word "Michelob," the word "cold," in the shop windows above her, her cheeks the same dappled violet as the sweat-stained silk shirt of the man who stopped to help her, who rolled up his sleeves and stuck his hairy-knuckled hands between her legs and who, she later learned, walked off with her pocketbook as payment, but not before handing screaming purple Penny, joyous gift, into her mother's strengthless arms, where she cried a first shrill cry that joined the honking taxi horns, the clicking heels, the screeches of birds, squirrels, rats, patrol cars, and other lower-level parasites, the faraway song of a wine-happy drunk, her mother's broken breaths—a cry that was, if you will believe me, melodious and full of hope.

Her father, like the man who would later sire for Penny a brat of her own, was nowhere to be found. Where was he? If it matters, he was three thousand miles away in a dry drainage canal that fed off the Los Angeles River, where a multitude of ants trod a well-worn trail through his cranium, a thoroughfare first opened by a tire iron, perhaps overhastily swung. But Penny would never learn this. Nor would her mother—and how could they? There were no telephones then. There was no Internet, no Morse code or ballpoint pens. Even feathers had not yet been invented. This was the immeasurable past, before words were spoken or thoughts thunk, before the seas receded and the earth was born. So much for patrimony.

When Penny was six her mother fell hard for a man whose pigmentation did not meet the local requirements, and was run out of town by the pitchfork brigade. She was not heard from again. Nor was he. Penny became a Ward of the State. The other girls at school wore identical uniforms of pink miniskirts, lamb's-wool twinsets, leg warmers, and patent-leather loafers, but Penny had nothing but laceless State tennis shoes and gray coveralls stenciled in brown: STATE PROPERTY SIZE 4–16. The other little girls waited for her at recess and pelted her with stones. They brought little bento boxes of sashimi to school for lunch and chattered happily about their fathers' speedboats and their mothers' lovers, clicking their chopsticks in the air. Penny brought State-loaned sandwiches made from stale bread-ends, crusty cold-cut ends and oily slabs of white government cheese. She picked her sandwiches in pieces, rolled the pieces in her palm, and threw the resulting spheres at the other girls. When she found them alone she pulled their hair, tore their twinsets, bloodied their noses, and crushed their dolls' plastic skulls. The boys were no better, so she threw dirt in their eyes and kicked them where it hurt.

The other little girls hated Penny for many reasons. Because she had no money and none of the many things necessary for girlhood (patent-leather shoes, sashimi lunches, dolls that wet themselves). Because she had no parents and no home. Because they could and wanted to, but also because, despite it all, Penny was gorgeous, shiningly, glowingly, screamingly so. As misshapen as her figure may have been, as slouched her posture and crooked her teeth, still, in muddied State coveralls, her green, green eyes black and sunken from blows and hunger and lack of sleep, her hair torn, a mess, her skin sullied with bruises and scabs, she still outshined them all. Though they never would have admitted it, even to themselves.

She was also, it need not be said, no dummy. So when the boys began to notice that she might be good for something other than beating and berating (at which time the other girls' cruelty reached a fever pitch), Penny saw in their panting, slack-jawed propositions an outlet for her rage. She acceded to the advances of only those boys, and nearly all those boys, who were already claimed by girls that she despised. She went down on them in movie theaters, in locker rooms, behind the bleachers, at home in their boyish bedrooms beneath posters of sweat-slicked basketball players. To their shock and delight she stripped before them and fucked them in the backseats of cars, in the cold beds of pickup trucks, on an old mattress in a gully in the woods.

It would be naive to pretend that Penny was motivated solely by vengeance. For while she did make sure that every boy's girlfriend learned that she had had him, and did not let the little boys pull their pants back up without first humiliating them, teasing them about the size of their adolescent pricks, for coming so quickly and fucking so clumsily, comparing them unfavorably to their best friends or their brothers—it cannot be said that their eagerness to touch her, and even at times to please her, meant nothing to her, nor that she never once fooled herself into thinking, just for a few seconds of quick-breathed teenage rutting, that the desire she saw in their eyes was something deeper and more lasting, something she'd read about in books. But she recovered herself quickly and, ashamed of her delusions, ashamed of her pleasure and her need, sickened by their boyish smells, by the slug-like trails of semen they deposited on her neck, breasts, or thighs, she let her words dig into them all the deeper, planting, she hoped, seeds of self-loathing that might bloom throughout their lives.

It's not that Penny felt nothing but hate, though hate was generally all that she let on. Pity at times crept like a rat into her heart, but she did all she could to chase it off, to plug all holes with steel wool, ground glass, and poison. When a boy, who in the end was just that, a helpless, naked boy, broke out in sobs beneath her rage, reduced, in the wake of the act that would supposedly make a man of him, to a blubbering imp, pity nonetheless slithered forth, and on its bony back it sneaked affection. Penny could feel her arms reach out to pull the boy to her, could feel his tear-streaked cheeks warm against her breast, the heat of a different kind of need. But disgust—at his weakness and at hers—overcame her, and she stayed her wayward limbs, dressed, and left in silence.

Now when Payne, a tender sixteen, arrived at pretty Penny's school, he was not only a budding superstar athlete and a born leader, as the coaches put it (within months he was captaining the football, ice hockey, lacrosse, water polo, basketball, archery, sailing, riflery, debate, track, and torture and interrogation teams), but a premier cocksman to boot.

He made it his stated goal to tumble every last girl in the school, from the most perky-breasted cheerleader to Agatha Shrug, she of the scoliosis, the harelip, and the squint. And he nearly succeeded. Every girl knew of his plan, knew he cared not a whit for them. They feigned disgust amongst their girlfriends and swore they wouldn't dream of it, but one after another fell to his advances nonetheless. Except Penny, who had no girlfriends and no need to feign disgust. She saw in Payne's conquests a denatured, lobotomized parody of her own, and had little trouble resolving that he would be the one boy she would never touch.

Payne, of course, gave it his all. He cornered her behind the gym one day, where she sat smoking, pulling the legs from a spider. "Everyone-says-you're-a-freak-but-I-think-you're-really-pretty-my-parents-don't-get-home-'til-six-and-we-can-drink-their-booze-if-you-wanna-come-over," he said, but this tried-and-true strategy went nowhere. She flicked her ash at him and walked away.

Too wise for his age, Payne knew that cruelty is the only way into certain well-guarded hearts, and changed his tactics to suit. He sat next to her on the bus, pulled her earphones from her ear, and hissed, "You're-such-a-dirty-slut-it-makes-me-sick-there's-no-one-as-nasty-as-you-just-from-sitting-here-I'm-gonna-need-to-be-hosed-down-later," but she smiled sweetly at him and got off at her stop in front of the State Home for Castoff Girls.

He wrote her letters, kind, cruel, and crass. He shoved

them through the slats in her locker door and lingered to watch her toss them to the floor, unread. When Penny passed him in the hallway, he'd grab a girl at random and shove his tongue down her throat. Penny didn't even look. He began to take all his conquests to the crabgrass lawn beneath Penny's barred window high in the highest of the State Home's stone towers, to mount them noisily in the early-morning hours, letting their cries and his rise like burnt offerings to her bed. Penny dropped lit cigarettes on his rising buttocks, emptied her chamber pot on the rutting pairs. Astink and horrified, the girls complained, but Payne insisted they finish, and finish loudly. "Enjoy it," he'd grunt through gritted teeth, and word got round that Payne had changed, that he was weird, that he wasn't *nice* like he used to be. And girls—pretty girls, ugly girls, average girls, girls whom everyone wanted and girls whom no one so much as noticed—began shunning his advances, ignoring his leers and ill-crafted come-ons.

Payne stopped sleeping. For the first time in his brief life, he had encountered something he couldn't have. For the first time, he really wanted something. Every other girl had been a passing whim—he hadn't even seen them. On the football field, did he really *want* every yard he ran? He just kept moving, the crowd cheered, and the yards passed beneath him. Well Payne stopped moving. He fumbled every pass, missed every goal and every basket, stumbled at the starting line, sunk his sailboat, stuttered his rebuttals, lost his nerve at testicular electroshock. Pimples began to sprout from pores that had never seen a blackhead. He began to wear the same soiled clothes day after day, and his hair hung heavy with grease. His varsity letters were stripped from his jacket. His friends beat him up. Teachers and guidance counselors clucked in disgust when he slumped past them in the halls.

After school he sat alone on the curb in the shadow of the State Home's highest tower and drank can after can of warm National Unity beer. In the mornings, Penny would sit at her window and watch him wake. Lying on a bed of crumpled cans, snails, gravel, and crabgrass, he would prop himself up on his elbows, clutch his temples, peel a slug from his neck, and look up at the tower, hoping to spot the ember of her cigarette glowing in her darkened room.

After a month of such mornings, Penny woke herself up before dawn, tied sheet-end to sheet-end, squeezed through the bars, and rappelled down the tower. She kicked a half-filled beer can at his head.

"What do you want?" she said.

Payne wiped beer from his eyes and looked up at her. "You."

"You can't have me. Go away."

He grabbed at her ankle as she turned to leave. "Wait," he said. "Please. I want you."

"Why?"

"I don't know."

"Bye," said Penny. She crossed the crabgrass lawn and shimmied up the sheets to her room.

I wish I could end this story here—what a happy tale it

might turn out to be: Penny and Payne suffering their hard-earned freedom, each off in the world alone!

But the demands of narrative are cruel. How best to describe that strange, sick process by which Penny's heart was turned? Let's put it this way—Penny had made such stringent efforts to armor her heart, testing it again and again in the fires of carnality, that, like iron that's been worked too long on the anvil, her defenses grew brittle and cracked. All of her efforts to kill her needs only caused them to bubble and expand. Suffice it to say that Payne's persistence paid.

He brought a sleeping bag and left the beer behind. Penny would sit up nights at her window, watching Payne warm his hands over a campfire, while he, below, glued his gaze to the orange trail made by her cigarette as it moved from hand to mouth. Once she saw him bathing in the drainage ditch and, despite herself, couldn't look away. She soon found that in the mornings she would walk from the cement slab of her bed to the window even before she lit the day's first cigarette. On cold mornings, Payne's sleeping bag was white with frost, and Penny laughed as he cursed and danced to keep from freezing. One day, after about a month of this, she rose from bed and saw no sign of Payne. To her horror, she was not only disappointed but concerned. She smoked three cigarettes, lighting each from the butt of the last, before she spotted him, not in his usual place across the road but directly beneath her, at the base of the tower. In a rage, she tied sheet-end to sheet-end, squeezed through the bars, and rappelled swiftly down the tower. With index finger and thumb, she flicked her cigarette at Payne's frost-encrusted head.

"What," Penny demanded, her green eyes burning, "do you want?"

Payne shook the ice from his hair, rubbed at the burn on his forehead, and tried to smile. "You," he said.

"Why? Do you know yet, why?"

"No."

Penny turned to go, reaching for the sheet-end that hung above her head, but Payne grabbed her once again by the ankle. She pulled back a steel-toed boot to kick him in the head, but before she could, he spoke again.

"What do you want?" he asked.

"I don't want you," she said.

"But what do you want?"

No one had ever asked her this before. Penny bit her lip, confused. She searched her pockets for the cigarettes she'd left upon the windowsill. "Why do you care?"

"Why, why, why," said Payne. "Just answer."

She thought about it. She thought about kicking him again. And then she answered. "I want to get out of here," she said. "I want to leave this place."

"The State Home?"

"No. All of it. This. Here. Everything. All of it."

Payne grinned. "Let's go," he said.

"Where?"

"Anywhere."

"What's different there?"

"Everything."

"Do you believe that?" Penny asked.

"Yes. Let's go. Now."

And so they went.

Oh teenage dreams of flight! Things were not, of course, different anywhere, or not in ways that mattered, so they put their faith in movement and got off Payne's motorcycle only to eat and sleep and shit. And in the rushing wind and the blur of asphalt that their lives became, Penny's arms around Payne's waist, something passed silently between them, up through the fleeing pavement, into Penny's clenched thighs, up through her spine, out her arms, into a place deep in Payne's gut, and out through his arms onto the road again.

This is not a love story—I'll say that again if you want— and it is certainly not *that* love story, the teen romance of Penny and Payne, but you can, I'm sure, imagine the wretched details, the gory depths that to their unending surprise they discovered for each other in themselves and coquettishly displayed each for the other. Enough of that for now. The bike broke down, the money ran out, and Penny and Payne were stranded, far away, bound only to one another. They agreed to call this new place Home.

This is of course just one version of the tale, and not, per-haps, the likeliest. The others are endless. And all of them are true. Penny, don't you know, was not an orphan or an outcast but a perfect little dream, a straight-A student beloved by teachers and peers alike, captain of the cheer-leading squad, and she and multilettered Payne, everyone agreed, were made for one another. They went steady freshman year and only got steadier as the years went by, king and queen of both junior and senior proms, royalty from the start. Payne worked afternoons and weekends at his old man's shop, and a month after graduation they got hitched. Payne put a down payment on a split-level with a three-acre lot a few towns over. They planted a sign on the lawn that said, "Home." He raked the yard, she dusted the curio cabinet, they shopped from catalogs, the rest you can imagine.

But really Penny was all that I've described, and Payne an outcast too, the new kid in town, all black denim and hair slicked back, a switchblade in his pocket and a joint behind his ear. From the wrong side of the tracks, rebels to the core, they took on the jocks and the debs. Payne bested them playing chicken with a stolen Camaro (hot-wired by nimble-fingered Penny) in the field behind the school. He slashed a lacrosse star's pretty face in a knife fight at the drive-in and was sent away for eighteen months. When he got out, Penny was waiting at the gate in a torn leather skirt, and they together hopped a Greyhound and got as far away as they knew how. When the bus driver at last kicked them off, they looked around and at each other, and the ditch they stood in they called Home.

And Penny was a bookish geek in kneesocks, Payne a

quiet nerd with a backpack. They passed shy notes in calculus class, read Rimbaud aloud together (in French!), dry-humped with the Smiths on the boom box when their parents thought they were off at college-prep. And Payne was a punk rocker and a stoner and a gangsta, gothic letters tattooed on his neck; and Penny was a black-lipped goth and a chola and a JAP; and they got drunk at a party and the first time they did it Payne knocked Penny up and her dad made them wed; and they fell instantly in love the first day of school right there in homeroom; and they never went to school at all but grew up shipwrecked on an island and swam naked in a hidden cove they called Home; and Payne was a Hasid and Penny an Arab and they loved against all odds, Penny's dad a grand wizard and Payne's a sharecropper; and they were indentured servants in neighboring households and saw each other only on market days until they escaped to a place they could call Home; and they were brother and sister and their love was unholy and they ran away to where nobody knew and that is the place they called Home; and in at least one version, the simplest and perhaps the loveliest and most true to fact, Payne and Penny never met, and never found a home.

But it's too late for that already.

3

In the Palace

or

The Gory Depths

or

Jumping Forward,
Leaning Back

"WHO ARE THEY?" Penny asks, sitting cross-legged on the bedspread, shaking the bottle's last drop into her glass. Her mate does not respond. He lies on his back and does not move, but his breath is uneven still, and not yet slow, so Penny knows he's not asleep. She pulls his eyemask from his eyes, lets the elastic snap back in his face. Payne sits up fast, tears off the mask, grabs Penny's wrist, then lets her go. He does not even bother to curse her.

"What?" he demands.

"You weren't sleeping," Penny says, swirling the ice in her drink.

Payne just stares.

Penny takes a sip. "Don't ignore me," she says.

Payne pulls the mask back on and lies down again, on his side this time and with his face to the wall.

"I asked you who they are," says Penny.

"Who who are?" answers Payne.

"You know, them. The only ones out there. I've seen them in the hills, hiding behind rocks, flitting about like scared little birds. They run away at the slightest sound. I see them out the window, watching you."

"And?"

"I want to know who they are, how they live."

"And you think I know?"

"You're out there all day."

"Working."

"That's what you call it, I know." Penny yawns and empties her drink. Her eyes catch on the gnarled wood of the headboard beside her, and the corners of her mouth drop in annoyance. She slips four fingers through the unbuttoned fly of Payne's flannel pajamas. "Sweetheart," she coos, conjuring perhaps a pint more sugar into her voice than the moment requires, "Honey bear, do me a favor, will you? Run downstairs and open me a bottle."

Payne slaps her hand away. "You're drunk enough," he says.

"No. Not yet I'm not. Not nearly." Spurned, Penny's hand retreats to the bedside table and again lifts her glass to her lips. She sucks on what little ice remains at the bottom. She gnaws a cuticle. "Don't you care who they are? Aren't you even curious?"

Payne rolls over and slides his mask up on his brow, which pushes his hair into a sudden pompadour. Penny laughs. He pries the glass from her fingers and sets it atop a coaster on the bedside table. "No, not curious," he says. "They're little animals. Rodents. They fuck behind rocks and sleep all day. They hide in the hills and scatter when they see me. Mice are more useful. Cleaner too. What's to know?"

Penny hugs herself and twists her lips into a smile. "You're a pig, my love," she whispers. "Your heart is a pine nut and your mind is a tomb. Now be a dear and go downstairs for me."

But Payne does not go. Instead he pulls his knees to his chest and yanks the covers up over his head. Penny stands on the mattress and kicks him where she thinks his ass might be. Not hard, but hard enough to make her point. Still, he doesn't stir. Something in her knees begins to give, but she recovers and steps, wobble-legged, to the floor. With shaking hands she strikes a match and lights a cigarette. She heads for the stairs but pauses in the doorway. "One day I'll leave you, Payne," says Penny, blowing smoke into the bedroom. "I'll join them out there. You'll see me fucking in the fields, sleeping my days away, skipping through the hills like a deer. And when you come calling, and you will come calling, I'll just float away."

And with that, Penny closes the door before Payne's silence can seep out into the hallway, invade her lungs, and soak the aching caverns of her heart.

But we're getting ahead of ourselves. It wasn't always like that. Can anything go sour if it wasn't once sweet? When we saw them last, Penny and Payne had run as far as they could run, in whatever sense you wish to take that, and when they ran out of breath or gas or cash, they declared the ground beneath them Home. Well here we are, Home at last. Let's look around.

Home at first is just a temporary lodging of the most ordinary sort. It's a motel room. Penny and Payne's room is on the second floor in the corner farthest from the pool, but the water is kind of murky so neither of them minds. More than murky really—Styrofoam cups bob like icebergs in a sea of twigs and leaves. The room, though, is clean enough. A double bed. A silent television. (Even with the volume up, it's all just snow and fuzz.) Beige walls and beiger carpet. A framed print on the wall: an island in an azure sea, gulls like double-u's, leaning palms and sand. The sheets and towels get changed every day, or sometimes every other, and there's hot coffee in the office if you don't mind spitting out the grounds. Sometimes there are donuts, free for the taking. How bright the world can be! The mustachioed manager is always there behind the desk and always good for a smile, though his accent preys on his words like some thick, exotic moss, so Penny and Payne just chew their donuts and hold their laughter until they've rushed back to their room and can let it out together, door closed and curtains pulled, their hands fumbling for buttons, clasps, and zippers.

Shall we spy on them there as they hurriedly unbutton, unclasp, unzip? Let's. Payne strips Penny to her socks. He kneels and starts to nibble at her thigh, but Penny stops him. She pushes him down on the bed. Penny bites Payne's chest. She licks a circle round his navel. She clamps a hand over his eyes, and when she lifts it and lets him see again she's scrunched a lock of hair between her upper lip and nose, flattened her chin into her neck, and bugged out her eyes in perfect mimicry of the man behind the manager's desk (to wit, the manager). Payne laughs and covers his eyes and tries to cover his ears before she starts in on the accent too, but laughter gets to her before she can get a word out, and they roll convulsing from one side of the bed to the other, then fall with a thump to the floor and laugh still harder until Payne looks up and finds Penny on top of him, mirth chased from her eyes by some profounder pleasure.

Shall we peek behind those eyes? Even here, amidst all this goof and bliss, were we so morbidly inclined, we might start . . . asking questions. And in the asking we might uncover the seeds, the saplings even, of that melancholy bedtime scene above (the competing demands of the eyemask and the bottle) that you recently had the indecency to observe and I the indiscretion to report. Can we ask what

Penny wants from Payne, what she, poppling on top of him there on the motel carpet, expects beyond this heated moment?

Penny wants what she has right now: the certainty of his desire. She wants his desperate concern for her pleasure, and hers in turn for his, to spread throughout her life, to smooth its edges, fill its gaps, buff it to a shine. She wants to rest in him, to dig a shelter inside herself for him to rest in, to pad its floors with throw rugs and deep foam pillows, a playroom of the heart, a palace in her soul. And though poor Penny learned long ago to expect little from the world, she is free nonetheless to want. She is damned to it, in fact.

Her partner there, young Payne, the one with his feet still tangled in the bedspread while rug burns blossom on his back—he's easy. Payne wants what he does not have. Rarely can a man be so tidily defined. For though she has surrendered herself to his grasp right now (he's turned her over, and holds her wrists tight above her head), Payne cannot congratulate himself. Whatever self-loss he briefly won through laughter has abandoned him. Penny's eyes are closed, and he can't know what she thinks or what she feels, what hides behind her moans and guttered sighs. Her eyes flash open, and if any other fool would see in that vast spread of green her broken and wide-open joy, Payne can see only meadows yet unmown, forests not yet logged, continents uncharted. But Payne expects to win, to conquer and contain. He pushes on, methodically. Though even in the calculated rhythm of his thrusts, Payne withholds from Penny the one thing that would permit her to yield every last acre of herself entirely to him: he surrenders nothing.

Perhaps it's not so simple. Almost, but not quite. Poor Payne. Like a guilty imperialist, vice-regent of some Baghdad of the heart, Payne desires not just conquest but to be welcomed in. He wants all past monuments to topple. He wants kisses from virgins and widows alike, bouquets stuffed into his hands, a constant victory parade. He wants precisely what Penny will not give him, and she wants the same from him—as fine a formula as any for the efficient production of . . . want. But satisfaction is the enemy of desire, and despite himself, Payne allows Penny glimpses of that one thing wanting, if only through his clumsiest gestures—a thumb that lingers too long on her nose or her chin, a misplaced stutter, some small uncertainty in his eyes. Those are enough, for now, to keep her by his side. More than that: to let her call what flows between them love.

They're standing when, with shared shudders and one long, rising moan, they finish. Penny is bent, hugging the television, and Payne clasps her from behind, his eyes closed and his teeth still dug into her shoulder. Penny's knees give out. She lets the television go and sits down on the carpet. Payne sits too. They cross their legs behind each other's backs and lean their foreheads against each other's foreheads. Penny crooks her elbows behind Payne's head. She grabs hold of his ears. "Are you okay?" she asks.

His eyes still shut, his breathing rough, Payne nods.

"You're quiet," Penny says.

Payne shakes his head. "I'm fine."

"Then why are you crying?" asks Penny, and swipes with her thumb at the droplet sliding down Payne's cheek.

"I'm not," Payne answers.

Maybe he's not lying. Maybe it's sweat. Maybe something's in his eye. Penny prefers not to believe him. "It's okay," she tells him, and strokes his jaw with her thumb. She kisses his mouth. Her voice breaks a little. "You can say it," she says, and clears her throat.

"Say what?" Payne asks.

Penny bites her lip. Her heart skips and her fingers shake. She wants to pin a name to it, to this, this pulsing thing between them, this push and pull, this thirst. She wants to speak the name aloud, to live in the light it casts. She leans in to Payne's ear and almost mouths three diminutive, over-burdened words. But her spine bows from their weight. Her shoulders slump. Her courage fails her. She drops her head against his chest.

Payne lifts her hair from the back of her neck. He drags his lips across the topmost knot of her spine and into the hollow just above it. His fingers wander up her thigh. He whispers in her ear, "Let's do that again."

Penny sucks in a breath and holds it as long as she can. She laughs and lets it out. Her fingers wander down his chest and down his stomach. "Okay," she says, and laughs once more.

Let's leap ahead again. Not so far this time. They've left the motel for more permanent digs. For now it's little more than a lonely shed in the middle of a yawning valley: four rough walls and a floor of poured concrete, room for a mattress on the floor, a table, sink, and hot plate. The shower is outdoors. Really it's a garden hose tied with twine to a high nail, but Payne has bigger plans. It's nighttime, and an oil lamp burns on the table, projecting abstract orange dramas on the flesh of Penny's back. She's standing in the cramped space between the table and the bed, naked in her boots. ("Let's be naked all the time!" Penny once exclaimed to Payne as he buckled up his jeans and stood.) Payne is on his knees (again!) before her, clutching at her calves, making promises.

"I'll build you a palace," swears Payne, and wanders into revery, guiding her through the marbled hallways, flipping channels on the giant-screened teevees, twisting golden spigots in the tub. Penny is bored, but Payne is so proud of these dreams that she doesn't have the heart to stop him, to tell him she wants none of it, that she doesn't mind the bare floors, the cold showers from the hose, the squirrels and sparrows that find their way indoors, that all she wants is him. She doesn't ask him from where these fantasies are coming, doesn't speculate aloud that this home he wants to build is not for her but against her. She doesn't voice her fear that he will pour its foundations and hammer its walls between himself and her, or protest that his vows are but flimsy material substitutes for the invisible domains she would so much rather rule with him.

Why is she so silent? Why does she not tell him what she fears, that he constructs these cantilevered dreams not merely to shield himself from her—from the mess of her heart and the greater mess of his surrender to it—but from all the swirling chaos on which the world depends, which is, the more daring ontologists among us might suggest, no more or less than the mess aswirl in Penny's breast, just rendered macrocosmic? She holds her tongue because she treasures his enthusiasm, even when it leans so far away. Because wherever else he is, he's on his knees before her, and she doesn't want to break this spell.

Penny suddenly feels her nakedness. The boots are not enough. Maybe it's just a draft, some corner of the night breezing through the plywood walls. She crosses her arms across her breasts. "I'm here!" she wants to say, and shake him by the ears. "Why are you so far away?" But she says nothing. She kneels beside him, silences his ravings with a kiss, and then another kiss. She tries to pull him to her, to bring him back, to make him see her, to vaporize his mad, domestic fantasies and lend him lodging in her breast. She fails. Payne is content to interpret her kisses as a sign that he has won, that his plans have her consent and her approval, that Penny wants what he wants: smooth walls, unspotted glass, warm water, and soft, and dust-free floors. A little more, perhaps: whatever he can get.

Don't be glum. It's not so bad. Better things have started worse. Aren't we lucky if, for all our blindness, we land here and there some glancing, diagonal caress? Well Payne and Penny do. They miss each other mainly. They shoot wide, and at different targets. But sometimes they hit. And isn't all of that, the hitting and the missing too, what we call love, its sweet give and bitter take, its tidal whims and tidal tortures?

Onward. In this scene Payne calls his wife a slut, and Penny implies that her husband's skills in the sack leave something lacking. Love is a curious critter: it pads its nest with the oddest bric-a-brac. Payne's palace is under way. Penny's is crumbling inside her. The kitchen is finished, the dishwasher installed, the microwave hums on demand. The den is carpeted, though there's no furniture yet. The bedroom is still just a mat on the floor, and the dining room smells of sawdust. Payne rises early, does his push-ups and his sit-ups, jogs five miles, chops down trees, attends to grout and drywall. Penny sits in the kitchen and smokes too much. She opens the window so she can listen to the squabbling of the birds hidden among the branches of the oak tree in the yard. Sometimes she climbs the hill behind the house and hikes to the old motel. She wanders through the empty rooms. She fingers the CLOSED sign on the office door. She draws faces in the dust of the office's windowed walls. Some of them are smiling. She paces the parking lot, gathers a pocketful of stones and tries to knock the letters VACANCY from the dim, unblinking sign. She walks home and runs a bath. She soaks until she fears the fibers of her muscles will actually dissolve. She naps a lot. She teaches herself French with a book and cassettes. She reads thick Russian novels and slender volumes of pornographic prose. She lies on the bedroom floor and stares out the window at the clouds. She tries to keep the vodka bottle in the freezer until it's nearly dusk, but she doesn't always succeed.

When Payne finishes up in the evenings, he pecks Penny on the lips, squeezes her ass, and announces that he's tired. He takes long showers and locks the bathroom door. He retreats to an armchair, an atlas on his lap. He warms his feet beside the fire and studies the crumpled contours of the world. He reads home-improvement manuals and engineering texts. Sometimes he reads books: *The Art of the Deal*, *To Hell and Back*, *The Greatest Generation*. Sometimes he smokes a pipe.

Penny stands beside him, rests her palm on his shoulder. "Put your book down," she says. "Come have a drink with me."

"Sure," says Payne. "In a minute."

A minute goes by, and then another ten. When Penny comes back to check on Payne, his book is shut, his chin is on his chest. He's fallen asleep. Again. Can you ever pinpoint exactly what went wrong, and when and how? What fled, and when it left, and why? What new beast has stepped into its skin? Sometimes you can, and are all the worse for that, but Penny can't. Eventually she has to let off wondering. So she empties the vodka from her glass into her mouth and pours the ice on her sleeping husband's lap.

A fight ensues. Do you really want to see it? I'll summarize. Payne calls Penny a bitch and barely stops himself from smacking her. Flattered by this sudden passion, Penny smiles and opens the freezer to pour another drink. She pours one for Payne too, but he throws it against the wall. The bricks are fake, so the glass falls intact to the linoleum, and bounces. Payne accuses Penny of not appreciating all that he has done for her. She confesses that she does not. He calls her an ingrate, and other things besides. She calls him a eunuch and suggests that she has little to be grateful for. Sinking a level or six, Payne reminds Penny that she was sucking off an entire county until he thought to rescue her. She throws her glass at his head (missing him but shattering the glass door of the new convection oven) and sinks another dozen notches: she lies, and implies that at least some of those boys knew how to satisfy a girl.

Shall we stop? Payne stops. He calls her a cunt and slams the door behind him.

Things are not so far gone. They are young yet. When Payne comes home he's made every effort to conceal the fact that tears have crossed his cheeks, but still his eyes are red and swollen. Penny has made no such attempt. She sits curled in his easy chair, her mascara a mess. Her lip bleeds where she's been biting it. They don't quite run to one another, but almost. They hold each other tight. They don't let go. For a while anyway. In a week or two they'll play this scene again. Thus they are to one another bound.

Step forward with me now again. Penny is upstairs. Payne's palace, in its current incarnation at least, is nearly done. Which is to say the bedroom is finished. The big bay window has been squeegeed to an extraordinary state of streaklessness, and Penny can see Payne way off in the valley below, digging trenches. His shirt is off and his chest is striped with dirt. Why trenches? Penny doesn't ask. The bed is unmade. The black silk sheets dangle onto the floor. Whatever else goes on in here, the bed is still well used. The clothes they wore yesterday—panties and bra, turquoise jockey shorts, argyled tights, a muscle tee—still litter the floor, lying where they landed, cast off in a rush.

Penny sits on the bed in her bathrobe, an ashtray on her knee. She leans against the headboard, a giant, tangled piece of polished wood that Payne cut from the roots and trunk of an ancient, leaning oak, the same one you've seen just outside the kitchen window. That tree was the occasion for another tiff. It was not the oak's age that Penny had admired, or even the birds that crowded its limbs, but its ambition. Its trunk twisted and turned upon itself. Its branches forked, stretched, dipped, and climbed as if it wanted at the same time to explore its own recesses, its extremities, the sky above and earth beneath. Its bark was gnarled and scarred, in some places smooth, in others torn and scaly. And for all the endless energy recorded in its flesh, the oak tree never moved. Every time Penny strolled around the house, there it was, shaking its leaves in greeting. And there it was when she looked up from sudsing dishes—right there out the window, its branches mobbed with sparrows, finches battling with crows. Until one morning when Penny, sucking at the day's first cigarette, stood in her flip-flops watering the gardenias and heard the whine of a chainsaw. She turned the corner of the house and saw Payne assaulting the oak's thick torso. What was he doing? she demanded. Its roots were all over the place, he said, and they'd crack the foundation for the garage.

"Garage?" she yelled. "We don't even have a car!"

"We will," Payne swore, as if she'd stung him. "We will."

When the dust cleared, Payne, in what he understood as a reconciliatory gesture, carved the corpse of the tree into a bed frame. He spent one week sanding and another rubbing lacquer into every knob and knot. After he'd pushed the frame in place, he fluffed the pillows and tucked the linens in himself. He ran to get Penny to show off his work. She refused to so much as look at it. She told him she would never sleep a wink beneath "that thing." But she did, even that same night.

That was months ago. Other squabbles have long since eclipsed the Incident of the Oak, other ecstatic reunions and tearful rapprochements. The silences grow more routine. The chill is felt by all. Certainly by Payne, who spends as much time as he can on one project or another, communicating with Penny, during the day at least, only with the distant thud of his pick and the scrape of his shovel. There are other noises too: the hammer's clanging, the groans of the saw, the wheelbarrow's insistent squeak. But today it's all thud and scrape as Payne extends his trenches.

Why trenches? Penny has ceased to wonder, but we can all the same. Payne is constructing a defensive perimeter. In inverse proportion to the presence of anything worth protecting within, Payne is increasingly concerned with what he calls security. Or what he would call security if anyone (i.e., Penny) ever bothered to ask. His dreamed-of palace is finished, and if its current state does not quite match the grandeur of his fantasies, it gnaws at him nonetheless that it is such a fragile thing, its contents guarded by nothing more than a few inches of plaster, plywood, and recycled vinyl siding. So he digs, and dreams of future fortifications.

In the bedroom, Penny sits and smokes. She taps her ashes into the ashtray on her knee. She's hitting the vodka early today. She watches Payne's shovel rise and fall. And she sees, just over the uneven berm of dirt that lines the outer edge of the trench, human faces peeking forth. They huddle in the shadows. They're far away, and smeared with grime, so she can't make out their features. Payne turns, and they all duck. He pretends he hasn't seen them, resumes his digging, but flings his shovel-loads of soil high over his shoulder so the dirt rains down over the berm where they are hiding. They stand, rubbing their eyes, shaking dirt from their hair and spitting it from their mouths until they realize that Payne has climbed from the trench and stands just yards away. He grips his shovel with both hands. They flee. They scamper up the hill, tripping over roots and stones. In the open, Penny can see that some are male and some are female. Some are fat but most are thin. Some are tall and some are short. One is very short. They disappear behind the rocks, over the hill, into narrow gullies and up the trunks of trees. Penny stubs out her cigarette. She catches herself tapping her fingers to the echoing thuds of Payne's busy shovel, and pours herself another glass.

4

Building

or

Early Myths Regarding
National Origins and
the Foundations of
Civilized Order

or

Paradise Lost
(or was it gained?)

WE WERE HUFFING GAS from paper bags when
Payne first came to us. We'd seen him around, chopping
down trees, paving meadows, quarrying stone for his
palace on top of the hill. Of course we'd seen Penny too,
just once, when they first rode in. We'd been here a
while, most of us. Can't say for sure how long. The early
stuff is all a fog. But we'd never seen anything like Penny

before. She was just a kid back then, barely out of her teens, but none of us was any older. And there wasn't one of us, boy or girl, who wasn't tormented straight off by those green eyes. They sent us into such confusion! One glance was enough, and a glance at first was all we got. It was like waking up all over again, not knowing we'd even been asleep and then not knowing where we were, like every single thing around for miles had been taken away and replaced with things identical but at the same time changed, unrecognizable. For the first time we knew we were where we should be. Where we were made sense. Everything now called out for her. Everything just cried her name, and in the clamor none of us could sleep.

The sunlight fell and we scurried along the ridgelines to watch Payne labor in the valleys below, hoping for a glimmer. It didn't come. The sun fell too. We tossed and turned all through the windy night in our beds of rocks and sand. The moon stared down at us, and each one of the stars, and they all seemed dim compared with the cruel and tender glow of her eyes, so green, and the black of the sky was bright with our desire. We lay there tangled in the silk of her hair, trapped beneath her slender wrists, impaled by the very thought of her toes, pinned to waking hunger by the imagined curve of her calf.

So when at last Payne strolled up and said, "You! Layabouts! Help me build a wall!" we put down the gas and complied. Well at first we ran and hid, but Payne kept yelling, so later we complied. Ursula stood and showed herself, then Hans and David holding hands, then Robert, and one by one the rest of us. Another glimpse of Penny, we hoped, might restore to us our sleep. We followed Payne to the quarry and banged rock out of that hole for months. We hauled it up the hill, piling rock atop rock, craning our necks at the palace, praying for a glance. Then one evening, as the sun fell between the hills, we laid down our picks for the day and Payne came down to pay us for our labor. "In appreciation of your sweat and toil," he said, standing on a stump, "I have stocked the sea with fish for you to eat, and seeded the clouds with the sweetest water for your thirst. And I brought you some paint thinner. And a new paper bag."

We rushed at the can of thinner and fought, pulling hair and bending fingers back: we hadn't inhaled anything but air and dust for weeks. Theo kept yelling, "Stop it! Cooperate! There's plenty to go around!" But all the while he was punching and scratching too, and grabbing for the can himself. In the end most of it spilled, and we split what little remained, passing the bag in a circle, counterclockwise and back again. Felix, on account of being small, was excluded. The decision was Theo's. "Sorry, little guy," he said. "There's just not enough for you."

Felix kicked him in the shins and ran. He kept running all the way down to the shore, where he dove into the sea and came back dripping, his arms filled with fish. At the sight of them, all wet and wriggling and wide-eyed like that, we leapt up screaming. What little thinner was left in the bag spilled out, and we scattered to hide in the rocks and scrub. When we crept back a few hours later, Felix was sitting in front of a fire. Beside him, perched on a log, sat Penny. They were smoking cigarettes and picking at the charred remains of a sea robin, now mainly spine and gills, laid out on a newspaper between them. Too awed to step forward, we cowered in the bushes and watched the firelight dancing on her forearms, her nose, on one extended ankle. Penny must have seen the flames reflected in our eyes, though, because she looked at us each, one by one, and smiled, showing off her gapped and crooked teeth. Then she stood, said something to Felix that we couldn't hear, flicked her cigarette into the flames, and walked off into the dark.

We leapt out and shook little Felix. "What did she say?" we demanded.

"She thanked me for the fish," he said.

"What else?"

"She said it was good."

"What else?"

"She offered me a cigarette."

"What else?"

"She told me I was cute."

We could have fallen down right then and rolled on the sand for hours moaning and pulling out our hair with jealous pleasure. Instead we stole what was left of Felix's cigarette and roughed him up a bit. We split the other fish he'd cooked. That night we slept at last, the memory of her smile caressing us like a great warm hand smoothing out the folds of our souls.

By winter we'd finished the wall. It stood ten meters high and three meters thick, with slits for small artillery every three meters and larger gun turrets every five. The last months were spent sanding: Payne wanted the outer wall mirror-smooth, he said, so the reflected sun would blind all comers. When we were done, Payne came down from the palace. He had a bottle of Wild Irish Rose beneath one arm and a plastic soda bottle half-filled with yellow liquid in the other. "My friends and fellow citizens," he said. "On this day, and for the past few hundred days, you have done your nation a great service."

Arthur removed his mouth from its usual spot on Zöe's breast long enough to interrupt. "Nation?" he said.

"That's me," Payne smiled, and went on. "To make a show of my gratitude, and to provide you with the sustenance necessary for the completion of your next noble task, I have sowed the fields with herbs and roots and fruit-bearing trees, and released upon them many fat and toothsome beasts for your consumption, including but not limited to: the rat, the snake, the snail, the salamander, and the larger nonpoisonous insects. And I brought some fortified wine. And gasoline."

As soon as Payne walked off, we all rushed the goodies, and in the melee that followed, little Felix slipped beneath Carl's legs and grabbed the wine. He ran off into the dunes before anyone noticed. Anyone but Carl, that is, who was too embarrassed by the whole episode to say a word. We patched up an old paper bag and passed the gasoline between us, wiping our noses and scratching ourselves, Arthur softly suckling Zöe, Hans and David kissing and cooing, Theo collapsed in Lily's lap, Katerina and Sally trading back rubs, Yves and Ollie teasing Robert, Nellie and Izzy groaning behind a bush, Carl, Xavier, Victoria, and Joseph watching and giggling and blinking a lot, Ursula pacing all alone, Queenie, Elizabeth, and Garth just lazing and huffing and sniffling too much.

It never took long for the image of green-eyed Penny to drill its way back into our skulls, for that one desire to chase away all others. So after a while we remembered Felix, who had last time attracted Penny, and who'd run off with the wine. All of us, except for Izzy and Nellie, who were busy, fanned out among the dunes to search him out. We spotted the glow of a fire, and our hearts leapt and echoed in our chests. We crouched at the edge of the dune, desperately hoping and desperately afraid that we'd catch him with Penny. But it was just Felix there alone. He was drinking from the bottle, half-empty now. Over the flames he held a branch on which he had impaled one rat, two lizards, and a tree frog. The lizards looked done. Felix sang in a slow, drowsy voice.

> *Just give me one penny,*
> *One penny will do.*
> *Shiny or tarnished,*
> *Don't care if it's new.*

Keep all your gold
And your nickels and dimes—
Just give me one penny
And something that rhymes.

We all stood at the same time, surrounding him. Felix dropped the stick in the fire and tried to run, but Joseph caught him by the neck and threw him back. While Joseph was shaking his head, apologizing and asking Felix if he was okay, the rest of us secured the bottle, then pushed Joseph aside, gave Felix a pounding, and split up the food.

The next morning we woke to a terrible clatter. Payne marched from bed to bed, kicking sand in our faces and beating away at a cast-iron skillet with a rusted length of rebar. "Idlers, slugabeds, faggot tramps!" he yelled. "Help me build my palace." But it wasn't the racket or Payne's shouting that got us up off the ground. It was that one word, "palace," which we all knew was nothing more than a dress that Penny wore.

Payne had already done a lot on his own. He'd built a three-bedroom split-level with a sunken den, eat-in kitchen, finished basement rec room, double garage, and two and a half baths. There was wall-to-wall carpeting in blue-beige shag, hand-painted daisies on the wallpaper, faux-distressed marble in the bathrooms, more closet space than any of us had ever seen, and a piece of drift-wood hanging over the door, painted with a sunset in faded pastels, garnished with the words "Home sweet Home."

Payne marched us through the wall to the end of the cul-de-sac he'd paved through the valley and on up to the end of the driveway. "Watch the lawn," he said. What he wanted was a palace, he continued, fit for a king of a free people. And however grand it was, what he had already built was just a house. A nice house, a real nice house, but not yet fit for a king of a free people.

Nellie interrupted. "Free people?" she asked.

"Quiet!" Payne snapped, and went on. What the palace lacked, he said, was a Great Hall, a place to entertain his guests, because he did intend to have guests, important ones, princes and pop stars and presidents, lots of them, and the kitchen was just too small. He would feast them on the bounty of his realm, huge joints of meat, flagons of the finest wine, camels stuffed with pheasants stuffed with quails stuffed with baby squids and tangerines, crystal decanters of ancient brandy, chocolaty Bundt cakes and moldy old cheeses. "There'll be dancing girls," Payne said, "revelry and song, bears on chains, poets declaiming, circus clowns and acrobats—I want it really, really big."

He wanted the ceilings ten meters high, with balconies for special events and overflow crowds. He wanted the lighting recessed and indirect and flattering but also spotlights and colored lasers for floor shows. He wanted polished marble floors and a parquet dance floor and niches on each side lined with carpets and pillows so the guests could rest or make out. He wanted a fountain big enough to swim in, that could be frozen for skating events or ice sculpture and heated for steam baths or soup. He wanted four separate storerooms: one for wine, one for weapons, one for gifts of tribute brought by guests, and one for servants on smoke breaks. He wanted a trapdoor and a secret tunnel that led to an undisclosed secret room in the house, and he wanted us all to be blindfolded while we built it. He wanted a turret, higher than the walls or the surrounding hills, where guards could keep watch on the borders of the realm.

And as he explained all this, there in the driveway, pointing up at the clouds to show us how high, Penny, in nothing but flip-flops and a bathrobe that didn't even cover her knees, came out through the door and sat on the steps. Her eyes were heavy-lidded, her hair matted with sleep. She lit a cigarette. She hugged her robe closed. She blew smoke out the corner of her mouth and picked at her foot with her thumb. Of course we agreed to build it.

The palace was done by the end of the summer. It took a little longer than planned because Payne kept getting ideas for add-ons: bullet-proof glass, a carport, a cactus garden, a moat with crocodiles, central air. He had us running all over the place looking for crocodiles, but we couldn't find one anywhere, and a moat filled with nothing more than water might as well be a birdbath, he said, a cute little fishpond. So as soon as we finished digging the trench, he sent us trekking miles over the hills to where there'd once been a polymer plant and a smelting plant and beside them a chroming shop, a paper mill, and a dry cleaner. He had us empty all the rusted old waste tanks and any stray barrel we found into jugs, and the jugs into wheelbarrows, and we carted it all back to the palace and filled in the moat with toxic sludge.

By the time we were done, Penny had exchanged at least a word or two with all of us, except Izzy, but he lied and said she'd kissed him and promised him a pair of shoes like Payne's, white leather slip-ons that all of us admired. She had given cigarettes to Arthur, David, Felix (twice!), Kate, Lily, Oliver, Robert, Theo, Ursula, Yves, and Zöe. She had poured glasses of water for everyone but Hans and Izzy. She had put her hand on Victoria's elbow, and brushed a bug from Theo's arm. Once Felix fell off the scaffold and Penny helped him up. When Arthur punched Robert and hit him with a wrench, Penny told him to put it down, and brought Robert some ice. She winked at Felix, shared a cheese sandwich with Nellie, and once got Garth a pencil from the house. Later Felix stole it, and Garth bloodied his eye, and the next day Penny asked Felix what happened, and Felix told her, and that night Garth beat him again. By the time it was all finished, everyone had a memory or two to fluff and mend and launder, except of course for Izzy, who had his lies to keep him warm.

Payne had us string blue ribbon around the door, and he invited us all up for the ceremony. He wore a black suit, three-button, and a dark blue shirt and tie. He was smiling cheek to cheek. He kept gazing up at the guard turret with pride. Penny wore a black silk strapless evening gown, torn up one thigh almost to her hip. She had three holes in her stockings. There was one above her left ankle, modestly sized, a larger one behind her right knee, and one big one on the inside of her left thigh that crawled up as far as we could see. Those holes sucked us right in, and the rest of the world faded straight away.

They stood on the steps, Payne beaming as Penny whacked a bottle of champagne against the lintel. It didn't break. "Again," Payne said. "Harder." So she held it by the neck with two hands and swung it like a bat. It burst, and the champagne sprayed everywhere, foaming all over her face and her neck and her bare shoulders, and when she wiped it off and licked her fingers we all cheered and jumped up and down with delight. "Bravo!" shouted Robert, and he immediately blushed. Then Payne cut the ribbon with a big pair of poultry shears. He bowed grandly, but we hardly noticed him—we couldn't get away from the shine of spit still wet on Penny's fingers, and from the flash of the white of her thigh.

Inside, Penny and Payne sat at the head of the long, polished wooden table. The rest of us stood because there were just the two chairs. Payne opened two bottles of champagne, shooting the corks in the air. One was for him and Penny, and the other one for us. He'd only brought two glasses, so we passed the bottle around from lip to lip. Payne asked Penny if she wanted to say a few words in honor of the occasion. She didn't say anything. She didn't even look at Payne. She just emptied her glass and winked at Felix. "Fine," Payne said. "I've prepared a little toast," and he started droning on, something about home and family and the bedrock of national pride.

We passed the champagne along and tried not to squirm too much or giggle, but when the bottle got to Felix it was empty. He upturned it but not even a drop came out, and when he started banging on the bottom we all couldn't help but laugh—even Penny laughed!—and interrupted Payne's speech. He was saying something about the everlasting glory of a nation founded on the vital principles of freedom and opportunity, of the responsibilities that accompany good fortune, the sacred obligation to boast of one's virtues and display one's wealth for all to see, and thereby, he said, spread freedom to the farthest corners of the globe. He cleared his throat and continued. "A free people always wins," he said, but he soon noticed that none of us was listening. We were all just staring at Penny's crossed knees and at her bobbing ankle, and even Penny wasn't paying attention to Payne. She was playing tic-tac-toe in the dust on the floor with Zöe.

Payne cleared his throat again and waited, then shrugged. "To hell with it," he said. He shook out a satin bag and two dozen tubes of modeling glue clattered onto the table. "Now get outta here."

That was the last time Payne invited us into the palace, except for guard duty, skylight-washing, and light-bulb replacement.

Payne gave us a day off. "Rest," he said. "Regroup." So we lay in the sand for hours immobilized by glue fumes and sticky dreams of Penny, interrupted only by Theo, who stripped off his clothes and kept stumbling about and insisting that we all strip too and hug him. No one would touch him, though, not even Lily, so eventually he threw a fit—"Comrades," he yelled. "You're not my comrades!"—and passed out in the dirt.

Payne showed up at dawn, rebar and frying pan in hand, kicking sand and banging away. "Derelicts, spongers, filthy trash!" he yelled. "To arms! To arms!" Having no idea what he meant, we stayed in bed.

"Up with you!" Red-faced, he screamed. "Bums!" he yelled. "Get up and build me an arsenal!" None of us knew what an arsenal was, but chances were it had something to do with Penny, or she would visit it now and again, so we got up and followed Payne. Again Ursula jumped up first, then Robert, then, one by one, the rest of us. Payne stood high on a rock and explained. He didn't look at us as he spoke, but at a point just above our heads.

"Freedom requires," he began, "in every instance, security and strength. That's what freedom is. To be a man at all, a man must walk straight, tall and free, certain in his power. He must know what's his is his. All the better, then, if everything is his. He must impose himself. He must hunt down fears like rodents. For a man to be a man, he must conquer every threat—only then will he know freedom. And just as a man must defend his home and everything that's his, a nation must secure its borders. Where it begins and where it ends—these facts must be sure. But it cannot rest at that, no more than a man can be content within a cage. A nation cannot stagnate. It must march ever onward, doling out force as a mother distributes caresses to her pups. All hostilities, within and without, must thus be rendered bland and soft. For its citizenry to freely breathe and thrive, a nation must at all times expand through conquest, free trade, and diplomatic subterfuge. And for these vital efforts to succeed, it requires arms and armor. The human body, in its nakedness, is oozy. It is weak. It has no scales, no horns or fangs or talons. A naked man is a useless bag of pulp. And a nation, undefended, is hardly worthy of the name. To stand and prosper it requires not just walls but catapults and cannon, not just shields but swords and spears and smart bombs, Kalashnikovs and cluster bombs. Also helicopters. And boats. With lots of guns on them. Ammo too. And fragmentation grenades. Also RPGs and napalm. Daisy-cutter bombs. And machetes, sharp ones. Go now, and build me these. Build me an arsenal worthy of a free people."

He gave us picks and shovels and had us dig ditches deep into the hills. We were pulling out ore all through the day and night 'til our arms and backs were knit as hard as the iron, copper, tin, and lead that we mined, and our sweat stank of sulfur and ran black as carbon down our brows. We scarred the hills with our efforts, pocked them through and through with abscesses and seeping boils.

Payne dug up some old textbooks and taught us to stoke fires that turned the sand of our beds into glass, and to smelt the rocks that we dug into steel. We stained the sky with great wandering plumes and blossoms of smoke. The sunsets were incredible. Queenie, to our surprise and hers, proved an able blacksmith. She banged out swords, shell casings, shiny brass belt buckles, and other items necessary for waging war, including semiautomatic rifles, medals of honor, and, after days of consultation and planning with Payne, one slightly misshapen but functional Black Hawk assault helicopter.

All through the many months that we labored mining in the hills, felling trees and splitting wood to fuel Queenie's fires and to carve into spear shafts and rifle butts and spare propeller blades for the chopper, Penny never came by to visit. All that time we never saw her, not once. And in the absence of the present Penny, the Penny of our imaginations gained strength and life and firmness. Her voice rang in our ears. Her touch kept every pore alert. So again we stopped sleeping, and when our muscles burned from toil, we threw ourselves harder into work, hoping that pain, at least, might distract us from our hungers, that our exhaustion might peak and allow us thereby a moment of rest.

It did not, so on we worked, building Payne an arsenal.

5

Fighting

or

The Growth of Empire

or

Before the War,
Other Wars

THE HELICOPTER ALONE USUALLY does the trick. Swoop down, raise some dust, empty a clip, break some windows, shoot a dog or a mule to make your point known. That should do it. Land, swords unsheathed, safeties off, be ready. A few shots in the air never hurts. Round up the men in the center of town and empty the homes of their goods. Sometimes they get brave and one or two start shooting. Nothing can be done. Shoot back. Sometimes they're ready and they're holed up inside, fanatics, the dark eyes of rifle barrels winking from every window. They want death, so kill them. Burn them out.

Throw bombs. Shoot them as they run. It doesn't feel good at first, but do it. Later you won't mind so much. Take the trucks and the livestock, the grain and the fruit. Take rope, take tools, take what there is to take. Take the cooking oil and the petrol, the jewelry, any pretty pictures on the walls. Take the books and the wine. Take liquor if you find it. Sometimes there's a stash of cocaine or methamphetamine or a cannabis crop in the yard. Take it. Take the sturdy boots, the silky underthings, the linens and the feather beds. Take a guitar if you see one, saxophones too. And of course take the weapons, every last knife and gun and shell, or they'll come back at you. Forget all the rest, take those first.

It's Payne's idea, the raiding. What he doesn't have, he wants. This is not unusual. Look out at the world, at what was and at what is: this is what men do. They take from one another. They fight for what they can. We praise the bold and by and by ignore the rest. Payne is simply human. Perhaps he's braver than you, more brazen. He doesn't wait, he takes. His brashness offends, but where would we be now if it weren't for men like Payne? Don't judge, he's just like you, only maybe not so shy, maybe less polite. Dig deep: Are his wishes far from yours? Are his fears? What is weakness, and what is strength, and where does virtue lie? Payne takes what he wants when he can.

"We don't have enough," Payne explains, prior to the raiding. "We simply do not have enough to get by." And who can judge, really, who has enough and who does not? Where are the borders of need?

"It's better this way," Payne adds. "All around. *Our hunger endangers everyone.* Better that we be full." And then he laughs. "Besides, stolen fruit tastes sweeter, no?"

The first time out, Payne kills. It's as if he's in a hurry to get it done, as if after that it'll all come easy. That first time out, the chopper lands and they fan out onto the ground, guns at the ready, Payne leading. A dog, hidden in the spiraling dust, whines, and snaps at Payne. He fires a shot, and the bark of his pistol is followed by a yelp. The dog's lungs rattle and it muddies the dust with its blood. The rest of them walk around it, give it a wide berth, like it still might bite, like death is a disease that catches.

Payne says, "That house first," and points to the biggest one on the street. His back is straight and his walk is certain, but they all hear his voice break when he speaks. He fires three shots at the door and kicks it open. There's no one inside. Each room is empty. Coffee still steams in two mugs on the kitchen table and burnt toast jams the toaster, but there's no one around. Payne sits and sips the coffee. Izzy takes a cup, and Joseph grabs an apple from the counter. Payne puts his finger to his lips. They hear a cough, then another. From below. Payne tears a throw rug from the floor and uncovers a trapdoor. He fires twice down through the linoleum. He motions to Izzy to open the trap, and when he does it, Payne says, "Come up outta there."

It's an old man, an old woman, and three shirtless children, wide-eyed and pale, their torsos a washboard of bone. The old man's sagging arm is bleeding from the bullet through the floor. "What nuts have you squirreled away?" says Payne, and he motions to Joseph to climb down the ladder and see. The old man steps between Joseph and the door, but his eyes are on Payne. "Thief," he says. "Be ashamed."

A vein pulses blue in Payne's neck. He nods to Joseph again. "Go," he says. And the old man spits in Payne's face. A yellowy gob, flecked with browning blood, drops from his cheek to his chin. Payne grabs the old man by his bleeding arm, and he cries out from the pain of it. Joseph steps back and Payne's free hand is shaking and the old man sees it and sees fear in all of their eyes and takes comfort from it, and says again, calmer now, certain that his command will be heeded, "Be ashamed." The barrel of Payne's pistol shivers this way and that until Payne can still his wayward hand. He sucks in a breath and shoots the old man in the chest. He lets go the limp arm and the old man falls down the trap and no one in the room has ever before heard a silence as complete as the one that follows that shot, that clattering fall.

Payne burns the house without searching the basement. The whole ride home he grips one hand with the other to stop its trembling, but after that day his hand never shakes again. After that it all comes easy. For Payne at least.

Everyone, he decides, must shed blood. A bond will thus be formed, he says. "And how can I trust you, otherwise?" He goes in order, from A to Z. Each will have their turn. Again, please, don't judge too harshly. Who wants to be alone in guilt? Who among you has not sinned? Is it still allowed to ask that question? There are not two brands of humans. What exists in any one exists in every one. After that it's all just scale. If Payne's transgressions are grander than yours, who is to blame? He for his boldness, or you for your timidity?

The next time out, they enter a house and find a chest hidden in an attic, an old wooden chest locked with a rusted padlock. A knock-kneed woman, hair thin and straight and brown, wears a starched yellow housedress and on her knees begs Payne not to touch the chest. He shoots off the padlock, and she hurls herself atop it. "Not this," she says. "Not this."

Payne calls for Arthur and tells him to open it, but when he tries to lift her off, she bites him on the wrist, drawing blood. Arthur backs off. "Let her keep it," he says, gesturing back to the helicopter, already overfilled with digital watches by the crate, with cakes and casks of wine and fuel. "We've got enough," he says. "Who cares?" But Payne shakes his head and hands him his pistol. Will you hate Arthur less if I tell you his knees buckle with the gun in his hand, that his trousers darken as he pisses himself? Will you hate Zöe less for allowing him in her bed that night if I tell you she does not sleep, and that as she wrestles with the sheets a skein

59

of bone fills the cracks in her heart, never to wear away? The wooden chest, it turns out, is empty save a sheaf of age-yellowed photographs and handwritten letters in thin envelopes labeled Par Avion, a single threadbare dress shirt, plastic child-sized sunglasses, and one green silk scarf now soaked in blood.

The next time out a young boy hides on a rooftop and shoots clumsily at the raiders with an old .22. He has only a handful of bullets, and none find their targets, and when he runs out, they drag him from the roof. He is crying, and so is Carl, who does as he is told.

And the next time out it's David, who ends the frenzied struggles of the huge man who has broken Robert's ribs with his fists, torn Garth's ear, and bloodied Lily's nose. When the giant's neighbor comes running with a kitchen knife in each fist, it's Elizabeth who, unblinking, does the honors. She never complains.

When his turn arrives, Felix tries to prepare himself. He's quiet the whole flight in, jaw clenched, foot tapping. As soon as it lands, he storms off the helicopter, gun raised and ready. He kicks down doors and drags children from their beds. He pushes men twice his size to their knees. He barks out orders and slaps a granny to the ground. His face is purple with fear and rage. He kicks a cat and shoots a squawking chicken, and when an eye-patched man grabs at his arm and says, "Hold it, Shortstack," Felix shoots him in his one remaining eye.

That night, as everyone sits around the fire, drinking brandy and eating pilfered chocolates, Felix stays in bed.

When they at last stumble off to slumber, they find him lying in a fever, and fear his brains will boil. Penny hears the news and, for the first time in many weeks, comes down from the palace. She sits on his bed and holds his head in her lap. She smooths his sweat-soaked hair and soothes his burning brow with a cloth chilled in ice water. Felix tosses his head and mutters dry-mouthed nonsense and then looks up, and through the fog of his fever he sees the wide-open green of Penny's eyes staring down at him, and the haze lifts for a moment from his own eyes, small and brown, and he squeezes them tight and cries.

"What did you do, little Felix," she whispers, "to make you feel so bad?"

He doesn't answer but lies curled in Penny's lap, bawling until the sun arrives, and then he finally falls asleep, and Penny slips away.

Felix sleeps until evening. When he awakes he asks for water and for Penny. Sally runs up the hill to get her, but when she rings the bell it's Payne who answers. "She's busy," he says. He gives Sally a bottle of aspirin. "Give him these," he says, "and go away."

At night, Penny comes down from the hill. Katerina, searching in the moonlight for an earring she maybe dropped beneath the palace windows, hears Payne yelling as Penny leaves. A door slams somewhere inside. The windows rattle in their panes. You bristle at his selfishness, but ask yourself, what man does not wish to guard his wife's affections? Especially when he has given them so much space in which to wander. Who does not fear to be alone? Have you never sought to bind a lover or even lovers to your side, to confine them and prune their growth so their hearts would never stray from yours?

Don't be ashamed, just honest. For if you are capable of such an act, of willing the bondage of one so dear to you, can you really, from where you stand, condemn Payne for any crime at all?

Penny spends the night at Felix's bedside, stroking his temples, drying his tears. Again Felix does not sleep 'til dawn, when Penny climbs home to the palace. That night, Katerina, searching for mushrooms in the moonlight beneath the palace windows, hears Payne and Penny fighting, and that night Penny does not come.

A week passes, and Felix recovers, but something in him has slowed and stiffened, not just in his pace but in his gaze and in his speech. He can sing still, but without music to cushion them, his words rattle and clank across the threshold of his lips. His limbs appear more tightly wound together. His smile, when it comes, sways as if hung tenuously from hooks. Soon Payne tells Queenie to fuel up the helicopter, and they all strap on their swords and their guns, and they go. Even Felix goes, shuffling, his eyes on the dirt at his feet.

But they go, and the storerooms fill with wine and grain. Garth, unbidden, cuts a man down with a sword. The pantries fill with spices, dried meats, and fragrant oils. Hans shoots a bent old woman in the lump of her back.

Gold chains hang coiled like garden hoses from nails on the walls. Silk shirts and CD players pile like leaves on the floor. Izzy, told by Payne to kill a child who has stabbed Yves in the thigh, takes the boy into the cellar, and in the dark hides him in a cardboard box, fires two shots at the floor, and tells Payne the child's dead. Only Nellie sees through Izzy's lie and doesn't know if she loves him more for it, or not at all. The pastures crowd with cows and sheep. Joseph, Katerina, and Lily each shoot a man in a firefight in which Victoria is killed. Pens must be built to house all the pigs, and coops for the chickens, ducks, and geese. Nellie shoots a screaming fat man in the gut and won't let Izzy in her bed for a month. Bricks of hashish rise in stacks in the closets. Ollie is jumped in the dark of a hallway and strangles a man. Cognac replaces gasoline as the stupefactory agent of choice. Queenie throws a grenade into a shed and never learns how many die. The shelves grow heavy with leather-bound volumes, and some are even read.

Poor Robert loses his head and beats a man to death when he won't give up his watch, and after that he shivers even in the sun. There are guns enough for everyone to have three, and Payne keeps the surplus from then on. Sally steals a car and drags its angry owner two kilometers down the road until he finally lets go of her leg. They sometimes eat with silver forks and sometimes drink from goblets of crystal, but usually they eat with their hands and drink directly from the bottle. Theo stabs a man once, can't believe what he's done, and stabs him sixteen more times to punish the insane permeability of his flesh until Payne has to kick him to make him stop. There are feather beds for everyone, futons for those who prefer them. Ursula is stung by loneliness and spite and burns two sleeping lovers in their bed. Cigarettes pile up by the carton, and no one has to bum a smoke again, except for Felix, who smokes too much. Xavier empties his pistol into the face of a man who reminds him of his father, turns the gun on himself, and weeps when he hears the hammer click. There are handkerchiefs of silk or linen in every pocket for eventualities such as this. Yves pushes a man from a roof. Cars outnumber drivers for a while, but Felix drives half of them into the sea, and Sally wrecks the rest. Zöe thinks of shooting Payne, or Arthur and herself, but instead shoots a toothless old man who begs her to do it and do it fast. Everyone's got all they need and more.

6

Rebellion

or

Interregnum Opens Wide

or

Only the Emperor
Wears Clothes

Theo:

Really, the world is rich and waste is nothing to be ashamed of. It's life's first principle, waste. And it can be fun. Drink a glass, spill a glass. Drink a glass, break a glass. Give something back. Don't hold on so tight. The world is rich with scent and color, with wind and sounds and silence, with soft and cold and pills and the most delightful itches. If a tree falls and you don't hear it, do you cry over the loss? That's waste. It's everywhere. And theft? So silly. Everything you have is stolen. You steal water from a spring, air from the sky, warmth from the air. You steal smells and sights and tastes. You steal laughter from a bottle, pleasure from a friend. You steal life from pigs and plants. Do you pay them? The whole world is free and everything is stolen. What could it mean even, for something to be yours? Empty your hands and take another bite.

I'm not justifying anything. I'm only trying to explain. Before the War, there were other wars. Those are the ones I'm talking about, and also what came after. They were little wars. For land, for fun, for all the stuff piled, by some sad trick of fortune, in other people's closets. Maybe to call them wars is too much. They never lasted long, a couple of days at most. Warlets. Sometimes we'd fight two or more a week. On our own, I'll admit, we never would have thought on a scale that big. We'd have whiled away our days enjoying what few vulgar pleasures we could find. At best we might have mugged a dog. It was Payne who pushed us, who inspired us to push ourselves. Payne led the charge each time. "Follow me," he said, and we all followed. And following doesn't come easy for us. But we didn't see Penny much in those days, and if Payne didn't look much like her, at least he smelled like her sometimes. In the mornings anyway. By noon he smelled like Payne.

So we followed. We armed ourselves and marched behind him. We sailed to this island and that one, near and far. We piled into the helicopter and flew low through the canyons and high over rivers, gorges, lakes, vast asphalt parking lots populated only by tumbleweeds, potholes, and puddles. And we got rich. Payne got richer. We spent and he just kept. Waste is life's first principle, have I mentioned that? It's hard to see the point of holding on to anything, much less producing things. Why add when there's so much to subtract? Why stop eating after just a few bites? Why not go on forever? But Payne held tight to everything. While we frittered through our fortunes, his grew and grew and grew. This wasn't something we regretted. We always had enough. Even before he came, when we had nothing. Maybe not then. But while we smoked and drank and snorted everything away, his storerooms filled. That was in part because the apportionment process was a little skewed. More than a little. But also because we made a point of acknowledging that nothing accords less with nature than to save. By nature I don't just mean trees and birds and all that. I mean it's part of nature too if I follow a squirrel to his tree and eat the nuts he stored, and then where is he? What will nature do for him? I mean that nothing can be protected, and nothing lost gets found again.

Don't get me wrong, I mean that in a good way.

Look at what happens to dead things—other live things eat them. Every last bit. And they get eaten too. Animal or vegetable, there's no distinction. Cows eat grass and grass grows from their skulls. We eat cows and will one day feed the grass, and then the cows. There's not much time, and time is all there is. Everything is waste, and nothing's ever wasted. The planet eats! That's all it does, consumes. Look at the excess, the hurricanes, the floods and epidemics. What idiot invented moderation? All there is is ecstasy! The cosmos is on an endless reeling binge! Think about black holes—even densest nothingness just eats and eats and eats. So how do we celebrate expenditure, make it the principle by which we live? We strip ourselves naked as the wind—the wind that chews away mountains and blows oceans where it wants—and we let it breathe through us. Wouldn't that be just like being free?

I tried to make a point of this. I printed up flyers, and Lily agreed to help me pass them out. "Get rid of everything!" they read. "Meet at Theo and Lily's! Bring all your stuff! Go home empty-handed! Naked! Free!" The idea was to come together through spending, giving, throwing away, to gain ourselves through loss. Lily was enthusiastic, or tried to be. We sat out all day long on the porch—it's nothing fancy, two rocking chairs on a concrete slab. We sat and rocked and held hands, with everything we owned laid out on the cement for the taking, even our clothes (we weren't wearing any). But none of our comrades came. That's not quite true. We drank all day (port, then gin, then Kahlúa, I think, then beer) and worked our way through a bag of fat pink pills, but I'm pretty sure I remember Felix dropping by, picking out a couple of fishhooks, a ball of twine, and a little blue perfume bottle, then running off without a word.

Later Lily confessed that she had forgotten to hand out the flyers. She didn't exactly forget. She drank too much with Sally and Kate and dropped the entire pile in a ditch.

"You're lucky I didn't fall in," she told me. And she was right. Ditches too are hungry.

While we were sitting there, rocking, drinking, watching the clouds drift by and listening to the wind chase sand across the rocks, Lily asked me what I had in mind. "I know, I know, waste is life's first principle," she said. "But when they show up with all their stuff, then what?"

"They can lay their stuff out with our stuff," I said. She hadn't told me yet about the ditch.

"And then what? Do we build a big bonfire, burn it all, and dance around a maypole?"

"That's not a bad idea. I hadn't thought of that."

"That's what I'm asking," Lily said. "What did you think?"

I hadn't really thought it through. I figured we would eat and drink and let our whims decide the rest. Planning out the details seemed a bad idea. "I don't know," I told her. "We'll have a party. After a while they'll go home."

"And leave their stuff with us?" asked Lily. She was grinning. Then her chin started shaking. "You devil," she cackled. "Waste is life's first principle! Go home empty-handed! Naked! Free!" Then she fell out of her chair.

"Don't be like that," I said, and reached for another pill.

In the end it didn't matter, of course, but Lily convinced me later that even though no one had shown up, it didn't mean they were not committed to the project. On their own, she said, wherever they were, our comrades were pursuing precisely the objectives I had laid out. So I felt a little better.

But that was all a long time before the day I'm talking about, the day when Payne put out the call for War. And by then we were tired, really, sick and tired of it. It was just so much effort, all that fighting and flying around. And we'd had enough of killing, most of us. It's easy enough for kids and for cats, but after a while, death begins to weigh on you. You wouldn't necessarily think it would. After all, it's someone else you're snuffing out. What's it got to do with you? I don't want to seem inconsistent here, but it's a violent act, killing. There's no getting around that. It takes a lot of effort. In the wet and the warmth of the moment, knife slippery in hand, you don't know whose blood is whose, who's killing and who's being killed, or if you even care.

We didn't mind at first. At least I didn't. Maybe I did, but what I mean to say is that Payne deserves some credit, because whether he intended to or not, he educated us. He brought us a certain amount of sophistication. I don't just mean that some of us really took to reading books and Robert started wearing ascots or that Felix learned a couple of jazz chords—because he didn't—or that we gave up huffing gas for cognac and cocaine. We still huff gas sometimes. What I mean is that our desires were no longer built on the cold bedrock of absolute want. We had more, and could pick and choose a little. Mainly we chose ease.

Of course some of us were killed, and that only made it worse. Nothing can be preserved, I know, and it's loss that spins the planet. But still, it can be discouraging sometimes to watch your comrades die. The first to go was Victoria, shot unsuspecting through the head with a hillbilly 30-30. She was bending to pick a flower when they got her. Really, that's true! That's how sweet she was, dreamy even with everything going to hell all around her. They were meth freaks, the ones who killed her, sitting tight on their lab, cranked up and crazy, ready to shoot and shoot all night, but my Lily tossed a fragmentation grenade into their lair with the most gorgeous flick of her wrist. That did it. Kabloom. She and Joseph and Kate went in blazing and each dragged out a fat and bleeding biker. What a come-down. We considered tying them to the helicopter to soften our landings, but even fresh-killed they stank too bad, so we fed them to the dogs they'd kept chained starving to their roof, then shot the dogs out of pity, burned them in the street, and flew dear Vicky home.

And then there was David. Poor Hans is still a mess. We raided an island about a three-hour ride to the south. The raid went easy—forewarned somehow, the inhabitants had fled and left most of their goodies behind. Among those goods, chained in a pool behind the poshest house on the island, was a crocodile with a snout as long as my leg. Alive. Payne had always wanted one for the moat, so he bribed Felix with double his share of the loot. Little Felix just leapt on the thing's back and looped a wire noose around its jaws. We wrestled it into the chopper and brought it home. Of course it died within an hour in that moat. That was the only time I ever saw Payne cry, when that big, awful lizard floated belly first to the top.

At night Payne came down to our camp and took David aside. He promised him his own share of the take on our next outing if he got rid of the reptile's corpse. David went up and poured a gallon of petrol on the critter right there where it bobbed in the muck. He dropped a match on it, and the whole moat, five meters wide, half a kilometer around, went up in flames. David burnt to ash in seconds. There wasn't anything left of him to bury, and Hans, ever gentle, who'd loved David since they were boys, got mean and stayed that way.

So we'd had enough of dying. And for a while before Payne even mentioned the big War, he'd been insisting that we "get serious." First that just meant uniforms. They weren't Payne's idea but Hans's, and Hans never thought to call them that. It was just after David died, and he didn't know what to do with himself. He started wearing black in mourning and a week or two later we all woke and found black pants and a black shirt folded beside our heads, a pair of black socks rolled up on top of them. None of it fit, not even the socks. I had to tie the pants with twine to keep them from falling to my knees, and Lily popped half the buttons from her shirt right off. She couldn't zip the fly at all, but out of respect for David, we all did what we could.

Payne was thrilled. We went out on a raid not long after that and we were all still wearing black. Though by then it was more like gray on some of us. Payne kept grinning the whole time. When we got home and divvied up the take, he yelled, "Report tomorrow! Oh-nine-hundred hours! Uniforms required!" But a while had passed since David's death, so by the time we'd all gathered at the palace gate the next afternoon, only about half of us were wearing our outfits. Payne was furious. He sent us all home, which was fine with everyone, but the next time we went out he started docking the shares of anyone not dressed in black.

Someone had to take a stand. No one else was willing, so I confronted Payne. I slipped a letter beneath the palace door. I didn't write anything I hadn't said a thousand times before (to Lily anyway). "Dear Payne," I wrote. "In formal objection to this business with the uniforms: I protest. Calm down a little. Don't you think it's better to be naked? Not just cooler when the wind is hot or when there's no wind at all, but that way we're not so guarded all the time. Maybe guarded is what you want when it comes to any old whoever we run up across with a pitchfork and a 12-gauge and coming for you now, but haven't you had enough of that? And what about each other? What about between us? That's all I'm trying to suggest. That only in our nakedness are we anything at all. To each other but also to ourselves. How else can we cut through all this stuff between us? We can strip ourselves naked as the stars and the sea and the birds who recline on the wind and make their homes in the barest empty air. Wouldn't that be just like being free? Also Penny could be naked too.

Most sincerely, A friend."

73

Payne didn't answer, never even mentioned if he read the letter, and a few days later he started with the drills. First he sent out memos. "Drill tomorrow. Oh-six-hundred hours. At the gate. Be there." Everyone ignored them, but there he was the next morning at the crack of noon, banging that frying pan of his, yelling his head off. He had us marching and about-facing and standing in the sun all day nearly every day after that.

Somehow it never occurred to us that we could refuse. Obeying just seemed like the easiest choice, the quickest way to shut him up. Of course it wasn't. But we were tired. We'd had enough. This was different too: it came not from our needs or whims but from something more abstract. Payne promised us loot, sure, riches beyond measure, but it all had more to do with his ambitions, with bizarre imperial fantasies that had nothing to do with us, and less with satisfying present needs. And I think I speak for all of us when I say that present need is something we have no interest in getting past. Excuse the pun.

From what little Payne did say, it seemed that there was a solid chance of defeat. Without any immediate reward, we could be walking right into some unpleasant, faraway death. It wouldn't be just us allied in arms against whichever hollow-eyed nobodies we stumbled across that day. No, it would be us allied in arms with other groups we'd never met, people from other lands, people we might not care for. Battling who? we asked. He wouldn't say. We could guess, though, that it would be someone we had nothing against, and who none of us stood anything to gain from, except maybe Payne, whose vision extended well beyond the next banquet, the next orgy, who was willing to deny himself—and us—in pursuit of something nameless and invisible, something he couldn't eat, drink, or caress, that wouldn't sing to him or hold him through the night, that would always back one step away with each step he took towards it. We had no use for it, this thing.

I called a meeting. No flyers this time. I went door to door. "Come as you are," I said. I even offered drinks and snacks. But no one came. Even Lily found an errand to run. "I dropped a button in the road, I think," she said, kissing my fingertips and backing out the door. "I have to find it." So I wrote another letter. I kept it short this time. "Dear Payne," I wrote. "What's this all about? The world is rich. Why go so far away? What's this got to do with us?

Most sincerely, A friend."

Of course he never answered, which, for me at least, was answer enough: Fuck off.

So we did.

Hans:

There's no point in talking about it now. I mean, how much do you get back? Jackshit. Fuck-all. Things come and go, but mainly they go. No point in waving bye-bye, one hand toodleooing, the other up your ass, thumb first and fingers spread. Wide. Mainly things don't come at all, but when they do, they go. Right quick, look fast and then they're gone. Don't blink. Cause what's left after? Pillars of salt. A whole world of salt, nothing sweet no more never and not enough ever to wash it all down. So who's waiting for what? Answer me that. Cause it ain't me. Nothing comes back, not never. Sing another song, I'm listening. I'm tapping my fucking toes.

Izzy:

Payne came to me early in the morning, before the sun had fully risen. He stood outside my window and whispered.

"Sir," he said. "Please, sir, I need your honest counsel." My dear Nellie clung to my neck. "Don't go," she implored me, her nails embedded in my tendermost parts. "Not now." But through a terrific effort of will I was able to tear myself from her side, promising her my full attention upon return. I bestowed a kiss upon her, dressed hurriedly, and joined Payne out of doors.

"My friend," I said, "what is so pressing that it cannot wait 'til evening?"

He clasped my hand and begged that I forgive him for rousing me at such an hour. He said again that he needed my advice. He had come to rely on me, you see, not only because I had aided him so many times in the past but because his wife, Penny, so favored me, and he deferred to her opinion in all matters of import. I should say that as much as I appreciated her esteem, and returned it triple-fold, I was rather tired of this role, as it made the others jealous and resentful and caused me undue trouble thereby. But I've never been able to deny a friend.

Payne was more anxious than I had ever seen him. He stuttered a bit and asked if I had ever heard the story of his birth. I told him I had not. He had just recently learned of his true origins himself, he said, after dredging an old family photo album from the attic and reading a letter that slipped out from beneath one of his circumcision photos. He had always thought he was the son of the man who had raised him—a kind and honest judge, or maybe an embezzler, I forget—and that his mother had died in childbirth. In fact, he said, this letter revealed that he'd been deceived since infancy.

"The story of Christ's final romance, which took place on the cross," he told me, "has not, for reasons which you, sir, will soon come to appreciate, been widely disseminated." I raised my eyebrows, intrigued. "You see," he said, "once he'd been pegged up there on the crossbeam, Christ began to have regrets, hence that infamous *Eloi, Eloi, lama sabachthani* outburst. It was the pleasures of the flesh that he regretted, or the lack thereof in his own short life. He'd experimented a little here and there as a youth but had never allowed his sensuality to bloom. And so he hung there, helpless now to fulfill desires so long bottled up, heaving with regret, recalling every woman, old or young, who had asked him to lay his healing hands upon her, every beardless boy who'd followed him through the streets, tugging at the corners of his cloak. In those final, agonized moments, he lived out gloriously impossible orgies, tormented, imagining himself making infinite permutations of love to nearly every living beast he had ever seen—boys and girls, crones and duffers, serpents and dolphins and mules. And in the heat of this final fantasy, a carrion bird landed on the great protruding branch of his godhood and tore a ribbon of meat from his chest. That simple caress, the tangible trace of another's desire on his lonely flesh, coming as it did at the very height of his arousal, pushed the son of god to climax. His perfect phallus spasmed mightily. The vulture lost its footing, slipped, and was impaled upon the man-god's prong. He came with such force and torrential joy that the bird was thrust miles into the air. It circled the earth twice before landing, immediately following which it laid the egg from which I hatched." Payne crossed his arms, his story told.

"Interesting," I said. "I never supposed."

In truth, at the time I didn't give much thought to his tale. I was impatient to return to Nellie's arms, and wondered with some irritation why'd he chosen that particular moment to relay his story. I suppose he was trying to impress me. But since then it's stuck in my mind with uncommon power, and though I have my doubts about some of the details, on the whole I believe Payne's tale. It does explain a lot. When all is said and done, though, it doesn't matter much. We find ourselves alone in the world, knowing not from whence we come, as if tossed here like kittens hurled through the rolled-down window of a speeding pickup truck.

But I wander. Eager to move things along, I prodded him. "You require my advice?"

Payne nodded gravely. He'd been approached, he said, by couriers and diplomats. They'd brought gifts, all manner of gold and gem-encrusted baubles, like nothing he'd ever come upon before. His eyes lit up at the thought of it. They had asked him, he said, to join their fight.

"What fight?" I asked.

He said he didn't know the details, but they were splitting up the world between them and had said we could be with them or against them. Those were the only choices. The world was changing fast, they claimed, there was a new order coming down. Out with the old, they exclaimed. A new day is dawning, they declared—are you in or are you out? They promised Payne a place of prominence in this new order, he said, with excellent possibilities for advancement. That meant deals on tanks and F-14s, or so they hinted. And what good came to him, of course, would come to all of us.

"What do they want?" I asked him.

"Our assistance in their struggle," he said.

"Against?"

"Against the old ways," he said. "I'm not sure exactly who."

"Where?" I asked him.

"They didn't say. Not near. Farther away than that," he said.

"How would we contribute?" I asked him, and he said we'd fight. That was all, just fight. It would be the same as always, he said, only we'd have a little help. There'd be more people involved, maybe a higher level of organization, and challenges to help us grow.

"My friend," I said, "forget it," I said. "We have enough right here."

But it turned out it was not my counsel he wanted but my assistance. His mind was made up. He asked me to help convince the others. "They'll listen to you, sir," he said. "They respect you like no one else."

I apologized and told him that in good conscience I thought it was unwise, and that I could not ask another to do what I would not. He was silent for a moment. Then, with a tear in his eye, he embraced me, kissed both my cheeks, and left.

Felix:

Up in the hills, in the mountains, in the evening the hills are blue no matter where you were. Except there'll be a bit when they're pink, when the world and all that's in it turned pink and the wind hums in the grass. It just lasts a minute but while it lasts everything's transformed. Pinker. And after that the hills get smaller, they shrank. In the day the hills are brown or green depending on the rain, the amount of it and when it comes. At night they go away, turn purple if there was moon. Penny asked me to tell her about the hills. The hills are like dogs, I tell Penny, like sleeping dogs, the

head of one on the rump of the other but as far as I can tell
they have no tongues. She laughs. Or tails, she said. And I
say I hate to contradict but they do have tails, some do.
They just don't wag. How sad, she said. Yes, sad. But they
are sleeping after all. In the afternoon when the air cools
the lizards slept on rocks. They soak up the heat left in the
rocks by the sun. The birds will pick them off the rocks. You
know about their tails. Once, out fishing, I caught a dog
instead, a floating dog, all done with barking. Up in the
hills, at night the hills were purple if you can see them at
all. Sometimes they go away, but sometimes in the moonlight when there's wind I want to tell Penny the tails do
wag, not in the day but in the night when the hills were like
dogs humping, and the wind pants and moans through the
grass, that's when they wag. I want to tell her that.

Nellie:

No matter what I say, I'm sure you won't believe me, so I
might as well tell you the truth. Not that there's anything
about any of this that I'm ashamed of. I might even be a little bit proud. It rid us of Payne, which is fine by me. I know
some of the boys were in his thrall, but he always sickened
me. He'd smile at me in that slightly sleazy way of his. It
made my teeth hurt. So why did I follow him all those
times? Why did I *obey* him? Maybe it was as simple as
hunger. Call it greed, but we never had anything. We slept
on the rocks before he came. The birds were better off. And
you can make a lot of excuses afterwards and during, but it's

not always easy to distinguish need from desire. Lately I'm not sure it's worth the effort. To separate them, that is. Of course there's also Penny. What started as infatuation became somehow something fixed, the way you get used to feeling pain even in a missing limb. Or so I hear.

But I was talking about Payne. I was describing how odious I found him. I can't speak for the others, but the greater my love for Penny grew, the more I hated Payne. There was never any room for the sort of romantic identification that kept some of the boys going for a while. Izzy anyway. How his fantasies exhausted me. Exhaust me. But no. The thought of him, Payne, *in her,* was repugnant to me. Still is. Each one of those braided muscles more repugnant than the last. There was some amount of fear as well, that if we lost Payne we'd lose her too, that to obey him would keep her close. Perhaps that was stupid, but so what.

Izzy had been sick for weeks, in that state of near-complete collapse and helplessness that he seems to love more than any other. He wouldn't talk to anyone but me, and I couldn't stand to be near him. There's something about his passivity that fills me with nausea. I can't be with him when he's like that. And I know he resents me for it. Maybe that's even what I love best about him, that extreme of vulnerability. But it's also what turns my stomach most—to be so *necessary.*

He was at death's door, he insisted. When the call came I left him there, laid out. I didn't hesitate to leave him. Not even as long as Payne, who had been waiting for him to recover, to have a full cast for his latest drama. He finally got impatient and ordered us all to meet him on the palace lawn armed and in uniform. We all went down except for Izzy, who would have been left behind. Not just by Payne, but by me. I was relieved to have a pretext to get away. Given the chance, I'd do it again. There: some truth.

We'd all heard rumors of War. Felix had muttered something in his usual way, and there was a little fireside chatter about "something big." I never took any of it seriously. Even when Payne started about freedom and all the rest, I didn't think it was anything new. But then he began to go on about "This Campaign." It would be different from the others, he said. This Campaign would require great and noble sacrifices. It would extend farther than we'd ever gone, and had no end in sight. "This is it," he said. "This is what we've all been training for."

Sally was the first to speak up. She asked what was in it for us. She put it more diplomatically than that, but not much more. She maybe gilded the question with a wink and a smile. Payne spilled a bit more tripe about fighting for freedom, against the forces of evil, about the common good and how glorious a thing it is to lay down your life for the nation, for freedom. "Your names," he swore, "will be etched across the stars." Then he promised us more loot than we'd ever imagined.

When Sally pressed him, though, asking in that Little Miss Innocent way of hers who precisely we'd be fighting, why and where and for how long, Payne got vague. He sputtered on about the enemies of order and of course of freedom and the new way coming down. "We will fight on many fronts," he said. "On all fronts if we must. And I know we shall prevail." He said something about sacrifice and loyalty and all he'd done for us. "When I first found you, you were little flightless swallows, hopping about in puddles of swill. And look at you now—ready to soar!" Then Theo got brave for a minute and asked him just what he meant by freedom, but Payne pretended he hadn't heard and shouted, "About face!" and ordered us to march. He began marching off to the docks. Ursula followed, but the rest of us stayed. Rifles on our shoulders, feet planted. Robert began to follow him too, until he saw that it was just him and Ursula.

Then Payne turned around. He must have noticed the silence where there should have been footfalls. He saw us still standing there behind him and this funny little smile flashed across his face, like it was a joke we were playing, like there was something cute about it, like we were toddlers trying to make their daddy mad, and he wasn't going to fall for it.

Again he ordered us to march. We stayed put. His face turned red and he kicked at the dirt and he yelled. He stamped his feet and screamed, "You don't deserve to be called soldiers! You're a bunch of little girls! All those who are not prepared to die in defense of freedom lay down your arms and take off your fucking uniforms now!"

Zöe was first. She dropped her rifle. She didn't place it on the ground and she didn't throw it down, she just opened her hands and let it fall. She threw her cap beside it and began unbuttoning her shirt. Before she reached the bottom button, Theo had stripped off his pants and tossed his shirt to the ground. We all did the same, though maybe not with Theo's eagerness. But after a minute of fumbling, we had all stripped to our underwear, except for Hans, who didn't undress but stood there crying, and Ollie, who wore no underpants. He hid his privates behind cupped hands. Sally, it turned out, wore a bra but no panties. Bony little Felix's shorts had more holes than cotton to them, and he squirmed in embarrassment. Our clothes lay scattered around us on the ground like crumpled crows. I've never been so proud.

Payne's face blanched. His eye began to twitch. I undid my bra and stepped out of my panties. Everyone around me did the same, except those who weren't wearing bras. (Yves was!) And except for Ursula, who stood at Payne's side, rifle slung on her shoulder, expressionless. Payne unholstered his pistol. With his thumb he clicked the safety off and cocked the hammer. We were afraid, but not so much as you might think. Something had happened. He'd never had to threaten us before, so we knew we must have won.

I looked around, startled to see everyone around me, self-conscious, like chickens plucked alive. Theo was beaming! Felix gawked at Lily's enormous hanging tits, at the puckered rolls of fat that overhung her massive pubic thatch. He pointed, covered his mouth with his hand,

and began to giggle. Lily pointed back at his shriveled prick and protruding nipples, clutched her rolling breasts, and laughed. And soon we were all doubled over, beholding Yves's paunch, the hairy mole marring Zöe's otherwise flawless buttock, the psoriasis speckling Joseph's back, Garth's uncircumcised dangle, Robert's chicken legs, Katerina's boyish chest. We were lost. Huge swells of laughter reeled over us. We fell to the ground, the grass and stones pocking our bare flesh. Even Hans, his face still stained with tears, sat bent in the dirt, shaking, a smile on his lips. What could be more ridiculous than a naked human being?

When at last we wiped our eyes and looked, Payne and Ursula were black specks in the distance, and the helicopter blade was spinning fast.

ii

7

Writing

or

Heroïd Reconfigured

or

Missin' You Too Much,
My Sweet

No sooner had Payne flown off than Penny learned that she was pregnant. She chewed her nails until her fingers bled and paced circuits of several hundred miles from bed to couch to bed again until she was at last able to sit still long enough to hunch over the typewriter and punch out this letter to Payne:

```
Dear Payne,
  Fuck you for leaving.
  Fuck you.
```

Fuck you.

Fuck you.

We've been through it all before, but I'll
ask you again—what was so important that it
was worth leaving Home? What could you hope
to find out there that you couldn't find
here too? What does the world have that
I can't give you? Maybe that's a dumb
question, but this one isn't: Do you really
expect me to wait?

Fuck you.

Every night it is the image of your
bloodied corpse that chases sleep away.
Do you know how many ways I've configured
that image? How many places I've put the
wounds? How I've stretched them, shrunk
them to cover every possibility? What
shapes and colors of metal and flame
I have imagined penetrating you? What
monsters might replace your face? What
will be left for the pyre or the casket?
Will I even see a piece? I recognize the
unrecognizable, sent home taped up in a
shoe box, oozing through its corners what
once was you. Every night.

It is a small step from fearing your
death in every which way to wishing it.

Perhaps there is nothing I fear now more

than your return. Then I'd have only
myself to hate.

I miss you. Please come Home, and come
Home soon.

Love Always,

Penny

p.s. I'm pregnant. I pray it's not a boy.

*Eight months later, the child was born. Penny wrote again to
Payne. This is what she wrote:*

Dear Payne,

I hear the war is going swimmingly. At
least that's the news that Felix brings,
picked up on his wanderings. But he brings
no news of you. And no news from you
either. So I don't know if you received my
last letter. If you did, I can't blame you
for not responding, though I will, and do.
Every waking moment I do. There are
several possibilities. The letter never
found its way to you. Either because it
was lost and has dissolved in the sea, or
served as fuel in someone's stove. Or
because you were not there to receive it.
Because the helicopter crashed as soon as
it disappeared over the horizon. Because
you arrived as planned and were betrayed

and murdered right then and there. Or
perhaps it found you, and found you in
another woman's arms, and you read it aloud
and mocked me together between gymnastic
fucks. Or it found you, somewhere beyond
caring, where my name is like the face of
someone you once passed in the street. Or
it found you somewhere unable to return,
defeated, desperate, and ashamed. Maybe you
did write and the mail boat sank, the plane
fell from the sky, and now your letter is
ash, or is skipping like a leaf in the dirt
of somebody else's yard. Maybe you're on
your way home right now and will open the
door before I fold this page.

I'm not sure which of these possibilities
tortures me most. I give them all an equal
chance.

The baby was born. You're a father. Even
from afar, you get your way—I bore you a
son. Your name, though, will die with you.
The greatest skill a child can have, I've
decided, is to keep afloat above the tides.
I call him Bobby. It's a bad pun, I know,
and perhaps too cruel, but I pray for him.
I don't know to what, I just pray: May he
be smarter than his father, or dumber, but
with a larger heart.

Zöe helped with the delivery. Seven
pounds, four ounces. It lasted eight and
three-quarter hours, and yes, it hurt.

What do I tell him about his father?
Should I tell him anything at all? Will
I be able to shield him from the hate
I feel for you? Should I even try? You've
got at least a year before he remembers
anything I say to him, so hurry. If you
come in time, I might even remember how
to love you.

Kind regards,

Penny

*About a year later, Penny folded the mound of sweaters and
socks which had gathered atop the typewriter and again
pecked at the unwilling keys. She paper-clipped to her letter
a Polaroid photo of an infant, blue-eyed and towheaded, its
tongue between its lips. This is what she wrote:*

Dear Payne,

I try to think about all the times we
fought, every moment of neglect and
carelessness, your lies, your greed, your
bottomless capacity to dissemble, and every
cruelty, every petty slight you ever threw
my way. I want to build as strong a crust
of hate around my heart as I know how. But

you bastard, you won't let me. I wake in
the morning after a night of sweat and
bitterness, and the first thing I see is
your eyes smiling on the pillow beside me,
and my every joint aches with longing. My
hand, on the wooden armrest of a chair,
feels your strong thigh in its grasp. The
other night, in the banquet hall, Xavier
and Carl brought a roasted pig to the
table—a *pig!*—and in the lines of its
browned foreleg, I saw your freckled
wrist. I drank myself stupid that night.
I smoked the opium that Izzy passed around
and confused everyone with my laughter
and my tears.

Yes, I've opened your grand banquet
hall. It wasn't doing anyone any good.
Do you know that after all that work, we
never once had guests? Of course you do.
It began gathering dust as soon as it was
finished. No more. Home is a lively place
now. We melted down the guns you left
behind and cast the metal into chairs so
we could sit while we toast your absence.
Every night I invite everyone up and we
feast on your livestock and drink up your
wine. There's enough to last us several

lifetimes, or at least until you return.
And they are so grateful for my every
word and gesture. All of them, so sweet.
I don't know what to do with their
affection, except perhaps to twirl it
tight and hone and sharpen it into a
blade with which to someday cut you.

Your son is growing strong. He's a strange
kid, quiet, almost never cries. He's got a
full head of hair already. It's blond, like
mine was when I was a girl. His eyes are
yours, and there are times when I can't bear
his gaze, when he's nursing, and he looks
up at me with such wonder, tenderness, and
need, and I can count the times when in my
arms you looked at me like that.

This morning, when he woke, I fed him and
burped him and bounced him on my knee. He
smiled and I cooed to him (I'm a mother
now, I've learned to coo)—"What's your
name?" I said. And just as I was about to
pronounce his name for him, I heard him
say, plainly, "Payne."

I was so startled I almost dropped him. I
asked him again, "What's your name?" Maybe
I forgot to coo, but he just stared at me,
drooling from his little mouth. I asked him

again, and he started to cry. What could
I do but hold him to me, stroke his palm-
sized back, and whisper in his tiny ear?

Felix met up with some sailors who told
tales of prison ships and seas in flames,
black flags snapping in the breeze, cities
melted from above. But they had never heard
of you.

Where are you, Payne? Come Home.

Cordially,

Your Wife

*Two years later, in a hand that was in places almost frightfully
precise, in others quivery and near illegible, Penny wrote these
words:*

Dear Payne,

Our son turned three today. Don't worry,
he's not waiting for your card. We had
a grand old time without you. Carl made
waffles for breakfast, and Xavier baked
a chocolate cake. He could only find two
candles, but Bobby didn't mind. We put on
funny hats and sang to him. It was a happy
birthday, I'd like to say. I really would.
I'd like to gloat and tell you that. I took
him down to the beach, a pleasant outing,
just the two of us. Children adore the

seashore, and he is a child. He wanted to
swim, but it was too cold and the sea too
rough, so I told him no. I would have loved
to swim with him, to frolic in the surf,
to throw him in the air and laugh together,
to fall and flounder and be tossed about by
the waves, clutching each other tight. But
more than that I would have loved it if
he'd thrown a fit when I refused him.
I would have shed tears of my own, but
joyful ones, if only he had cried and
wailed, punched at my thighs, and stamped
his little feet. That's what children are
supposed to do.

That's what you would have done if I had
denied you something. But he didn't even
ask again.

He just stood there and stared at the
sea, at the breakers rolling in. An osprey
could have swooped from the sky and
carried him away and I don't believe he
would've blinked. I tried to distract him.
I sang to him, but he would not sing
with me. I tried to teach him to build
a sandcastle, but he of course ignored me.
So I built one myself. I'd brought down
pails and trowels and a little pink
plastic wheelbarrow and with them I built

such a gorgeous thing, Payne. It was as if
gravity had pardoned me somehow, granted
me some brief reprieve. My towers rose as
tall as I could reach. Some were narrow at
the base—just a single grain in width—and
grew fatter higher up, then thin again, then
fat. Others bent and dipped and twisted all
around. I built freestanding parapets and
buttresses, windows so thin they were
actually transparent, curving sheets and
skeins of sand. I built no walls around it.
I wanted no defenses, nothing fortified,
just height and grace and sweep. It was
not the sort of castle in which anyone
could live. It was the one in which I wish
to live.

Will you believe me if I tell you that it
hurt me to build it, not my hands or my
knees, but that it hurt me almost in the
same way you hurt me, Payne, that it took
something away? Unlike you, though, it was
there, and it was mine, and it was perfect.
Until Bobby knocked it down.

There was no tantrum. He was very calm
about it. Methodical, to the extent that
a three-year-old can be. No words, no
tears. Not even a sniffle. He walked over
and kicked a tower down and then stomped

down the rest. It all fell, just sand.
I had forgotten, but of course it was all
just sand.

Husband, I beat our son. I didn't slap
him. I thrashed him. On his birthday.
I made him cry at last. I made him need
something from me.

I can't ask him to forgive me, and
I wouldn't dream of asking you.

Tonight, he did something he's never done
before. He crawled into my bed. He
wouldn't touch me, but he wouldn't leave
my side. He is asleep beside me now. His
little blond eyelashes are fluttering.
A dream. His tiny chest rises and falls.
His cheeks are bruised.

May this letter be lost at sea. May you
not live to read it.
P.

*Penny let a year go by before she wrote again. She paper-
clipped to her letter a snapshot of a little boy with long blond
curls, frowning, and dressed in a royal-blue sailor suit
trimmed with white. This is what she wrote:*

Dear Payne,
I wish I could say I've forgotten you.
How long is it supposed to take? I forget

everything else: my dreams, my keys, my age, birthdays, the promises I make, my sunglasses, other people's names, the stories they've just finished telling me, the ones they told me last time, the lyrics of songs I've sung a hundred times. I forget the ends of jokes just before I get to them. I forget tasks in the middle of attempting them, and I forget what I was doing before I began the forgotten task, and I stand where I am, lost. I forget to turn off the lights, to take out the trash, to turn off the oven. I have lived through very few things that I have not forgotten. I've forgotten my mother's face and the name of the first boy I kissed, and what he looked like. I've forgotten how I got that scar beneath my knee. I've forgotten most of the first ten years of my life, and recall only the foggiest details of the next ten. I don't mourn this, I only wish I understood the process. Who decides what stays? What mad sifter? Who's in charge of all this throwing away?

There's little that I want to remember. I have most of what I need at hand. But there are things I want to forget, and

you, my love, are one of them. Not that
some of the memories aren't sweet, but
Payne, they break me again and again.

We've heard news of you. Felix, out
fishing, came across some traders with news
of the War. It's still raging, they say.
And yes, they'd heard of you. You've made
quite a name for yourself. Felix brought
home tale after tale of your valor. He
scrambled them all, of course, but the
point was that you're alive. I can't tell
you how happy I was, and how disgusted
I was with my joy.

A month later Felix came in crying,
inconsolable. He had come across a troop
convoy, sailing reinforcements to the
front, and the crew had heard of you, and
one man said he had seen you die. We did
mourn you, Payne, but I've been mourning
all this time. Two months passed and Felix
came across a trawler. There was a soldier
on board who said he'd fought at your side
just days before. What am I to do with
this? Die or don't die, come Home or fade
away. Be at my side or not at all.

How dare you never write me?

Your son has learned your name. I tried
to keep it from him, but someone told him

all about you. No one would admit to it,
despite my demands to know, or perhaps
because of them. He asks after you every
day, and I don't know what to tell him,
so I don't tell him anything.
　　Let me go, Payne. Let me go.
　　Penny

Penny received no reply. Some years later, she learned that the War had ended. Other men had returned to their homes, but Payne had not. No front existed to which she might mail her missives, no headquarters, base camps, or foxholes, so Penny sent no more.

(What about Payne? You've not forgotten him? Well he's not dead, as Penny fears and hopes. Perhaps he should be, who's to say? He's sent many to their graves these last few years, but all is fair, they say, in at least two notoriously difficult situations.

He excelled at War as few men do. Arriving at the front alone, with only Ursula in tow, he was assigned initially to a counterterrorism-covert-op brigade. Payne learned fast. His exploits were legendary. He could slit your throat with a fish-hook, garrote you with a single loose thread from your collar, stop your heart by jabbing just one stiffened finger into any of thirty-six lethal pressure points known only to him. He could shoot the ash off a cigarette from a mile away in the midst of a tornado, and hit it again before it fell to earth. Disguised as a squirrel or a monkey or a crow, he sat motionless in the sway-ing peaks of palm trees for days on end and picked off rebel commanders with his rifle, one by one. He skipped and danced through minefields and scaled the walls into enemy headquarters in broad daylight, emerging with purloined bat-tle plans and strings of ears as souvenirs. Posing as an old woman, with sagging breasts, jowls, and dewlap crafted from plastique and a machine pistol dressed up as a swaddled child, he rescued a captured allied general from a cell in an underground bunker a half-mile beneath the slums of the enemy capital.

Ursula stayed back and kept his boots and buckles shined, his guns oiled, his daggers sharp as the creases in his trousers. Need I mention that she loved him? She rubbed his face with greasepaint before missions and cleaned the blood from under his nails when he returned. She sutured his wounds, massaged aloe vera lotion into his powder-burned hands, bathed him, and greased his battle-tired legs with scented oils. She found him food and cooked his meals—in the third month of a siege and the second week of famine she served him seared foie gras with pears stewed in pomegranate wine. The next night he ate leg of lamb and pan-roasted parsnips. Ursula shot him up with penicillin when he came home with the clap after a night at the admiral's bordel. She lanced Payne's boils, popped his blackheads, trimmed his cuticles, buffed the fungus from his toes, and never expected a word of thanks. One night, after a marathon seventy-two-hour session of wrestling secrets from captive would-be teenaged suicide bombers, Payne got filthy drunk and asked her to suck him off. When she was done, he belched and fell asleep without so much as touching her.

Two weeks later, returning from a covert raid of her own on the enemy officers' commissary, whence she made off with a goose, a tin of fresh white truffles, and a magnum of Chateau Lafitte, Ursula tripped a wire and lost both legs to a land mine. Her cries were silenced by a sniper whose heart had not yet been entirely stripped of mercy. Payne had her court-martialed in absentia for failing to appear on time with his dinner, and replaced her with a downy-lipped boy valet before the sun had time to rise.

He was harsh, yes, but there's no room for swishy sentiment when a war is on. Military discipline can allow no laxity. Lest *you feel too bad about it, it's worth mentioning that it was Ursula who opened Payne's mail and who used Penny's unread letters to buff his boots that lustrous black. Also that she lay awake each night of the last year of her life, in fantasy dying again and again for Payne. Some dreams do come true.)*

8

Mourning

or

Various Stripes of Lament

or

Ain't Always Easy,
Sayin' Goodbye

STRANGE AS IT MAY SEEM, Penny told the truth
when she wrote to Payne that he'd been mourned. Back
at the palace, his health and whereabouts had been the
subject of much speculation, and an abundant source of
anxiety for his onetime followers. At the very least, they
knew his return would mean their expulsion from the
palace, where they had quickly become accustomed to
spending most of their time. It had become, for them, a
Home. They had made it theirs. They carved their names
in the oak of the banquet table and etched enough graf-
fiti into the palace walls to deprive them for good of their

mimetic luster. The once-green lawns were weedy and overgrown in some spots, dead and brown in others, dotted here and there with patches of cannabis and poppies gone to seed, planted by Theo in a lazy stab at horticulture.

Payne's reappearance would surely mean that the slightly depleted bounty of his storerooms would be closed to them for good. Their daily sustenance would once again be a burden all their own, and all the more difficult to bear given the bloating of their livers and the attendant swell of their guts. More than that, though, they feared that Payne, hardened as war hardens men, would not forgive them for abandoning him, and might, accompanied by various unimaginably terrifying comrades in arms, visit some immense violence upon them, that they might all come to join David in the still-burning moat. Even worse, they knew that Payne's return would bring their permanent banishment from all proximity to Penny.

And yet they mourned him. For some, there was surely some real affection there, if only of the sort that a beaten dog develops for its master, who, after all, gives it bones as well as blows. (But this, too, is a form of love and no less real or worthy than the rest.) For others, what Nellie termed "romantic identification" proved quite strong—they knew no other way of imagining themselves men, or at least men capable and deserving of commanding Penny's love, than through the image of Payne. With him gone, they were set free in a most uncomfortable way. Nothing stood between them and Penny, and they were left with only their own impoverished wills and stunted imaginations to bridge that vast divide. And some, bless them (but please bless the others too), saw Penny grieving, and grieved her grief, caring little for the spring from which it flowed, wishing only that it be plugged and she be soothed.

Motives aside, within an hour of Felix's tearful delivery of the news, word had spread that in place of the usual dinner, all would gather the next evening in memory of Payne. Some malicious soul (Izzy) added on to this the claim (false) that Penny had ordered a day of fasting until the event, so for the first time since shortly after Payne and Ursula's departure, they did not all gather at dusk in the banquet hall to bid the day farewell with a few hours of conviviality and fine repast. Carl and Xavier, who had assumed all culinary responsibilities with exceptional enthusiasm, took the day off. The others were left sneaking to the bathroom or the bushes to nosh on leftover drumsticks and kaiser rolls, snort a thumbnailful of speed, or guzzle down a quick plastic pint of gin, half-assedly hiding from each other the crumbs on their shirtfronts, the powder in their nose hairs, and the booze on their breath.

A night of sheet-clenching anxiety and the odd tear passed as slowly as such nights always do, and all spent the daylight hours searching out the remnants of the mourning clothes which the man they were to mourn had at one time so admired. Hans, who was always already mourning, didn't have to search. He openly flouted the fast, announced he would not waste so much as a breath of grief on Payne, and passed the day emptying can after can of malt liquor. The hour arrived, and all save Hans and Elizabeth (who was watching over Bobby) gathered, garbed in the tatters of their long-forgotten uniforms, or in some serviceable substitute thereof, washed and pressed as well as they could manage.

Beneath the vaulted and chandeliered ceilings of the Great Hall, they took seats around the long wooden table, polished to a shine and scattered with hundreds of dandelions and pink carnations. (Felix had been put in charge of the floral arrangements.) They sat quietly, tugging at their buttoned collars, shifting in their seats with discomfort. Carl cleared his throat. Katerina coughed. Felix closed his eyes and hummed a tune beneath his breath until Ollie slapped him in the back of the head. They heard footsteps on the staircase, and turned to see Penny, led along the banister by Zöe, who had spent the night at her side, wiping her tears with silken hankies, stroking her brow, nursing her with warm hibiscus tea and lukewarm Percocets to numb the pain of Paynelessness made permanent.

Penny wore her grief well. She had on the same torn black dress she wore the night they celebrated the completion of the Great Hall in which they sat. Tailored from a clinging, almost sheer, black fabric, unfaded yet by age, it hugged her a touch more snugly now over hips widened by Bobby's precipitous emergence into this dry world of air and light. To this she added a matching veil of a stuff still sheerer, and pinned that up above her furrowed brow. Despite her slightly altered shape, the runnels care had etched between her temples and carved in more diminutive tributaries around her mouth and eyes, Penny looked ravishing. Her hair hung limp. Her mascara streaked black along her cheeks. Her pallor, the hazy painkiller sheen, the blown-out capillaries in the whites of her eyes and the inky rings around them—all only served to deepen her eyes' emerald glow and to further entrance her assembled guests. She sat, and Zöe, after bringing her a tumbler filled with vodka, sat beside her.

A minute passed, and another one. They waited, twitching, for Penny to speak. To take charge somehow. To corral this awful silence. But she didn't even stir to touch her drink.

At long last, Robert found the strength to stand. With shaking hands, he pulled his glasses from one pocket of a black blazer, its shoulders pinched and sleeves too short. From another pocket, he produced a single sheet of paper, which he had already crumpled and worried almost to shreds. He cleared his throat. He swallowed. His Adam's apple bobbed and bobbed again. In a barely audible voice, he announced, "I wrote this poem." And he read:

> *Payne bled?*
> *Could he be dead?*
> *Shot through the head?*
> *With burning lead?*

The earth his bed?
Worms fed?
Is that what they said?

The paper slipped from his quivering hands. He bent to pick it up, shook a tear from his eye, and continued, his voice cracking:

Why couldn't it have been me, instead?

Robert sat, changed his mind and stood, scurried to Penny's side, tripped over his own shoe, changed his mind again, and crawled back to his seat. "Thank you, Robert," Penny said and, with perhaps more grace than he deserved to witness, shaped her lips into a smile.

Arthur took the floor. He pulled himself to his feet with the help of the tabletop, the back of his chair, and a supportive hand from Zöe. His chair scraped against the marble. Tucking his wrinkled shirttails into his wrinkled trousers, he stroked his mustache with all the gravity the occasion demanded, and raised his glass. He struck it three times with a small silver spoon, calling, redundantly, for silence.

"A toast," he said, and with those words Xavier popped from his seat, hustled off to a corner of the room, and wheeled back to the table a brass-and-walnut bar cart. Faces brightened all across the room. While Arthur stood in wait, somewhat unsteadily, a grayish liquid sloshing onto his shirt from his upraised tumbler, Xavier displayed his mixologic genius, the result of many months of self-training, aided, of course, by many an eager, sotted volunteer. With all due somberness, he decanted precise measures of many-shaded liquors into twelve cocktail shakers already filled with ice. He tossed the shakers in tight orbits around his head and—the rest still circling in the air—strained each one into waiting crystal goblets with a steady, skillful hand. Miraculously, the spirits so combined did not blend their hues in any sloggy brownish mix but recombined in even brighter shades. Each retained its chromatic integrity and poured off in distinct prismatic layers. Arthur whistled tunelessly. Penny squinched her eyes. Carl produced a silver serving tray and placed a rainbow-colored cocktail in front of every guest, while Xavier refilled Penny's glass with vodka and refreshed Arthur's drink from an opaque plastic bottle he kept stashed in a low cabinet labeled "Art."

Arthur dipped a pinky into his glass, then licked the finger. He bowed deeply to Penny, who was now staring at her hands. He thanked Xavier and Carl, and looked questioningly to Zöe, who smiled reassuringly back. He began.

"We all knew Payne," he said, and paused to sip his drink.

"Payne was a man," he continued. "Who married Penny." Arthur rubbed at his eye.

"And then he went away. Far away." His voice trailed off into the frothy surface of his beverage. It hissed audibly back at him. Arthur took another swallow and gazed from face to face.

"Now," he went on, "he's dead."

Arthur, roused, stamped his foot and said it again. "He's dead." He spelled it out. "D-E-A-D, dead. Dead as a box of hammers. Dead as a doorknob. Dead as a mouse after you stomp it good and throw it in the fire and piss on the fire to put it out and use the ashes to make soap and wash with it 'til there's just a sliver left that gets stuck between your toes and you find it later in your sock. Just like that. Dead." He stood, swaying slightly, nursing his drink and clawing at his stomach through his shirt, considering the profundity of all he'd said. He had just begun to spell the word again, "D-E-A- . . . " when Zöe came to his side and, with a yank and a gentle shove, sat him down.

"Thank you, Art," she said, and everyone drank, and courteously applauded. Except for Penny, who did not move at all, except to rearrange her lips into a tense and distant smile.

Izzy was the next to rise. He wore a crimson velvet dinner jacket and had pinned one of Felix's carnations to his lapel. He hooked his thumbs through his suspenders and began. "I'll never forget the first time I met Payne. I had gotten up at just before dawn to hike in the hills and clear my mind for a spell, to ready myself for a brand-new day. I scaled a steep and crumbling cliff and, perched atop a boulder, let my legs dangle and watched the antelope frolic in the meadows as I skimmed through my pocket Rilke. The shriek of a goshawk inspired me to compose a few verses of my own, and I had just put pen to paper when I saw him there crouching in the reeds. 'My friend,' I said, 'show yourself.' But he didn't stand. How rude, I thought, and I strolled over, intending to correct his manners in a way he'd not forget. I grabbed him by the shoulder and spun him around, 'Sir,' I said, 'do not insult me.'

"What I saw shocked me—Payne's fine-boned but rough and masculine face was streaked with tears of pity. In his hand he held a wounded bird. It was just a little birdie, a sapling of a bird. Its wing was broken, its delicate feathers matted with dew, and it peeped in a most pathetic way. To see an innocent creature suffering always brings out the fire in me, and I embraced Payne and said, 'Friend, we must find the villain who harmed this suckling birdie and punish him posthaste!'

"Payne took my arm with a manly grasp and said, 'No, sir, please, calm yourself, and let pity fill your heart. For if a man was cruel enough to bring such misery to this sinless seedling of a birdie, if any man's heart be so vacant of charity and feeling, be assured he suffers sufficiently and needs no further punishment from us.'

"I can tell you now without embarrassment that I was so moved by his compassion that I burst out in tears myself. 'Curse me, so quick to find fault in other men!' I said. 'More likely it was the unthinking viciousness of Nature that has damaged this adorable twig of a bird. Unable yet to fly, it must have fallen from its mother's nest and limped and wandered in mortal anguish to the spot in which you found it.' And we wept at the thought and hugged each other tight with tender manliness.

"'No, kind sir,' said Payne, tears of fellow feeling streaming down his bronzed, bewhiskered cheek, 'I would not have you resent this world. Truly, it would break my heart right here beneath my ribs,' and he put my palm on his firm, well-muscled breast, 'to know that as good a man as you had lost faith in the gentle beneficence of nature. For nature is generosity herself. She provides all good and comely things for all her creatures in harmony and grace. No, do not blame the gods or the sacred generative powers of the earth, for nature is beauty and beauty is goodness and no evil can spring forth from her.'

"And he paused to behold the tiny creature peeping so miserably in his cupped hand, its little eyes glassy with pain, and a tear streamed down his face and fell from the tip of his nose onto the birdie's little head, where it burst into droplets like a shower of grace. And he took my hand in his and said, 'No, good sir, we cannot blame our fellow men for the suffering of this lambkin bird, for they are good as the gods that spawned them, and we cannot blame the truly first-rate forces of nature, unsurpassable in her benevolence. No, sir, if anyone is to blame, it is this wretched, ingrate bird itself,' and Payne closed his virile fist around it until we heard its little bones crack and the pathetic peeping stopped. And we embraced again with mannish vigor and wept there together until the sun was high in the sky."

Nellie feigned a cough and emptied her drink down the front of Izzy's trousers. "Sorry, dear," she said. She looked around. "Maybe someone has a paper towel." No one volunteered.

Izzy patted at his crotch with a balled-up Kleenex, leaving globelets of shredded white tissue all along the black fabric of his fly. "It's cold," he said, and smiled stiffly.

Izzy sat, and all was quiet save the rattling of ice in empty glasses. Penny stared off into an unlit corner of the hall. Her gaze was sharp, as if she were trying hard to make out the contours of the dim. Xavier mixed another round of cocktails. Carl served them, and no one said a word until Lily hoisted herself to her feet, which spilled out of a delicate pair of patent-leather pumps. Her little black dress could barely contain her breasts, and the flesh of her rounded shoulders fought to snap its narrow straps. She leaned on Theo for support. "I'll never forget the first time I met Payne either," she said, and paused for a long, meditative sip of her drink. "Always a gentleman. He called me fat."

Cries of exaggerated bafflement tumbled from every mouth but Penny's. "No!" said Felix. "No!" said Kate. "No!" said Ollie and Zöe and Garth. "No!" cried Theo, loudest of all.

"Yes," said Lily, sliding her empty glass across the table in Xavier's direction. "What he actually said was, 'Fatty, get off your ass.' I was shoveling coal for Queenie's fires, all day every day. Black from head to toe with coal dust—even my sweat was black. When I brushed my teeth at night the toothpaste I spat out was black."

Lily reached for her glass. Finding it still empty, she banged it on the tabletop, prompting Xavier to spin eight bottles in the air. A moment later, Carl stood behind Lily with her drink on a tray. She took it. "In the morning my eyes were crusted shut with black. But that day I was working. I was shoveling and shoveling and I put down my shovel for just a second, sat down to have a snort. Then Payne came by, dressed all in white. Golf shirt to tassel loafers, all bleach-stain white. I'll never forget that man. 'Get off your ass,' he said. Called me 'Fatty.'" She raised her glass above her head and nodded in Penny's direction.

But Penny's eyes had closed.

"To Payne," said Lily, and slapped her ass and drank.

When the applause died down, Sally rose to speak. Before she could get a word out, though, Carl and Xavier arrived at the head of the table, wheeling in a carving cart bearing a roasted pig reclining on an enormous silver platter. In the pig's mouth was an apple, peeled and carved into a near-perfect semblance of Payne's face. The roast had green grapes in place of eyes, on each of which Carl had drawn an iris and pupil with red magic marker. It wore a garland of pink carnations around the crisped flesh of its neck, and its ears were singed an ashy black. The pig was lavishly garnished with apples Cockaigne, tomatoes Florentine, Brussels sprouts, and tiny roasted songbirds, unplucked. Its snout rested on its forelegs, browned and stretched out before it, trotters and all.

Xavier honed a three-foot blade, more sword than carving knife, with an equally oversized steel and commenced slicing off, on first the right side, then the left, the foreleg and the ham. Penny's face crumpled like an old paper bag. A low groan rumbled from her throat. She shut her eyes.

"Take it away," she said, her voice hardly a whisper.

"Pardon?" said Carl.

And Penny yelled, "Take the pig away!"

Carl and Xavier blanched. "As you wish," muttered Carl, and they wheeled the creature back to the kitchen.

All was silent for one long moment in which every muscle in the room contracted. Even the air itself seemed pinched. Then Penny, her face red, the tendons in her neck taut, hurled the glass in her hand through the stained-glass window directly above the door, smashing a panel depicting Payne dispensing bow-tied gifts.

"Idiots!" she yelled.

She grabbed Arthur's glass and tossed it through another window, this one an image of her reclining languidly on a couch, legs crossed but slightly open, arms behind her head. It fractured into a rain of a thousand colored shards, which hung in the air for one extended moment before clattering all at once to the ground.

"Idiots!"

She smacked Izzy in the back of the neck and yanked Art's chair out from under him.

"How dare you!" she yelled. "How dare you even imagine you have earned the right to say even one word about that man, much less sully him and stain my grief with these stupid, stupid, stupid . . ." She grabbed wildly at the air, groping for an adequate word. Finding none, she twisted Izzy's collar. "You wretch! You miserable, useless, lying wretch!" She twirled around and smacked the drink from Lily's fist. "And you! Dainty thing, he called you fat. Imagine!" She glared across the table at Robert, but he did not raise his downcast eyes. "All of you—you drink and you eat and you leer and you fuck and that's all you're fucking good for!"

The flush had left Penny's face. She appeared almost calm as she reached behind Xavier's abandoned bar cart, brought out a bottle of some syrupy, scarlet liqueur, and lobbed it upwards, immediately following it with what came next to hand: a bottle of chartreuse, a liter of purple Pucker, flasks of bright blueberry and banana schnapps. All eyes rose to the vaulted ceiling. The first bottle collided in a brilliant, shimmering explosion with the chandelier that hung above the table, beneath which everyone leapt for cover, hands over their heads to shield themselves from the downpour of crimson-stained hailstones and icicles of crystal that crashed down all around them. The next bottle dislodged the sturdy brass armature of the chandelier from its bolt on the ceiling, and the third, fourth, and fifth bottles aided one another in knocking the fixture free from its mooring until, with a squeal and a groan of relief, it hastened to chase the ornaments which had so suddenly fled from its arms, and fell like an anchor onto the polished tabletop. The old oak table collapsed in a great splintering burst, flattening the refugees gathered beneath it.

Lily was the first to crawl out. She shook a sticky mist of blended liquors from her fingers, kicked off a broken heel, and helped Theo to his feet. He in turn helped Penny up, attempted to brush off her dress but was rebuked with a shove that almost sent him sliding to the floor again as the others one by one dragged themselves out and upright. Lily scouted out an unbroken bottle and an unbroken glass, and poured herself a measure. Sipping, she surveyed the wreckage around her, the shattered crystal and ragged wood, everywhere splashed and puddled with polychromatic booze. She regarded Penny, who stood apart from the rest, dabbing her forehead with a folded paper napkin. Lily looked around at the others, who were all gazing at Penny too, a gritty admixture of sheepishness, fear, and desperate expectation sticking to their faces.

"She's right, you know," said Lily, as if speaking to herself. "About us." And swaying her shoulders and hips in a slow and mournful rhythm, Lily began to sing, her voice breaking at first but growing fuller and more confident with every word: "We drink and we eat and we leer and we fuck." She pulled Theo to her. He joined his small, nasal voice to Lily's by now throaty lament, and soon all were on their feet, hands clasped, heads hanging heavy with contrition, dancing in a wide ring around Penny, who stood alone, blank-eyed and leaden, spent by her outburst, emptied out. Her arms hanging at her sides, she stared at the ground, littered with glass, at her own broken image as, their voices echoing now with almost earnest mournfulness, they crooned her words back to her: "We drink and we eat and we leer and we fuck and we drink and we eat and we leer and we fuck . . . "

After a few rounds, the rhythm began to waver. Voices fell off here and there, and the ring of dancers began to dissolve as one or another dancer, distracted, unclasped a partner's hand to brush away some previously unnoticed but suddenly itching mote of debris. Without the chandelier the hall was dim. Only three weak bulbs remained, perched in imitation torches bolted to the columns that lined the room. The night air whistled in through the broken windows. It bounced about the vaulted ceiling, rising to a low and hollow moan, competing with the murmur of voices and footfalls below. Lily's voice dropped almost to a whisper. The shadows of the few remaining dancers stretched and flickered in the thin yellow light as they crunched across the glittering carpet of glass beneath their feet.

Felix broke away and tapped Penny on the shoulder. "I," he stuttered, "I—I wrote a song for you." He crawled under the now severely truncated table, and, emerging with an accordion strapped around his shoulder, rushed back to Penny's side. A disco ball crashed to the ground beside him. Most of the others had wandered off, converging in a dark corner to fight over the few remaining intact bottles. Someone moaned from beneath the wreckage of the table. Whether it was in agony or delight was not clear. Neither Felix nor Penny paid any attention. Felix blew a lock of hair from his eyes and pumped his instrument gently, releasing one soft, plaintive note. He led it fade entirely, and then, tapping one diminutive foot on the floor, commenced to play.

His song was very simple, just three slow and quavering chords, jerked out by his clumsy fingering but echoing nonetheless with all the sad and broken optimism that only that noble instrument can convey. Accompanied by the ambient percussion of smashes and crashes, moans and crunches and thuds, Felix sang:

> *Penny you're so pretty,*
> *I don't know what to do.*
> *Don't want you to be sad,*
> *Anyone but you.*
> *Penny you're so pretty,*
> *Why dontcha come with me?*
> *I'll wipe the tears from your eyes,*
> *And you can be with me.*

Felix swung the heavy accordion in front of him. A calm smile took over his face as he arrived at the chorus.

> *Don't cryyyy, pretty Penny,*
> *Don't waaiiil, pretty Penny,*
> *Don't grooaaan or pull your hair.*
> *Don't cryyyy, pretty Penny,*
> *Don't waaiiil, pretty Penny,*
> *Don't mooaaan or kick the chair.*

Felix shook his hips. He shimmied across the floor, pumping all the while. The others noticed his playing not at all, nor that moisture had begun to pool in Penny's eyes, and the slightest, softest, saddest of smiles was only barely, almost undetectably beginning to deform her cracking lips.

Was it Felix who won that smile? Or was it the sight of little Bobby standing on the stairs, escaped from Elizabeth's perhaps excessively opiated watch, his face framed by the bars of the banister, a study in blankness with sailor cap askew? Penny didn't stick around to say, but climbed the stairs to put her boy to bed.

——— ———

A Brief Addendum
to Chapter 8:
Morning

MORNINGS, DAMN THEM, ALWAYS ARRIVE, and most often precisely when they are welcome least—following the night. And so the morning came. It greeted Penny with a rap to each of her temples, another behind her eyes, and a fourth to the tender bottom of her brainpan, perversely tempering these assaults by caressing every crease and curl of her intestines and by blowing a long, thirsty, vodka-flavored kiss up her trachea to the roots of her tonsils. Lest it be judged too severely, morning took mercy and decreed that these discomforts would, for a little while, be permitted to upstage the agony and ambivalence that might accompany any wakeful recollection of her recent widowhood. Ungrateful for this dispensation, Penny pulled a pillow over her head, and did her best to snatch herself some sleep.

As for the others, sleep had eluded all of them (save Bobby, who lay curled and dreaming beneath his twin-sized covers; Elizabeth, his sometime keeper, who snored softly at his feet; and Hans, who had sat out the preceding night's proceedings in favor of a solitary jag). Shortly after Penny had retreated to her bed the night before, Oliver had produced a plump baggie of methamphetamine, mysteriously brown in hue ("Cut with cocoa," opined Izzy), from an inner pocket of his coat. Lines were methodically cut and sucked into awaiting nose-holes. Feet tapped. Knees jumped. Teeth gnawed at gums. Eyelids twitched and twitched some more. Felix crooned up-tempo versions of his Penny-centric love ballads until Lily, at Theo's urging, again took up her eating-drinking-leering-fucking chorus. All clasped hands once more, and skipped quick rings around the ruins of the table. If earlier, in Penny's presence, some small degree of penitent self-awareness had pervaded their singing, now, in her absence, a rebellious note prevailed. They had outlived Payne! And so they sang, grinning and mugging, their every footfall boastful as they belted out the words, an unanswerable rebuke to their departed host.

The tempo gathered speed. They danced in tight circles for what well may have been an hour, or longer still, until at last they began to tire and grow irritable, not to mention dizzy. They began tripping over one another, falling and shoving. A fight broke out here, predictably enough, and another there. Lily landed a fist in Robert's belly. Felix tore at Joseph's hair. Their semirhythmic chanting was soon replaced by the sounds—all exclamation points, number signs, ampersands, and question marks—of garments tearing, crockery shattering, fists colliding with ribs and chins and cheekbones. Robert winged a salad plate at his assailant. Improbably, he missed her. Echoing Penny's earlier efforts, the plate took out a window. They were all so thrilled by the resulting cascade of glass that they forgot about fighting and took to smashing things. Theo and Ollie aimed soup spoons and butter knives at the lights left on the ceiling. Sally, perched on Katherine's shoulders, an upended gin bottle in her fist, methodically smashed every windowpane within reach that Penny had left whole. Nellie waded into the murky fountain and kicked the heads off seven marble putti. Yves wrenched off a bat-sized section of banister and wrecked everything he could.

This went on—rugs torn to ribbons, cushions slashed, and drywall shattered—until there was nearly nothing left to destroy, which happened to be almost precisely the moment that Penny surrendered to morning's insistent heckles, slipped on her robe, swallowed three aspirin and, on second thought, another Percocet, and walked stiffly down the stairs.

The dust had only just begun to settle. The banquet hall of which Payne had been so proud was now a tangled mess of rubble, broken glass, and floating pillow down. The faces of his onetime followers were white with powdered plaster. Their hands were bloodied, their clothes in shreds. Theo was naked. They slumped speechless before Penny. She descended the last two steps of the staircase and gazed from face to face, her own eyes red-rimmed and blank. She kicked at a severed marble wing.

"You'll clean this up," she said.

She turned to leave. But before she had climbed a single stair, the heavy door at the other end of the hall swung open. Hans stumbled in. He was a sight—unshaven, bug-eyed, hair matted with ash—but he looked a shade better than all the others present (save Penny, of course). He staggered across the room, taking no notice of its state, pausing only to trip on a broken floorboard. When he reached the base of the staircase, Hans dropped to one knee. He squeezed Penny's hands between his own trembling fingers. His eyes bloated with tears, his throat dry and rattling, he uttered just two words: "Marry me."

Penny brushed his hands from hers but didn't say a word. Her face revealed nothing, not surprise, anger, or disgust. Not even exhaustion. Hans gripped her ankles and pleaded, "Please, Penny . . ." Before he could get another sentence out, Ollie shoved his way between them.

"Don't pay him any mind," he said, his voice a throaty whisper. "It's too soon, I know. You need time." Ollie reached out to smooth her hair, and went on undiscouraged when, with eyes still empty of emotion, Penny slapped his hand away. "And please, when you feel ready, please turn your thoughts to me." But Kate was already standing behind Penny, massaging her shoulders and the nape of her neck and murmuring unintelligibly in her ear. And Felix dropped his accordion with an echoing crash and thrust himself between Ollie and Penny's knee. "Me!" he shrieked. "I love you more!" And Nellie elbowed him aside and yelled, "Me!" And Lily threw Kate to the ground and roared in Penny's ear, "Me!" And Izzy clamped his hand over Nellie's mouth so he too could yell, "Me!" And Arthur and Zöe pulled at each other's hair to be the first one at Penny's side to yell, "Me!" And Carl shoved the apple-carved visage of Payne into Xavier's mouth to prevent him from also yelling, "Me!" And Garth and Joseph, somber Queenie, shivery Robert, dizzy Sally, swooshy Yves, all of them, there in the shambles they had made of her Home, threw themselves at Penny's feet to yell, "Me!"

And so concerned were they to get there first and yell the loudest and mute each other's cries that not one of them noticed when Penny, without a word, walked off. They kept on shouting and shoving one another until it was undeniably evident that the object of their desire was no longer within reach, if ever she had been. Then, following a brief exchange of furtive, bashful glances, Penny's suitors dispersed.

(How does the saying go—don't count your chickens 'til they come home to roost? All those obituary excesses were premature, it seems, and vain, for Payne still walked and breathed, a hero now, at loose. When, after all the years of bloodshed, a treaty was at last negotiated, Payne was among the luminaries packed along the dais to sign it, the stars on his epaulettes gleaming, his chest a forest of ribbons, bars, and medals. He took comfort in the knowledge that should anyone try anything funny in lieu of surrendering, he could slaughter the lot of them with just the nib of his pen. He set sail for home in a tall gray battleship, its holds overflowing with enough gold bricks to build a stadium, enough silk to tent a continent, a quantity of rare and fragrant spices sufficient to corner the world market on flavor for a century or more. He had the afterdeck cleared of the cannons and stacked chests of gems that cluttered its surface, which he then devoted to horticulture so as to have an acre of fresh flowers ready for Penny upon his return. After all, he did love her, for what that's worth, and, having done what he set out to do, fully intended to return to her side and make up for the long years' absence with riches and a reputation won.

But things did not work out. Payne did not count on the sea's cruel whimsy, its arsenal of gales, waterspouts, and whales. He did not count on the ocean's vastness, nor on the sparse distribution of habitable land. He did not expect his crew to rebel, nor did he calculate the wiles of giants, witches, or proud and peevish gods, all of which delayed him further. Someone else may see fit to one day relay the full story of those oafish misadventures. Not I. For me, it will suffice to say that Payne went to hell and back, and still could not find Home.

And now? Well Payne's not lost, not really lost, in the spatial-relations sort of sense. He knows where he is. He's neither Gilligan nor Crusoe, not trapped on some deserted island, barefoot and bearded, lighting fires to attract passing planes. He could get back Home. In fact, he wants to, if he only knew how. There he is, beneath us, in the chaise longue by the pool, refilling his gin and tonic from the pitcher beside him. He's wearing sunglasses and a visor, and his nose is white with zinc because the sun is bright and strong, so bright, in fact, that he cannot see us for its glare as we hover here above him in the sky. Payne wears gauzy white boxers and an open terry-cloth robe, and a pair of bedroom slippers sits beside him on the ground. An inflatable goose floats listlessly in the blue water of the pool.

His drink refreshed and just as quickly drained, Payne rubs lotion from a bottle into the bronzed skin of his chest. He has some scars you haven't seen before. Recall: the human body in its nakedness is oozy and weak. It has no scales or horns or talons. So a thicket of white lines courses across Payne's knee where it was pierced by shards of burning metal from a frag-mentation grenade. A long, diagonal welt carved by a scimitar traverses his chest, his nipples on each side of it like the opposing circles of a percent sign. There's a keloid on his jaw where a bullet grazed it, and a slash from a bayonet remains imprinted on his face, snaking from his temple to his cheek. His *zinc-caked nose, once straight, is crooked, but Payne is still a handsome man. He removes his shades to rub his eye, and there's an undeniable power—and at the moment an uncharacteristic tenderness—to those eyes, blurred by gin though they may now be. But look closer, before he returns his glasses to his face. Payne's eyes are tearing. Is it the sun? Could it be hay fever? Has he rubbed them with suntan lotion? Or squirted them with lime? No, listen carefully. Hear that soft whimper? It seems that Payne, strong Payne, is crying. Can this be?)*

9

An Arrival

or

First Flotsam

or

This Bright New World

BENEATH THE DUNES, on the sand, in the foaming yellowed surf below the sinking sun, among other castaways, including three wave-worn two-by-fours; the remains of 81 plastic shopping bags of varying dimensions; one human hand, missing ring finger and thumb; a rusted hammer; 21 syringes; most of an eyeless halibut; 139 beer cans, their labels bleached by sun and salt; the bloated carcass of a dog; two glass crack stems, one of them still usable; 48 billowing condoms; four and one-half quivering gobs of purplish ectoplasm, perhaps once jellyfish, squid, or biochemical waste; one corked bottle, inside it a note (blank); the spine of a moray eel; six dead birds, five gulls and one cormorant; a four-carat diamond ring; 319 bottle caps—among these other items, tossed up on the shore by the combined calculations of fate, gods, and tide, Felix also finds a man. Crumpled and battered, but nonetheless a man. He floats listlessly in a tide pool, faceup but with eyes closed, bobbing with the tedious comings and goings of the sea. He wears only banners of kelp, a crust of salt, and his own matted hair. There is very little left of him. Bones poke almost through his flesh, which is blue and taut and thin. Felix at first is certain he is dead. He attempts to reunite him with the three-fingered hand he discovered down the beach, but is foiled, as the man already has two hands, each one five-fingered and complete.

"Hey, mister," Felix says, but the man does not respond. Felix kicks him in the ribs. This too elicits no response. Felix drops his bag of bottle caps on the sand and puts his ear to the man's bare chest. It's like listening to a conch shell—Felix hears the low rushing of waves, water scraping through the rocks, and decides the man is breathing. He places his hand on the man's heart and feels a faint and broken rhythm there.

"Mister," he says again, "get up."

Felix's entreaties are ignored, so he tries to hoist the man up on his shoulders. But, skeletal and famished though he is, the man is too heavy for Felix to lift alone. He ties his bag to his belt, grabs the man by the ankles, and drags him, his hair gathering sandy clumps of tar, his head bouncing off driftwood and rocks, back to Felix's plywood and tarpaper home in the hills. There he lays him out on the bed, props a pillow beneath his head, and lights a fire. As it crackles and sparks, Felix sits on his one broken-backed chair and rolls himself a cigarette. He lights it from an ember in the stove, empties his bag of bottle caps into the barrel with the others, and pulls his ukulele from its hook on the wall. With his cigarette stuck to his bottom lip, he tunes his instrument, strikes a few exploratory chords, and sings to his guest:

> *Hey mister, you sure aren't a fish,*
> *Hey mister, you sure ain't a crab,*
> *Hey mister, I hope you ain't a jellyfish,*
> *A giant lobster, a shark or a man-eating*
>   *squid,*
> *But mister, I know you aren't a fish.*

He rehooks the ukulele, unsatisfied, and puffs at his cigarette, wondering what to do.

By evening, the man has still not stirred, and Felix leaves for dinner without him. At the now rather Frankensteinian dining-room table—jerry-rigged back into service with twisted clothes hangers, duct tape, wood screws, and several pounds of putty—Felix slices into his steak and mentions to Sally that he's come upon an unusual animal washed up on the shore.

"Is it a whale?" Sally asks.

"Nope," says Felix.

"Not a whale, huh? Is it a baby seal?"

"Nope."

"Not a whale or a baby seal? A sea cucumber?"

"Nope."

"Not a whale or a baby seal or a sea cucumber?" Sally asks, flummoxed. "Was it maybe a giraffe?"

"Not that either," Felix mumbles, his mouth filled with beef. "Found a man."

"A what?"

"Man."

"A man?"

"Yep."

Sally's eyes swell and she sucks in her breath. "Is it him?" she whispers.

"Him?"

"You know," Sally says, leaning forward. *"Him."*

"Nope," says Felix, but Sally's not convinced. She balls up her napkin and tosses it across the table at Katerina to get her attention and tell her about this man. It hits Kate in the eye, though. On nearly any other evening such a provocation would likely be answered in kind—with a hurled potato, say, a slab of meat or a bubbling tureen of melted cheese—but tonight no one's in the mood, and Katerina just shrugs it off and looks away. They're no more hungover than usual, and nothing in particular has happened to get them all depressed, but tonight everyone's sick of everything, and especially of each other. So they sit in crowded silence like a big collective scowl. Sally gets peeved when her Katinka ignores her, so she forgets to whisper, "Felix found a *man!*" and instead sits sulking and stabbing at her sirloin.

Feeling something tugging at his foot, Felix peeks beneath the table to investigate. Bobby's crouching there, fumbling with the laces on Felix's right shoe. Felix yanks his foot away and sees that Bobby has loosed every lace in the house and knotted each to the shoe beside it, forming a vast daisy chain of footwear beneath the table, binding each and all to the tablemates beside them. He's exempted his mother, and anchored one of Arthur's laces to a chair. Felix winks at Bobby, and puts a finger to his mouth. When he's swallowed the last of his steak, he pushes out his chair, liberates his laces, and taps Penny on the shoulder.

"I found a man," he says.

Penny's spine stiffens. "Where?" she demands.

"The beach," Felix says.

"Take me to him," Penny says.

"Now?" asks Felix, but Penny is already walking to the door.

There is no moon, but Felix knows the path. His feet make their way instinctively around rocks and broken bottles and oil-slicked shreds of tire. Penny, in sandals, stumbles behind him, and takes his hand for guidance. An incomparable warmth, a luminous inner softness, radiates through his wrist and up and down his trunk. He walks more slowly, partly out of concern for Penny's unclad feet, mainly to prolong her touch. But Penny's thoughts are elsewhere, if they can even be termed thoughts, so fractured are they, spliced with hope and fear and loathing—hope that it will be Payne he's found, and hope that it will not; fear that he'll be hurt or dead, and fear that he will not; loathing of Payne for leaving, and of herself for caring still.

Though Felix can plainly feel the too-quick pulsing of blood in her palm, he senses none of this, and doesn't think to wonder. Grateful that his fingers are intertwined with hers, he doesn't think at all. But as soon as they've pushed aside the door to Felix's hillside hovel, and Felix has lit a kerosene lamp, Penny lets drop his hand as you might let go the guardrail on the bus once your stop's been reached and the brakes have finished squealing. She kneels before the stranger. She takes a breath and brushes the sand and hair from his brow. Penny sees a face she's never seen before, and when she at last exhales her whole body deflates like a child's ball that's been kicked too hard. It's not Payne. The anticipation and anger hiss out of her, leaving only familiar ache. She lets her head fall to the man's ribs, half out of exhaustion, half to listen to the arrhythmic wobbling of his heart.

"Do you have water here?" she asks. Felix sorts through the clutter on the table and produces a yellow plastic pitcher, half-full.

"No," Penny says, "I mean running water, faucets, a tub." Felix shakes his head.

"Help me take him, then, Home."

From a doubled-over sheet tied at the corners to a broom and to a mop handle (which otherwise would both go entirely unused), Felix crafts a makeshift stretcher. They carry the man back to the palace, dropping him only once. Chemical fires still burn green and blue and pink in the moat, lighting their way across and in through a back gate, thus avoiding the banquet hall, from which thuds and helpless shouts have just begun to echo.

Penny changes into an old pair of corduroys. Felix tries to look away. She runs a bath and tests the water with her elbow. Felix helps her lift the man into the tub. The water darkens with dried blood, kelp, and sand. A shriveled sea slug and a small school of brine shrimp float to the surface. Penny squirts baby shampoo into the running water and bubbles foam forth, concealing the muck. She rubs a washcloth with soap and washes the stranger entirely, taking great and gentle care between the bruised furrows of his ribs, on the long raised welts along his shoulders and thighs, between his fingers and his toes, and in other nooks and corners that bring a blush to Felix's cheeks. She shampoos and conditions his hair, cuts away insoluble knots and tangles, trims his beard, and shaves his face.

Felix helps her dry him, and as they carry him into the guest room, the stranger's eyes flutter and then stay open, glassy and scared. The first thing he sees in this bright new world is something unnamable at the very bottom of the bottomless green of Penny's eyes as she stares down at him, something beyond her immediate fear and concern, beyond anything she feels at this second or any other. And if he remembered anything before this moment—his name, the various syllables and numerals that tie him to the world, his favorite color, his subcultural allegiances and ideological commitments, the number of candles on his last birthday cake, any of the endless and endlessly banal statistics of selfhood—he has already forgotten it. His limbs are limp, unmovable, and his temples burn with fever. Penny and Felix lay him out on the bed. His cracked lips twitch, and bleed a little, but he says nothing. "Shhh," says Penny. "Don't try to speak."

She sends Felix to get a pitcher of water and a glass, layers the bed with dry towels, and rolls the stranger onto them. She squeezes oil into her hand from a bottle beside the bed and warms it between her palms. She rubs it into his shins and flaccid calves, awakening with her hands the desiccated skin of his ankles and his cut and callused feet. Felix returns with the water. She lifts the glass to the stranger's lips as he drinks one glass and then another. When it spills out of the corners of his mouth, she wipes him dry with a cloth, then sends Felix to the kitchen for a cup of broth, and squirts more oil into her palm. She works her hands up the shrunken muscles of his thighs, and reaches under him, to rub to life his wasted buttocks. Will it shock you if I reveal that Penny, left so long alone, lingers on the stranger's upper thighs, rubbing oil into his jutting hip bones and the plains below his navel and then, holding her breath, into his drooping penis, which, miracle of miracles, proves livelier than its owner, and stands? A flutter of arousal, long forgotten, wiggles in her gut. She refreshes the oil in her hand and rubs the length of it from crown to root and up again, watching it shimmer. But sadness, and revulsion—not for this body here in front of her, but for herself and her own desire—overcome her, and she lifts her hands, moving quickly to his concave stomach and scarred and hillocked ribs.

When Felix returns, the stranger's gone soft again, and Penny has dried the tear that dropped from her eye onto his throat and is rubbing his joyless forearms with professional disinterest. But Felix is as jealous as he's ever been, watching Penny's hands caress another man, even one half or nearly dead, wishing he'd left him in the foam with the syringes, the hand, and the rotting dog.

(We left Payne crying by the pool. Even Payne, you see, has feelings. In fact, larger ones than most swell beneath his breast, supersized to match the scale of such a life. And if he lets them show, allows sadness to creep forth from the caverns of his heart and unveil itself on his face in full view of sun and sky, rest assured he's feeling something Big. Poor Payne is sick with longing. He shifts in the chaise longue and regards the ripples in the chlorinated water of the pool, the noiseless bobbing of the blow-up rubber goose. He watches wavelets beat stupidly and without end against the blue-tiled walls, and he feels himself swallowed in the infinity of repetition. How many years has it been since he's lain in his own bed, at home in Penny's arms, swaddled safely in her gaze? And how many days has he passed here in waste and idleness, up to his red-rimmed eyeballs in gin and quinine beside this pool, awaiting the return of the mistress of the house from work?

Yes, there's another woman here. That should not be surprising. And no, I won't reveal her name. It shall remain hidden, covered up. She's got a life of her own to live and ought not be publicly smeared for her misfortune, for falling for a married man. The revelation of her dalliance with one so illustrious as Payne would only bring the wolves to her door, and rob her forever of the privacy of memory, which is all, in the end, that Payne will leave her. It's enough to say that she adores him, that she knows he loves another but has learned through patient endurance of repeated disappointments to take what she can get. She asks little of Payne, and does all she can to lure him to her, to pad for him a nest, to shake from his mind all remembrance of Penny.

Clearly, she fails. But Payne, it should be said, is a willing participant in his own amnesia. In the late afternoon, he removes his robe and boxers and swims laps in the pool for an hour to sweat off the gin and, through pure exertion, shed his homesick anguish. He sweats in the hot tub to cast out the day's last tears before going indoors to shower, shave, and dress.

His keeper arrives. She kisses him and rubs his shoulders. She opens a bottle of wine, rolls a joint, and orders in for dinner. Before the food arrives, she undresses Payne and, right there on the couch, coaxes him to climb into the corporeal caverns which they together carve. They finish just moments before the buzzer rings, and she pulls Payne's shirt over her shoulders and tips the delivery boy with a flush and a smile. When dinner's done, she uncorks another bottle, lights another joint, and leads him to her silk-sheeted bed, where together they chase away all discontent, reveling in mutual wants immediately satisfied.

Every day is the same, though the food changes and the lovemaking varies according to their whims. Payne leads a life for which most men would kill, but when he wakes in the morning alone, hours after she's left for work, the sun streaming through the vertical blinds directly into his eyes, Payne again begins to grieve. He stumbles from the bed, its sheets still warm with last night's pleasures, and, before he has finished rubbing the sleep from his eyes, commences sobbing. Strange as it may seem, this life of simple gratification does not agree with Payne, poor slouched and sobbing Payne, one-time champion of freedom, of walking straight and tall. Here, where all is homey, where nothing but leisure and delight reside, he chafes and yearns for Home. When the sun is shining, without the immediacy of her body present, Payne quickly forgets his mistress and dwells on what he lacks. He gets out of bed, brushes his teeth, and shits. He fills a pitcher with ice and gin, a splash of tonic and a squeeze of lime. He dons his visor, hides his tears behind his shades, and heads poolside to begin the day again.)

10

Welcoming

or

A Name-Day Feast

or

Platypus Perhaps

THE STRANGER NEVER DID REMEMBER his name, his geographical origins, or any of the details of the past we laboriously accumulate as a dung beetle collects the ball it rolls before it. If the fever that for three days burned within him provoked any revealing visions or in any way jogged the striking neurons in the barricaded corners of his brain, he did not let on. He lay glassy-eyed and still, uncurious. It was as if he had been sired by the sea and sand themselves, and spit out after a gestation a couple of decades tardy, as if the wounds on his body were but recent scars of that slow and painful birthing. He could, however, speak.

This was discovered first of all by Zöe, who tended him while Penny slept (Felix was dismissed from that duty when

Penny caught him encouraging young Bobby to pinch the sleeping patient's nostrils shut, a task to which the boy required little prodding). She was sitting in a chair beside his bed when his fever broke. He woke from a day-long sleep and opened eyes which were, for the first time, unglazed. Zöe, it should be mentioned, is no eyesore. Many men, and not a few women, would be more than glad to awake to the sight of her round brown eyes and clear dark skin, though it is Arthur who generally has that privilege. To our sleeping beauty, however, she might as well have been dwarfish Felix. His first words:

"Where is she?"

"Who?" Zöe asked. "Penny?"

"Where?" he said.

"Penny. She's sleeping now. You rest too. When you wake up, she'll be here."

And so it was. He next awoke with Penny's hand on his brow. She shushed him, and stuck a thermometer beneath his tongue. The fever was gone. Shaking out the thermometer, Penny showered him with questions. She asked him his name, where he'd come from, how he'd gotten there, if he'd been at War, if he knew Payne or had heard news of him or knew anyone who might have known him or if the name even sounded familiar. But the stranger shook his head.

Penny crossed and recrossed her legs. She stared at her ankles and pulled up her socks. She asked him what he remembered last.

"Waking," he said. "Here. Without you."

"And before that?"

"You. Waking here. With you."

And before that there was nothing at all, a wall, a well, an egg. Sweet Fanny Adams.

"Who is Payne?" he asked.

"My husband," answered Penny. With the tips of her fingers she traced the course of the long, raised scar on his shoulder. "What happened here?" she said. He shook his head, a blank.

In two days he was eating solid food. In another two, his arm around Penny's shoulders for (perhaps more than just) support, he walked twice around the bed. She gave him one of her old nightshirts to wear, and it hung from his fleshless limbs like a curtain. Each day he walked a little farther, treading the carpeted halls, the tiled kitchen floor, and the linoleumed back stairs. "Let's go for a little walk, you and I," Penny would say, and the stranger would swing his legs over the side of the bed and reach smiling for her hand. With Penny nearby, some ill-adjusted part within him seemed to snap back into place, and he could laugh and talk like anyone else. When she was gone, though, he barely spoke at all. He moped and mooned, and had hardly more presence than a cloud.

As vague and incomplete as he felt every other hour of the day, like a vast parcel left unwrapped, contents poised to be scattered by the slightest breeze, with each knock at his door Penny bound him into something like a man. By the time she had him padding down the hall, her fingers wrapped around his elbow, he was practically overbubbling with solidity and delight. A little spacey, sure, still not all there perhaps, but more or less almost coherent as a person.

Penny too, to her surprise, found herself looking forward to their halting perambulations. She liked that he seemed to want nothing from her, save to have her near. She liked to know that she was helping him, and that he would let her help. She liked that when he tripped over the coffee table, as he invariably did, he apologized for falling. She liked that each day he said more and more—no great discourses or revelations, but conversation of a sort. He asked her how she was, and she tried to answer honestly. She asked him the same question and he always said, "I'm fine." When she pressed him for specifics, he would admit to no complaints. "You're here," he'd say. "Everything is fine."

Penny tried other questions, just to get him talking, mostly of the primitive first-date-interrogation sort (Where did you grow up? Do you have any siblings? How old are you? What's your favorite sport? Are you close with your mother?), with limited success. (Don't know. Don't know. Don't know. Badminton. Don't know.) She tried testing his memory, naming objects, asking him to describe them, hoping to jog something, or at least unearth some clues. "Saguaro," she would say, and he would laugh and answer, "Green and spiky, tall. Lots of elbows. Always waiting." Or Penny would say, "Cormorant," and the stranger would smile and respond, "Black. Webbed feet. Eats fish. Dries its wings in the sun. Like it's hanging laundry from itself." And Penny would try "battery," or "butterfly," "shotgun" or "sirocco," but would end up none the wiser. Every now and again, though, he made her laugh.

After a couple of weeks of such extended fishing, and ever more extensive promenades, when he proved himself able to walk ten laps unassisted from the upstairs guest bedroom to the sunken den downstairs, Penny decided to end her guest's seclusion. She found to her surprise that she missed his company during the hour or two each evening she spent attending to the others. So she brought him down for dinner.

Word had traveled fast, and all the citizens of what was left of Payne's small kingdom were alarmed at the presence of this new man, who had already won more of Penny's concentrated attention than any of them had ever at any time enjoyed. Arthur was doubly suspicious, as the new arrival had for a week of evenings also deprived him of Zöe, without whom he was able to do little more than pace and blubber. And of course drink. (When she *was* around, it must be admitted, he was rarely able to do much more.) Now, to top it all, Penny planned to impose this interloper on the rest of them.

Sitting at the banquet table, waiting for Penny to arrive, Zöe was once more at Arthur's side, but he was so dejected he did not even seek the customary comfort of a suckle. He sat stooped and sulking, his shirtfront stained and reeking of booze. Felix's chair stood empty. Many months had passed since Payne's perhaps overpassionate memorial, but the dining room remained unimproved. Most of the glass had been swept up. The floor, though, was still dusted here and there with shattered marble and splinters of wood, bits of shriveled meat and grape-sized turds left by the rats that scuttled among the ruins. The windows had been taped over with black plastic, which nonetheless let in the rain— and bugs and birds—and rustled up a racket in the wind. A single hanging fluorescent bulb stood in for the chandelier. Even a hint of a breath of a breeze was enough to set it swaying, causing every shadow in the room to shrink and lengthen with hypnotic regularity.

Arthur was not the only one unhappy. As Penny's admirers sat awaiting the introduction of her new guest, not a single cheek was dimpled by a smile. Throughout the room, at every corner of the damaged table, the mood was somber, the air dully abuzz with grumbling, none of it worth repeating, all amounting to the same senseless and purely rhetorical question: "Just who does he think he is?"

The answer, in which all were equally uninterested, would not have satisfied anyone even if they were. *He* had no idea.

(Perhaps this is unfair, and you feel slighted: if they know nothing, and she knows nothing, and even he knows nothing, at least *you* should know a little bit. You've come this far. You deserve that much, at least. Let us travel then, through time and space, far from this well-set table. I'll whisper in your ear these brief parentheses: some background on a certain someone.

Let's begin with a setting. For what is man but first of all location, a thing in space, that moves or doesn't move? Look around at the place to which I've brought you. Hard to see, isn't it, in this half-light? But it's not the light that's wanting. If it were brighter, you'd only be blinded more. It's the fog, the murk, the mist, so thick you can't see anything! What is this place?

This is a point of origin. This is where things begin. For our stranger anyway. For now. Of course behind each beginning endless beginnings lurk in this funhouse world of ours, and Penny's new companion lazed somewhere else before—somewhere sharp-shadowed and bright, where the air was thin and clear, where light followed dark and dark light in dull succession. But he left that place. He dove headlong into the drisk and dew, abandoning all those taut borders for this nubescent soup. Why would he flee such firmness and surety, all those handholds, for this oozy nimbic realm? It's cold here, and wet, and you can't see for shit. It's far from comfortable. But then there are no crags here on which to stumble, no treachery of tides, just floating and unease. So was it cowardice or valor that led him to leap? Shall we call it suicide or stoicism? Hard to say, isn't it, in this realm without edges, where antinomies intermingle and alternatives collapse?

Never mind. That's all behind us now, for there he is, the man himself, Penny's latest plaything! You don't see him? Of course not—you can't see anything. Step forward, then, be brave. A little to the left. And down. Two steps. It's slippery, take care. Now reach out. A little more. Do you feel him? It's our man, standing there alone, here in the heaving haze. Don't worry, he can't feel you and there's no one around to see—grab hold wherever you like. Can you tell it's him? It's not easy, I know, when you can't see the nose on your own face, much less on his, and the only scent is shoreless damp. But you can feel his scars at least. So feel them. Touch his shoulders and his face. Does he seem tense? Can you find knots in his muscles? Can you hear his stomach rumbling? Are there any signs of panic at being here alone? There are none. His belly's silent, his body loose. He's quite at ease.

But something happens. Even in this nephic gloom, things happen. The wisdom of the streets holds here too: everybody's got a hustle, even fog. And love's a hustle like any other grift. The fog is not insensitive to our man's arrival. How could she be, with all those hard corners on him, elbows, knees and ankles, jutting nose, and scarry ribs? [Forgive me, if you can, for genderizing limbo—she's no more she than any Western Avenue transsexual, which is to say: at least halfway. Remember, it's cloudy in here.] So at first she is incensed by this intrusion—the nerve, thinking he might fit in here! And without the courtesy to ask permission first! She is wounded, even, by the abrasions he has caused her. Clouds, after all, are easily torn. So she wraps herself around him close, the better to inspect him. Vaporous particles and banklets of mist drift between his hairs, under his nails, down the helix of his ear. They stroke his every scar and hanging flap of skin. They seep in through his mouth and nose. They tickle cilia and bronchi. And when they report back to their mistress all that they have found—his extraordinary courage, his cravenness, his sorrow, his triumph and despair—she softens towards him, if such a thing can be. Any softer, that is.

It would be a lie to suggest that he does not return her affections. [Not that lies and truth look so different here.] He dove in willingly, after all. He embraced her and gave away all else. But he asks himself, and she herself, what, in the end, they can offer one another. She wonders how to keep him, she who is incapable of offering even momentary comfort. He wonders how to please her, can't accept that she requires nothing from him, nothing but that he open himself to her.

She's right: she cannot keep him. No one stays in limbo. Not for long. Time goes by and he feels himself disintegrating. He loses sight of all the markers that once made of him a man. They float away. They sink into the brume. He lets them go, gives himself up to her embrace. She deprives him of the very notion of outlines, of being as a bounded thing. But she gives him nothing in return, nothing but an amorphous sort of soggy freedom. In the end it's not enough, and she knows that better than he, and lets him go. She kicks him out preemptively, before he can find the wherewithal to leave. She hands him over to her wild cousin, the sea, who can't stand the taste of him and spits him up to Felix, who in turn gives him to Penny, and to us.

But old lovers never let you go entirely. Everyone's got a hustle, and takes what they can get. His old girl keeps her cloudy claws afloat around his heart. She slips beneath his eyelids each time he blinks. She sings in his ear when he's not listening. She dances round his bed when he's asleep.

So now you know precisely who he is and where he's from: our stranger is the fallen groom of drift.)

At last (*at long last!*) Penny brought him down to dinner. A cigarette affixed to her lower lip, she descended the stairs, the stranger walking stiffly but steadily beside her, long-haired, sunken-eyed, and barefoot, his nightgown freshly laundered and gleaming white. At the sight of him so attired, the suitors' grumbling gave way to snickering and, following a flash of rage from Penny's eyes, to silence. Bobby appeared briefly at the head of the staircase, a slingshot in one hand. He did not snicker, but stepped down onto the topmost stair, as if to follow his mother and her new companion. He began to lower his foot to the next one, then thought better of it, arrested his foot in midair, and scuttered up and out the door. Penny did not turn to look for him. She took her seat at the table's head and, Arthur and Sally already having taken the chairs beside hers, asked Carl to set another place at her side. She didn't mention Bobby, perhaps was unaware he had been with her at all. The hall was silent save the nervous twitter of silver and crystal, the sloshing of wine from glass to gullet, and Arthur's labored breathing.

Penny had asked Carl and Xavier to prepare something special to welcome their guest, and, always eager to please her, they had complied. Some measure of rebelliousness, though, could be read in their menu by those who care to try. Which is not to say that their cooking was anything other than flawless. They consulted, as always, the estimable Escoffier, which volume they had ransacked several near-forgotten years before from the termite-sagging shelves of an abandoned junior high school library. The binding was now broken, the pages here translucent with butter, there spattered with sauce. Only in the inclusion of eel, a regrettably common creature, did their menu slip from the officially sanctioned heights of culinary sophistication. But Felix had not been fishing in days, or if he had, he'd not been back, and there was nothing else around.

Penny nodded to Xavier, who at her signal stubbed out his cigarette, upended his wine glass into his mouth, pulled a pair of white gloves from his pocket, and rushed off to the kitchen. He and Carl returned a moment later with the hors d'oeuvre course, each balancing three silver platters on one arm and carrying a fourth above their heads. "Cervelles Robert," Xavier announced. He laid a steaming tray between Penny and her new guest and carefully spooned a portion onto Penny's plate. She eyed the strangely coiled yellow substance with one raised brow.

"What is this?" she asked Xavier.

"It's got nothing to do with Robert," he said, bringing a blush to the latter's cheeks with the mere mention of his name. "It's lambs' brains, sliced and sauced with a mustard cream."

Noses wrinkled all around the room. A draft blew through the windows, and the bulb above them swayed. Robert's shoulders, never exactly loose, stiffened noticeably. Arthur stirred from his sulk and served himself, dragging his cuff through Penny's plate as he reached across the table. He grunted an apology, then shoveled half the platter's contents onto his own plate, spraying mustard sauce and bits of brain across both Penny's and the stranger's laps as he dug in. Zöe elbowed him in the ribs. He looked up from his plate, cerebellum protruding from between his teeth and lodged in the thicket of his mustache. "'Sgood," he muttered, and filled his mouth again.

As Carl cleared away the brain-stained china and Xavier rolled in a barrel-sized tureen of *velouté aux grenouilles,* a delicate frog soup, Penny rose from her seat and tapped her glass with her fork. All heads turned in her direction. "You have noticed, I'm sure, that we have a guest among us," she began. "He has been ill, and will be with us at least until he fully recovers. I expect you to treat him with all the consideration you routinely show each other." She paused, realizing that this was perhaps not enough, and added, "And all the respect and affection you show to me."

Not a single "Aye" or even a humble nod of acquiescence greeted Penny's announcement, only the resumed slurping of the soup and Arthur's outraged exclamation, "Frog? Did he say frog?" Art filled his glass again and declared to all interested parties—a group composed only of himself and the nameless newcomer, who listened heedfully—that being neither fish nor foul nor reptile, blurring all known categories, or at least those known to Art, "Frog is shit!" and therefore not fit to be consumed. Not everyone's at home with ambiguity.

Robert stuck his neck out. "It's an amphibian," he interjected. "That means they can live on land or in the water depending on the stage of their development."

"Frog is shit!" Arthur cut him off, and scornfully shoved his bowl to the middle of the table. After a reassuring glance from Penny, the stranger ate. He tried not to, but slurped a little.

The fish course soon arrived, the aforementioned eel, served cold in quivering molds of aspic. Arthur sprang from his seat. "Eel!" he yelled. No one, again save the stranger, even looked up. Glad of an audience, Arthur addressed himself to Penny's guest. "Let a fish be a fish, man. Let a snake be a snake, and a worm a worm!" he roared. "Eel is an outrage! An abomination! Is bat next? Platypus perhaps?" He spat, shook his head with what indignation he could muster, given his habitual distance from anything that might be called dignity, and swayed where he stood.

"Sit," Zöe said, tugging at the pocket of his trousers. "Behave."

Arthur sat with a thud, sending the bulb above them swinging again, casting one side of the table and then the other into shadow. Arthur's chin collapsed into his chest and he fell asleep, white bubbles frothing from his mouth into his mustache with each long, wheezy breath. Penny served her guest a wedge of eel, then served herself and, smiling, took a bite to put him at ease. No one else said a word, or even looked at one another, or did anything at all save lift fork to mouth and shift weight from thigh to thigh.

Arthur dozed until the arrival of the meat course, with which he was far more satisfied: four enormous platters of *tête de veau en tortue*. On each plate sat a single steaming calf's head, cooked whole and garnished with sumptuous heaps of cock's combs and kidneys, mushrooms and olives, tiny gherkins, crawfish tails, fried quail's eggs, boiled tongue thinly sliced, and yet more calf's brain, all of it dressed in a *sauce tortue,* which, despite its suggestive name, and to Arthur's great relief, contains no turtle and no genre-defying elements at all—just tomatoes, veal stock, sherry, and a pinch of cayenne.

Everyone else, however, Penny and her guest included, regarded the staring calves' heads with horror. The calves, unimpressed, stared back. Arthur helped himself, piling his plate with jowls and brain and maw, twisting his knife to pop an eyeball from its socket. The others had only begun to pick at their small, polite portions when Arthur was ready for seconds. His fork clattered to his plate and he sucked the last remnants of *sauce tortue* from his thumb. He refilled his glass and just as quickly emptied it again. Pointing a shaky index finger at the lumped globes surrounding the head like a crown, he nodded with sunny expectancy to the white-gowned newcomer, who by virtue of the fact that he alone had not ignored him, Art was now convinced was a warm and likely lifelong friend.

"Miss," said Art, "Could you please pass the brains?"

Robert, who had not for a moment forgotten the hors d'oeuvres, the horrid cervelles Robert, and had been trembling all this time in anticipation of the gags that would surely be had at his expense—the jocular attempts to uncover and remove his own cervelles, hee-haw, the raw lambs' brains he would undoubtedly find concealed in his slippers the next morning, and in his shampoo bottle and his pockets and his hat—could not have been more relieved. With Arthur's slip, the pressure building within him swiftly and suddenly departed. In the resulting vacuum, he was thrust from his seat like a champagne cork and, firing a partially masticated gob of cock's comb from his mouth across the table directly into Ollie's forehead, shouted, "*Miss!* HA! He called him *Miss!*"

Stunned by Robert's outburst, no one said a word. Until, that is, Ollie peeled the slippery nugget of half-chewed wattle from his brow, inspected it, grinned broadly, and popped it into his mouth, at which point everyone, with the exception of the newly christened Miss, who now looked tired and confused, collapsed in what can only be described as a gale of laughter, the winds of which blew a goblet from Yves's hand, tumbled both Arthur and Lily backwards from their chairs, and provoked a gherkin to lodge in Garth's windpipe, causing him to turn a surprising shade of violet which blanched and dimmed with the lightbulb's to and fro. Hans smacked him between the shoulder blades, the gherkin was dislodged and Garth's habitual pallid tone restored. Arthur and Lily righted themselves (Arthur not without a hand from Zöe, Ollie, and Hans), and Robert repeated, *"Miss, he called him Miss,"* while chuckling softly into his palm. Penny, who had not been able to prevent herself from daintily regurgitating some well-chewed calf's brain, wiped her chin and helped herself to the creamed carrots.

For dessert they had peach melba, without further incident. Even Bobby came down for a bite.

(Do you think Payne pathetic down there, watering his self-pity with gin? Why doesn't this consummate man of action get up, you ask, and do something, fight his way home to Penny, write her a note at least?

Don't be so smug. Is love such a simple thing? Elemental and unmixed, incapable of bonding itself to fear and self-hate? Is its call so clear as that? Does it come with printed instructions in unsmudged and lasting type? Are your eyes so sharp and your ears so free of wax that you know just what to do, where love is, how to follow it, what to do when you get there, how to keep it clean and fresh, to preserve it from the assaults of dust and grime and time? If you know all that, and know how to put your knowledge to good use, and have done so, then feel free to judge Payne. Piss on him for all I care. He won't know, he'll think it's rain. But if you have never loved someone who loves you back, and not known how to reach her side—even when she was right there next to you—then you haven't loved at all, or are uncommon blessed. So listen now, and look beneath you, beneath Payne's visor, on the far side of his mirrored shades.

It is not at this moment the image of Penny that flutters before Payne's shuttered eyelids, but something much older. He's a little boy again, sitting on the broad expanse of the front bench seat of his father's gray Caprice. He's wearing shorts, and the pale, hairless skin of his legs sticks to the vinyl. His father smokes a thin cigar, and his right arm is extended over the seat back in halfhearted mimicry of affection. Its bulk behind him prevents Payne from resting his head on the headrest, and he squirms in his seat and wishes the old man would move the hand at least. Outside the window the scrub of the landscape pulses by. There are plastic bags stuck in the trees. Yellowed newspapers and hamburger wrappers leap from one clump of dead and drying grass to the next in the wake of each passing car. A bird falls from the sky, and the chain of white painted dashes dividing the lanes twists off into an infinity of asphalt. The car swallows the road beneath it, but there is always more road ahead. Payne wonders if every road is ultimately connected to every other road and how long you could go without driving over the same pavement twice. In the backseats of every car they pass, Payne sees other children, lost like him and staring, but they do not return his gaze and there is no solidarity between them. He thinks of how little of his own brief life he can remember and wonders if he will remember even this unmemorable moment if he thinks about it really hard, if he'll be able to mark it somehow so that it sticks, imprint it with the weight of his desire that it last, and in lasting mean something, and not be allowed to pass unnoted.

Payne succeeded. Today, decades later, as he grieves poolside, he can recall that very moment in all of its detail. But he knows that so many others, even just that afternoon, were left unmarked, and were forgotten, and lie cast off behind him, dead and irretrievable as the white painted dashes on that long-ago highway. He knows the future holds more of the same, and this is too much to endure. Payne wonders if there is not a way to mark every passing second and fragment thereof, to hold tight to time, to lend it solidity and mass. He thinks of Penny's embrace, and the riches he has gained and lost, and pours himself another drink.)

11

Testimony

or

Sums and Ciphers

or

More Lies About Birds

Robert:

My inveterate cowardice should not get in the way of my filing an accurate report on this matter. At least not much. I've done the numbers and the numbers speak for themselves, so how I feel or don't feel should not come into it. I cannot pretend the results surprise me. In point of fact they confirm what I suspected all along, since the first time I was able to observe the subject in question, now known to all as Miss. There was something surely disingenuous about his amnesia, so-called, something highly slippery about his demeanor. A fine bit of playacting this, I thought. I have nothing against the fellow, but I have a good nose for deception, and I could have sniffed him out from across the yard. In point of fact, I did.

I will put my instincts and premonitions aside, for such intangibles cannot of course be quantified or verified, however infallible they may in this case have proved to be. My methods are entirely mathematical and follow strict logical and arithmetic rules. They rely on the alphabetical value of relevant numerical elements, and are simple and accessible to all, though they do require some practice and a small degree of ingenuity. Call it a gift. Every letter in the alphabet is assigned a numerical equivalent according to its ordinal value. Take my name, for instance. *R* is the eighteenth letter in the alphabet, *o* the fifteenth, *b* the second, *e* the fifth, *r*, once more, the eighteenth, and *t* the twentieth. My name can thus be reduced to the sequence: 18, 15, 2, 5, 18, 20, and thence discovered in the number 78, the sum of all those numbers. It can also be found in 15, the sum of the digits 7 and 8; or in the single number 8, the sum of 3 and 5, which are the divisors of 15; or even in the numeral 6, the sum of the digits 1 and 5. Through the careful analysis of the numerals attached to any individual or event, the divine code hidden in all things can be deciphered. We can uncover what is covered and act according to the knowledge so gained.

Now. The individual in question, called Miss, washed up on our shores on the fourth day of the fifth month, which in North American notation is abbreviated 5/4, which gives us the number 54, which is the sum of the numbers 2, 5, 23, 1, 18, and 5, which together spell out the word *Beware*. Precisely 50 hours passed before he was able to rise from his bed and walk, and 50 is the sum of 19, 14, 1, 11, and 5, which spells *snake*. His heart rate upon arrival was 48 beats per minute. This numeral is doubly important given that precisely 48 condoms were found on the stretch of beach on which the subject was discovered, according to Felix an unusually abundant crop. Forty-eight can be easily split into the numbers 5, 22, 9, and 12, which together spell *evil*. An alternate configuration produces the word *vile*.

All of this is still quite vague. But if we take the height in inches of Felix, who first encountered the subject, in thick-soled boots and standing on his tippy-toes, which is to say 66, the digits add up to 12, which is the number of hours between the first time the subject opened his eyes and the second instance of the same (as well as the sum of the digits 4 and 8, already discussed). If we consider that there are also 66 millimeters between the knuckle and the second joint of the subject's pinky finger and a total of 66 moles on his arms and back, we are led inevitably to the sequence 12, 9, 22, 5, 18, which of course spells the word *liver*, an anagram of *revile,* almost.

Furthermore, if we consider the measurement of his right leg from ankle to groin, 123 centimeters, and keep in mind that on that leg he has 6 scars (1 + 2 + 3 = 6) with a combined length of 36 (12 x 3 = 36) centimeters, as well as an estimated 1,728 hairs ($12^3 = 1728$), and finally, that he weighed 123 pounds after the tar was cut from his hair and the kelp and sand were scraped from his body, we can be fairly certain that the numeral 123 is crucial to understanding his identity, if not, in fact, its keystone. 123, of course, is the sum of 9, 11, 9, 12, 12, 5, 4, 16, 1, 25, 14, and 5, which together spell out the nonsense word *ikilledpayne*, or the sentence *I killed Payne*.

Certainly there is some ambiguity remaining, as those numerals represent only one possible equation with 123 as its sum. Why not choose the far simpler sequence 25, 25, 25, 25, 23? Because *yyyyw* is not a word in any language of which I am aware, for one. But any remaining doubters will likely be satisfied by the following evidence. Ten hours passed before the individual in question spoke. He has 10 fingers and 10 toes, which, admittedly, is fairly common but, given the overall condition of his body upon arrival, is in this case something to wonder at. There is just one of him (1, of course, being the sum of the digits of the numeral 10). By my count, he took 10 small bites of cervelles Robert at his first formal dinner, and seemed to enjoy it, which gives me at least 10 reasons to despise him (though that judgment should in no way color the objectivity of these calculations). Ten, as is well known, is the sum of the numbers 1, 1, and 8, which digits form 118, the precise number of times the individual in question blinked during the first *10* minutes of that first dinner, a sign, I might add, of severe shiftiness.

118 = 16 + 1 + 25 + 14 + 5 + 11 + 9 + 12 + 12 + 5 + 18, which confirms my earlier finding, spelling out as it does the single word *Paynekiller.*

Individually, each of these facts is merely suggestive, but together they form a narrative, the veracity of which we can accept as conclusive. We are to beware this Miss, snake that he is, at the same time evil and vile. With his own right leg, he took the life of our dear Payne, presumably with repeated kicks to the area of the liver.

[Robert's soliloquy is here interrupted, as the thought of Payne's death induces in him a fit of shivers so violent he cannot speak, and precisely 8 tears run in trembling trails down his bony face, 8 being the sum of 2 and 6, and therefore of 2 and 0 and 6, as in the numeral 206, itself the sum of 16, 15, 15, 18, 16, 15, 15, 18, 18, 15, 2, 5, 18, 20, in which sequence can be read the words *Poor, poor Robert.*]

I was saying. It is my conviction that the subject, called Miss, fought in the War with our beloved leader and, as he is clearly no match for him in open battle, was not an enemy but an ally, or thought to be by Payne, such that he was able to take advantage of Payne's trusting nature and caught him unsuspecting, or perhaps drugged him, and then set upon him, animalistically beating him with naught but his hands and feet and teeth, and in this cruel manner took his life, and thereby deprived us all of the one hope that lights our future, that Payne might one day return and redeem us. And now this so-called Miss has come here, feigning amnesia to win Penny's pity, which he intends to use to gain her hand. Not content with having taken Payne's life, he further endeavors to take his wife, his home, his land. This cannot be allowed to pass. There is only one solution possible.

Sally:
I was in bed the other night with Kate. Not in bed, exactly. She has a hammock, and we lay in that. Entwined. Her place is set up really nice, with pillows all over the floor and things hanging from the wall and the ceiling. Everything's soft. There's no edges in her whole place. We lit some candles and drank some wine and smoked a little hash, and we were just lying there, rocking, trying not to spill the wine, maybe kissing a little, maybe doing a little something with an alligator clip here and there, I can't really say what all. A little something here and there.

"I wish," I told her, "I was a kangaroo."

"Why?" Katya said.

"I like to jump," I said. "All day. Hop jump hop. And kick. I could really kick if I were a kangaroo."

"What would you kick?" she asked.

I thought about it. "Art," I said. "Big, fat, mustachioed Art. Right in the belly. Pow. Maybe I'd kick Zöe too, for putting up with him. But not so hard. And Hans. Definitely Hans." And we raised our arms in salute and shouted, "Heil Hans!"

"I'd kick Hans so far he wouldn't land for days. *Pow!*—like that. Off he'd go, then splat. We wouldn't even hear it, he'd be so far away."

"Who else?" she asked.

I thought some more. "Payne," I said. "If he ever came back, and I happened to be a kangaroo, I'd kick him good—hop jump *Pow!*—send him right back to wherever he may be, or farther. Bless his tender soul."

We clinked glasses. "Tenderize his blessed soul," agreed Katka.

"Also," I said, "I want a pouch."

"You already have one," Katushka said, and touched it. I closed my eyes and for a little while said, "Mmmm." And then I said, "Not that kind of pouch."

"What kind?" Kathy asked.

"Something more convenient," I said. "For holding things."

"Things?" she said, and tickled me inside just so.

"Mmmm," I said again. "Things. Like maybe a book. A sandwich. Maybe a bottle of wine. Maybe a corkscrew. A lighter. A snack. Sunscreen. A change of clothes. Maybe a pack of cigarettes, or Felix when he's blue. Flowers. A hat."

"Wouldn't it fall out?" Katinka asked. "With all that kicking?"

"Nope," I said. "Not this pouch." And then I just said, "Mmmm" some more until she got up for another glass of wine.

"What about the new one?" Katerina asked.

"The new one?"

"Miss. Would you kick him?"

"No," I said. "He's got those pretty eyes. It's hard to imagine anything too terrible coming from a man with eyes like that. But men will surprise you. Women too." And I did my best to surprise her, a little something here and there. It worked. She was surprised.

When I was done and she was done and the hammock's swaying slowed, Katie bit my lower lip. "I think it's Payne," she said.

"What is?" I asked.

"Him. I think he's Payne. I think Miss is Payne. In disguise. To test us."

"So what should we do?" I said.

She stopped smiling. "Kick him. Kick him far away."

But I'm not a kangaroo, not yet, so I bit her back and made the hammock swing.

Felix:

There's a field where I go on the hill up past the other hill between that hill and the next one. Where the car wash was. The field is flat and I can see the clouds. Sometimes the clouds fell low and fill the field. If I was in the field I can't see anything but cloud. Also there's birds. Never any people. Sometimes I saw three birds. Sometimes none. One time the sky is filled with little birds maybe sparrows or swallows but definitely not geese. There were so many so I couldn't see the clouds. So many it got dark, or darker. What they are doing, the birds, was flying in a square, not a circle, a square. They turned in corners, like they reached the edge of the sky and there's no choice but turning sharp, but really there was plenty of sky left and still they turn. Left left left left. All the same way. Four corners. The square moved across the sky and there are so many birds the clouds I couldn't see them. A box of birds. I pick a flower and pulled the petals off. The hills are like a spreading stain. This time today I can't see even a one single bird. I picked the grass from the cracked cement from where the car wash was. The wind gets sucked across the sky. My hands are green from the grass and Penny I miss you. I rub my knuckles against the cement until they bleed from broken glass. My hands were red with blood and Penny how could you? The hills they're like a spreading stain.

Joseph:

We drew straws and I lost. Actually Izzy drew the shortest straw. The whole thing was his idea, but he balked. He muttered something about an appointment and ran off. So it was up to me to do it. "Just tell him the situation," Theo said, and it sounded easy enough. But then I thought about it, and I couldn't figure out where the situation begins and where it ends, who is inside it and what it includes. Do I mention the weather, the phase of the moon, the three-legged cats I saw last night, a tune I heard in a supermarket when I was nine? "Tell him he's last in line," Theo said, so I figured I'd tell him that.

He was almost never alone, always either with Penny or with Zöe looking over him, and sometimes with Bobby there too, but Ollie said he'd take care of that. He came to my place later when I was sleeping and woke me up. He told me the time to come and where to go. "It's all set up," he said, and winked.

When the appointed time came I crossed the moat and opened the front gate, then walked through the weeds around the wall and went into the house from the back. I had never been in the house before, so I got lost at first and opened the wrong door. The first thing I saw was my own reflection. I looked terrible, flabby and pale, the top of my head cut off by the door frame. The room was a bathroom, tiled in pink. The shower stall was mirrored, and I was so surprised to see me there that I almost didn't notice Ollie, leaning up against the sink with Zöe's legs wrapped around his back. "Sorry," I said, and left.

I tried the next door, but it was wrong too. It was Bobby's room. He was sitting cross-legged on the floor. All around him were dolls, baby dolls, both black and white, stuffed bears in yellow slickers and in striped engineers' coveralls, rag dolls and dolls with plastic faces and oversized army dolls with jelly-filled arms that you could stretch. They were all naked and their heads were scattered about the room. Everywhere you looked was heads and frozen button eyes. The stuffing from the rag dolls covered the floor like snow. The jelly from the stretchy dolls seeped out in sticky puddles here and there about the carpet. In a corner of the room, beside the bunk bed, a gilded bird cage lay on its side. Its door hung open. Bobby had the bird in his fist. Just its head poked out from his little hand. It was too scared to even chirp. He looked up at me. The bird did too. "It won't come off," Bobby said.

"Here," I said, "let me try." He thought about it for a second, then handed me the bird. It was a tiny yellow thing, with just the teeniest black eyes. I could feel its heart pounding in my hand. I walked to the corner of the room and opened the window. I opened my fingers so the bird could fly away, but it wouldn't go. It just sat there on my palm. I put it on the sill. "Go," I said. "Fly away." But it wouldn't go. I blew at it, but it just sat on the sill and cheeped. I could feel Bobby's eyes on my back. I shrugged at him. "Sorry," I said, and closed the door behind me.

The next door was the right one. He was lying in bed on his back with just a sheet over him. I could almost see his ribs through the sheet. His eyes were closed, and if it wasn't for the vein pulsing in his eyelid I might have thought he was dead. I sat at the foot of the bed. After a couple of minutes he opened his eyes. He smiled. "My name is Joseph," I said, and I gave him my hand to shake. His grip was tired and limp, but for some reason that made me like him more. I didn't feel like he expected me to say anything, so for a while I didn't. I just sat and looked at the floor. The shadows cast by a tree branch out the window jumped about in the wind. Then I remembered.

"I'm here to tell you the situation," I said. He lay still, like I'd told him it was a beautiful day, and he agreed, and there was nothing more to say. I told him a little bit about Payne, and about how he left and how we didn't know but we didn't think he was coming back. I told him about Penny, how she would one day have to choose. He didn't say anything, but he looked like he understood and he really seemed happy that I was there, so I just kept talking. I told him about how the night before I saw three cats, all with just three legs, and one was to my right and two to my left and I didn't know what it meant, if it was a good omen or bad and did he know? He shook his head. I told him I was hoping it would rain soon because I was thinking of planting a garden so I could grow flowers and bring them to Penny and did he think that was a good idea? He nodded. I told him when I was a kid I was afraid of the wind, isn't that funny? I was afraid I'd get blown away, but now I really like it and I like the idea of getting carried off by the wind, it would be almost like flying, but better because it wouldn't be up to you how long you flew and where you landed, so you could just sit back and enjoy it and wherever you landed would be however it was and it would be fine. I told him sometimes I couldn't tell lust from hunger and it drove me crazy because I'd eat when I was horny and masturbate when I was hungry and I could never satisfy myself. He laughed, and I did too. I told him I was afraid of earthquakes because I didn't like the idea of being swallowed up by the earth and getting stuck somewhere and sometimes I felt kind of like that had already happened and the earth had swallowed me to my knees and I couldn't go anywhere or do anything except reach out for what was already in front of me but most of what I wanted leaned away as soon as I reached for it so I was just stuck there and reaching and did he know what I meant? He shook his head, no, but I'm pretty sure he understood. I told him about Bobby and the little bird that wouldn't fly away and did I do the right thing? He nodded, so I guess I did. And I remembered to tell him what Theo said. I said, "Don't forget, you're last in line." He smiled again, and we both laughed about it. I shook his hand again, and his grip was still soft and weak, but that was okay by me, it was fine. "It's been a real pleasure talking with you," I told him, and said if he ever wants to talk some more he should feel free to drop by my place anytime. "Just ask for Joseph and you're sure to find me, I never go too far," I said.

Later on, Theo and Ollie and the others cornered me. Theo asked me, "Did you make him understand?" and I said yes and Ollie asked me, "Did he give you any trouble? Did you have to get rough?" and I said no, it all went okay, it was fine.

(It's been raining all morning, but by the time Payne peels the sheets from his chest, the sun has burned through the clouds and a mist of steam is rising from the rain-soaked leaves. When he parks himself poolside there is no sign left of the weather's A.M. indiscretion. The puddles have dried. The plants are crisp and curling in the heat. The ice in Payne's cocktail melts in seconds, and he can barely drink fast enough to keep up with his thirst. He sits at the shallow end of the pool, the water up to his chin but still only slightly cooler than the air, and considerably warmer than Payne's own blood. He's on his second pitcher when the inflatable goose explodes. The pop sounds [to Payne at least] like nothing other than a .50-caliber sniper's shot, and Payne dives for cover to the bottom of the pool. He knows from long experience that he'll be lucky if he hears the next one. He swims erratically around the pool to make himself a moving target, turning suddenly and arrhythmically, counting on the refraction of the water to foul the shooter's aim. He's out of shape, but he knows he can swim like this for ten or twelve minutes without a breath while he figures out what to do. After just half that time, though, his lungs only beginning to burn, he thinks, fuck it, let 'em shoot me, and floats to the surface for air. As he fills his lungs again his eyes scan the treetops, the roofs of surrounding condos, the radio and cell-phone transmission towers. At least let me see the fucker first. But there's no one. No glint of rifle-barrel steel or tinted sunglass, no twitching balaclava'd head. And Payne realizes there's no one there—it was the heat, the fucking blow-up goose exploded from the heat. He tosses its deflated rubber carcass from the pool. It begins to melt into the cement just so, a goose-shaped stain, and Payne can't bear to look at it. He pulls himself out. He doesn't need a towel, the sun takes care of that. Every drop of water on his body evaporates before he pulls shut the sliding door into the cool cave of the dark and air-conditioned condo. He shaves, dresses, and combs his hair. He breaks open the drawer on her side of the bed, using a letter opener to bust the lock. He pockets the credit cards and the emergency cash. Sometimes stolen fruit tastes sweeter, but not this time. He calls a cab, pours himself one last gin, no tonic, and waits. Payne is heading Home.)

iii

12

Moving Along

or

A Few Vignettes

or

Ebbing and Flowing,
To-ing and Fro-ing,
Hither and Thither and
Home Again

GROWTH IS A FUNNY THING: that things get bigger. Change is funny, period: that nothing stays the same, not ever. Somehow it's not what you'd expect. (Cf. Wittgenstein: "I expected to be surprised, and I was not, and in that I was surprised.") But things don't just move around and switch places, that would be odd enough. They change in size as well. They stretch and shrink and bloat and shrivel.

They change shape, drastically. An egg becomes a bird, or an omelet, hence a turd. Turd becomes dirt becomes worm becomes dirt becomes tree becomes ash becomes dirt. What is worm and what is tree? What is cloud and what is sky? Or you or I? The thingness of things is a question. They are not this and not that. Is a whale a fish? Is a fish the sea? Is the sea inside of me or out? Where one thing begins and another ends is anybody's guess. So it's no wonder, really, that so many over time have denied the permanence of death. If nothing else is fixed, how can death be lasting? If nothing ends but shape-shifts, mutates, modifies, why should we be the only ones?

The other day on the bus, I saw a baby. Held in its mother's arms, the critter stared intently at the collapsed face of the ancient and toothless man sitting beside it, a weird, rickety old coot in orange cowboy boots, tattered Dickies, a ten-gallon straw hat, and a belt buckle that read, "Herm." The kid's mother kept trying to turn its little head away, but it always swiveled back, gawking, not innocently at all, but with a wisdom that was uncanny. The infant appeared not unconscious of its fate, not perplexed or scared but interested. And if such a thing as that bright child can become such a thing as that wreck Herm, why should we not join Pythagoras in supposing that when our eyes are shut for us that final time, it will be to reawaken as a pea?

But things do end, and end for good. That's what change means: growth and shrinkage, disappearance and death. Don't worry about thingness, or the bounds of your shriveling self: all things die, and selves dissolve. Nothing stays the same, not ever.

This is a long way of saying that Miss is getting fat.

Doing little but lying in bed and eating, he's putting weight on fast. Penny is pleased with his progress, if you want to call it that. She is every day more conscious of her own body's slow mutations, its glacial, almost imperceptible (to anyone but her) surrender to a conspiracy of gravity and age. But Miss just grows and grows. After only two weeks, his ribs fell back and the furrows between them filled. The caverns around his eyes puffed outwards. He sprouted buttocks. Then a tiny berm of a belly piled up below his chest. Now he has befriended Xavier, not by saying much of anything, but by hanging around the kitchen counter and eating whatever he's given, which means, by and large, the bits Xavier would ordinarily reserve for scrapple, or for Arthur's late-night snacks: brain, kidney, udder, tripe. Especially tripe. He eats it by the steaming bowlful, and (talk about transmigration!) the coiled and honeycombed guts of many a cow, sheep, and pig arrive inside the similarly coiled gut of Miss, where they are metamorphosed from foreign substance to indigenous fat, most of it lining the same part of Miss on which it previously sat on the body of its previous owner, roundabout the gaster.

He's gone through two sleep shirts, and won't fit into any of Payne's clothes. Penny sews him a new nightgown from a folded-over sheet. His once sunken chest now boasts a bust that would be the envy of many an impatient teenaged girl. There's a slight crease where his ankles meet his feet, and his knuckles are indented. Penny still makes him walk, not just around his bed anymore, but outside the palace, sometimes beyond the walls, down the driveway, and through the ravaged hills.

They stroll out past the suitors' jumbled huts, Miss struggling in flip-flops over cinder blocks, twists of rebar, and shattered pint bottles of gin. They cut through the valley where Queenie's smithy stood and stop to rest atop a fire-blackened boulder. Penny shuts her eyes, and rubs them. "What do you see," Miss asks, "when your eyes are closed?"

Penny shakes her head. "Nothing."

Miss lifts her chin with an index finger, redirecting her sightless gaze. "Look at the sun," he says. "Now what do you see?"

"Orange. Red. Sunspots. Swirling black."

"That's all?"

With her fingertips, she brushes his eyelids closed. She takes his face between her palms and points it at the sun. "What about you? What do you see?"

Miss smiles. "I see you." He opens his eyes and, seeing her still, his smile grows wider.

For a while neither of them says a word. A breeze picks up, and Penny hugs herself. She's about to stand, to suggest that they head home, when a cloud covers the sun, and a sheet of dim spreads across the hills.

"Look how bright the world is!" Miss exclaims and grabs her arm. He stretches his hand out before him as if to stroke the gray earth, the broken rocks and leafless scrub.

"Bright?" says Penny.

Miss laughs. "Look how it shines."

In the tree above them, a crow chases a sparrow from its nest. A buzzard caws grotesquely. "Listen," says Miss, "to the warbling birds."

"Warbling?" asks Penny.

Miss tugs her ear. "Birds," he says.

Penny nods. "Right. Birds."

The sky grows suddenly dark and thunder shivers through the clouds. A light rain begins to fall. Miss will take near any excuse to touch Penny's face. He nudges her chin sky-ward. She squints. "The world is bright," Miss says, "and beautiful."

Penny can't stop herself from laughing now. "No one ever told you that you shouldn't look directly at the sun?"

"I don't remember," he grins.

She pushes Miss's hair from his eyes. "Your hair's too long," she says. "I'll cut it for you." She pokes him in the gut with an extended middle finger. "You're getting fat," she adds.

"Too fat?" Miss asks, his eyebrows raised.

"No," Penny says. "Not too fat. There's more of you, that's all. There was almost none of you at first." And though he no longer needs her help to walk, she takes his newly chubby hand in hers. The sun reappears, low now, to their right and just above the hills. The rain still falls on

Miss and Penny, but the sky is newly orange and the rain-soaked earth glows purple and gold and almost green. The world is bright, and beautiful. Penny smiles, her green eyes glowing, and leads him home.

Crouched on the slope above them, Sally watches Penny walk off and Miss stumble slightly beside her. She hasn't climbed this hill to spy on them, but takes the opportunity when it comes. She's out looking for Felix. She's checked his hilltop perches, on which he sits to watch the lizards sun themselves on the rocks as the gulls fight and the occasional tanker cruises past in the distant sea. Climbing one hill, then another, took Sally half the day. Now, at dusk, she decides to check the caves. She doesn't know them all, and knows there are lots that Felix never showed her, but she's got a feeling he wants to be found, and goes first to the cave she knows he likes best. It's not a cave, really, but a collapsed mine shaft, one they had dug for Payne, for lead, she thinks, or maybe tin or tungsten. (Payne never told them anything.) They dug an airshaft through the top, and when Felix brought her there once before, he made a fire pit and stocked the place with canned sardines and cognac.

She's right. Before she even arrives at the mouth, she can see the smoke snaking up black through the darkening sky. She clambers up through the rocks and rotting fallen trees and then she's there.

The cave's got a waxy, plasticky smell, and Felix is bent over the fire. The flames skip up and down his face. He's sucking from a thin glass tube, one end blackened from contact with the flames. His hands are shaking. Not just his hands but all of him. He's lost weight, and his nose is running. He sucks and sucks, but there's nothing left to smoke, and no reward for all his prodding at the stem. Sally pushes aside some empty bottles and sits beside him. A rat rustles through the piled trash. Sally runs her hand through Felix's hair, which is greasy and matted with sand. His forehead is damp with sweat. It shivers like the rest of him. His eyes are sunken. There's white stuff in the corners of his mouth.

"Oh, baby," Sally says, "you are a sight." She takes the empty stem from his hand and puts her arms around him. "Did you just finish it?" she asks, and among his trembles she can distinguish a lateral shaking of his head before he looks up at her with questioning eyes.

"No," Sally says. She digs two white pills from her pocket and drops them in his hand. "They'll help," she says.

Felix chokes the pills down. Sally takes off her sweatshirt and wraps it around his bony shoulders. Felix swallows hard. "Penny sent you?" he asks through lips burnt and cracking from the pipe.

"Yes, baby," Sally lies. "She's been worried. Everyone's asking about you."

"She's coming?"

"No. She didn't know where you went. She wants you to come back. She wants you to sing her a song. She misses you."

"Liar," Felix says.

Sally hugs him and asks him to sing for her, but Felix shakes his head and she just holds him. After a long while he stops trembling. The fire burns out, Felix falls asleep, and it's Sally who lies awake shivering, holding his brittle body tight for warmth.

"Can you breathe okay?" Penny asks Miss as she pats down the sand covering his chest.

Miss coughs. A fissure opens in the sand beneath his chin. "I think so," he says. "Will breathing be required?"

"It's usually not a bad idea." Penny pushes one last scoop of sand to cover up the dome of Miss's belly. Now his head and squirming toes are the only parts of him unburied.

"There," Penny says, still kneeling, brushing the sand from her fingers and glancing over her shoulder at the swelling sea behind her. "I've got you just where I want you. The tide is coming in. Now I can ask you anything I like."

"Ask," says Miss.

"Tell me where you came from."

Miss smiles sadly, and shakes his head as best he can.

"You have to answer me," says Penny with an evil grin, "or I'll leave you here for the hermit crabs. And don't tell me you don't remember. If you don't know, make something up."

Miss does make something up, or tries to, and he almost tells the truth. "I was born," he begins, "at the bottom of the sea." But he stalls out and lies there looking lost.

"Your parents," Penny hints.

"My mother," Miss begins, but he can't come up with anything.

"Okay," says Penny. "Your mother. Was she a mermaid? A fish? A barnacle?"

"She was a barnacle." Miss grins. "A hardworking barnacle."

"Your dad?"

Miss thinks about it. "I never knew him. He didn't stick around."

"Just a sperm whale passing through," Penny suggests.

"Don't make me laugh. I'll have to breathe."

"Go on."

Miss is getting the hang of this. "My childhood was ordinary enough," he says. "The usual juvenile pursuits: molting, spawning. But no school would accept me, because I wasn't a fish. So I left home and let the tides take me where they willed. Eventually I got bored of drifting. I resolved to make something of myself. So I came here."

Penny's covering his hair with sand now so that just his face shows above the beach as if in bas-relief. "Why here?" she asks.

Miss lifts himself up on his elbows. The sand runs off him in dozens of small cascades. "For you," he says. "Because you're here."

Penny looks vexed. "You can't do that," she says. "You're buried. Play fair."

She makes him help her dig a deeper hole, then has him lie in it and pushes sand over him again. This time his toes don't show. "Can you move?" she asks him when she's done.

He cranes his neck around. "No," he says.

"Really?"

"Really."

"Good. Where were we?"

"My turn," says Miss. "You answer me. Tell me about Payne."

Penny stands. "No," she whispers. But in her way she answers nonetheless: she walks away. She stops just a dozen feet behind him, but Miss can't turn his head, and for all he knows she's gone for good.

"Hey!" Miss yells, but Penny doesn't turn around. She stands facing the dunes, chewing a thumbnail, kicking the sand at her feet.

"Hey!" Miss yells again.

Penny walks back quietly and kneels above him. She runs her fingers through his hair. "You didn't really think I'd leave you?" she asks.

"That wasn't funny," says Miss.

"No," Penny agrees, and starts to dig him out. When she's done, and he's stood, brushed himself off, and shaken the sand from his dress, Miss leans in to kiss her. She turns away, and his lips land on her cheek.

"What was that for?" Penny asks.

"For digging me out," answers Miss.

"But I was the one who buried you."

Miss leans in again, and she leans away again, and he gets her nose this time. "For that too," he says. "For burying me."

Lily's just started snoring when Theo nudges her awake. "I wasn't," she snorts.

"Wasn't what?" asks Theo.

"I wasn't snoring," Lily says, her voice muffled by the pillow. "I wasn't even sleeping yet."

Theo's propped up on one elbow, the sheets around his waist. He asks her, "Do you ever miss the old days?"

Lily rubs her eyes and asks him when he means.

"When Payne was around," he says.

She rolls onto her side. "Not for a second. Do you?"

Theo nods. "All the time."

"Really?" says Lily, eyebrows raised. "They were terrible."

Theo lays his head back on the pillow and shuts his eyes. "I know."

Payne shuffles his feet in tiny steps as the line inches forward. The man in front of him shifts his laptop bag from one polar-fleeced shoulder to the other. He nudges a garment bag ahead with his foot. Payne hates these tiny, chicken-feed steps. He decides he'll stand still until the line moves sufficiently that he can step freely forward and walk like a man. He's been waiting all day, led from one line to another, choking on the canned airport air. The lighting is fluorescent, the color of nausea, and the gray institutional carpet makes his feet itch through his shoes. The guy with the laptop kicks his garment bag forward again. Payne can sense the restlessness of the people behind him, their desperation for another quick baby step, but he holds his ground until the garment bag slides another three feet, and he takes two full steps forward.

Payne's at the head of the line now. Laptop is at the counter, taking his time. He's groveling for an upgrade, and Payne imagines snipping off his head between two shiny steel blades, watching the blood fountain forth from his stumped neck as the head, eyes confused and blinking yet, rolls like a nickel to the gate.

"Can I help you, sir?" asks the girl behind the counter. She's got a funny getup on, a red polyester suit with a name tag and a little satin ascot thing, and her smile has all the luster of the rug beneath her feet. Payne puts his ticket in her hand.

"I'll just need your ID," she says.

"ID?" asks Payne, the war-gloried king of a faraway people.

"Driver's license, passport, or military ID," she explains, her voice rising in pitch at the end of each word, as if questioning the very propriety of speech.

Payne shakes his head.

"I'm sorry, sir. I can't let you board without proper ID."

Payne sees blood falling in sheets down the walls, every passenger and janitor and red-suited check-in girl slipping and falling in gore, carried off flailing like flies in a whirlpool. He sees this woman in front of him belching knots of clotted blood, ichor loose and streaming from her ears and surprised eyes, staining her jacket a darker red.

"I'm sorry, sir," she says. "Next."

Penny's sitting on the rug with Bobby when Miss comes to the door. Bobby's got an entire box of crayons, sixty-four colors and a sharpener, but he only uses two. He's worn them down to stubs by now, and even the white cuffs of his sailor suit are scribbled red and black. He takes a sheet of construction paper, and, with his crayon clutched in his little fist, covers it entirely with red. Then he goes over that with black until you can see neither the original color of the paper nor the red with which he's covered it. Then he starts again on a new sheet. Penny draws a flock of birds flying in formation, and offers Bobby other shades. "Look how pretty this magenta is," she says, her voice almost trembling, but he ignores her and scribbles over another page.

She beholds the boy seated cross-legged before her, so contained, discrete, entire, and yet once part of her, a troublesome extra organ gone insanely agrow, its constant metastasis malforming her body from within, demanding she eat clay, that she pee every fourteen minutes and vomit between meals. Then the violent separation, the tearing and the blood and the loosing of the bowels. And now this, this little alien who seems to recognize in her no kinship and wish from her neither affection nor aid, this solitary boy. Penny takes the red crayon nub when Bobby's done with it and above the birds she's drawn already adds a wide-winged eagle, its talons outstretched.

Miss stands in the doorway, filling most of it. He knocks. Penny looks up. She covers her composition with another sheet. She lays what's left of her crayon on the rug and says, "Hi."

Even that one syllable is enough for Miss to be able to tell that something's gone stiff in her voice since last he saw her. A screen has dropped behind her eyes. Miss tries to see past it, but she won't look at him. He steps into the room.

"I like your drawings, Bobby," Miss says, his eyes not on the drawings, but on the artist's mother.

Bobby doesn't notice Miss's inattention. He doesn't even look up, just colors as intently as before. "My name's not Bobby," he says.

"Oh," says Miss, and smiles pained at Penny.

Penny glances up and just as quickly turns away, ignoring Miss's silent plea for sympathy. "I can't walk today," she says. "You go on without me."

Miss lifts his dress from his thighs and crouches, looks at Bobby's drawings, nods. He tries to uncover Penny's composition, but she shoves his hand away. "Are you okay?" he asks.

"I'm fine," she says.

"Will you cut my hair later?"

Penny turns to him. She rests her hand on his. Now it's her turn to plead. "I can't," she says. "Not today. I don't know when."

"Oh," says Miss, and stands and walks away.

Nellie licks her thumb and slides it up to the knuckle into Izzy's asshole. He moans.

"Do you like that?" she asks.

"No," Izzy says, and pushes her in deeper. She tightens her grip on his balls and lets a gob of spit fall from her lips onto the head of his cock.

"Does that feel good?" she asks.

"No," he moans again.

"Then I'll stop," Nellie says. She pulls her finger out of him, lets go his scrotum, and rolls to the other side of the bed.

"Yes," says Izzy, grabbing her wrist and pulling her back. "Please stop."

When Bobby has used up all the construction paper, Penny gets two bars of soap from under the bathroom sink, and two dull knives from the kitchen to teach her son to carve a boat. Bobby carves a narrow prow, a flat stern with slender keel, a forecastle and bridge. He asks Penny for a sharper knife and whittles portholes and cannon, a mast complete with crow's nest and a delicate skein of rigging, even a wheel for the bridge that turns. He traces oak grain into the wainscoting, and adds a barnacle or two. He carves a figurehead for the bow, a bare-breasted woman with wings outstretched. Her face is the size of a match head, smaller, but recognizable as his mother's.

The boat she crafts is a crude pointed wedge of soap. She cheats and shoves in a toothpick for a mast. "That's beautiful, honey," she says. "That's really nice. It looks just like me, only prettier."

Bobby shakes his head. "It's not you," he says.

Penny runs a bath to form a sea on which to sail their boats. They squat on their knees and race them around the tub. Penny tries to sink hers, but it floats and won't stay sunk. She hears the doorbell ring. "I'll be right back," she says, and pushes back his sailor's cap to kiss him on the forehead.

Downstairs she finds Sally, standing on the stoop with one leg crossed behind the other, biting her bottom lip. "Felix is sick," she says. "He keeps asking for you."

Penny frowns. "What's wrong with him?"

"He's weak." Sally shrugs, not sure how much to say. "He's not eating. I don't know. He's sick."

"Get Zöe. Tell her not to leave until I say. And tell Felix I'll try to be there later if I can."

When Penny returns to the bathroom the tub's been drained. Her soap boat is gone and Bobby is kneeling in front of the toilet, reaching up to flush it again. His boat buoys about in the resulting whirlpool, then founders and disappears.

Theo sits on Lily's knee and feeds her corned beef hash from the can. She's clothed, in big blue men's pajamas, but Theo is naked, and from behind his jutting scapulae look like the folded wings of a fresh-plucked pigeon. Lily licks the proffered spoon, washes it down with vodka. Theo opens another tin, but this time Lily pushes away the spoon. She asks a question.

"Do you think he'll come back?"

"Who?" mumbles Theo, his own mouth full.

"You know. Him."

Theo thinks a moment, peels a banana, dips it in the cold canned hash. He bites a little off, wrinkles his nose, swallows. "No," he says.

"Why not?"

"Think about it," Theo says, taking the vodka from her hand. "Wherever he is, *if* he still is, before he came all the way home, he'd have to make it halfway home."

Lily interrupts, takes a bite of the banana, scoops up some hash. "I think I've heard this somewhere."

"And before he made it halfway home," Theo continues, "he'd have to come half of *that* distance."

Lily bobs her giant knee, and Theo spills vodka down his ribs. She runs an index finger up from his belly, licks it clean. "A quarter of the original," she says.

"Fine. But before he could travel that quarter-way back, he'd have to go half of that distance too."

"An eighth."

"Okay. An eighth. But he'd never make it. He'd always have more to go. He doesn't have a chance. He's stuck."

Lily takes the glass back from Theo, fills it from the bottle, empties it again. "But what if he did it in one big step," she says, "and walked right over all those halves and quarters and all that other stuff?"

Theo's eyes widen. "Do you think he could?"

"I'm asking you," she says, and bobs her knee again.

Penny sleeps on the floor because she still can't stand to lie in the bed she shared with Payne. Only now she's not sleeping. Truth be told, she doesn't sleep much. The sun won't rise for a couple hours yet, but Penny is sitting on the floor, the sheets twisted around her, and she's punching herself in the arm, her middle knuckle extended to maximize the pain, to dig deep at that one bruised spot in the futile hope that the pain she feels right there might overwhelm the rest of it. And, perhaps, might punish her.

How many times, Penny asks herself, have I sworn I'd never shed another tear? And still they come. Not so often anymore, but they come. And more come these last few weeks than had for many months, as if whatever tiny tenderness she has to her surprise allowed herself to exchange with Miss has softened up her scabs. On nights like this one, when he—not Miss, the other one—visits her in dreams, laughing or silent or dead, she wakes conscious that it's all still there, the unfathomed well of hurt in her gut, right there in that old familiar spot beneath her navel. And she knows what little effort it would take, or rather the obverse of effort—she knows what little effort she would need to abandon, what little resistance she would need to let slacken, for that hurt to be free to expand and spread throughout her limbs, rising in her throat until it chokes her and death seems preferable to any recovery, for recovery, she knows, is always only partial, vitality always crippled, health diseased. The mere acknowledgment of the possibility of such a fall, of the power Payne holds over her yet, and the hatred with which she thus regards him and herself and their sulking offspring and all the others alike, is enough to loose a single tear. That one drop drags others in its wake until the flesh of her face pulls back from them as if fleeing from this sudden rain, convulsing as if to escape her body entire and the great big sucking hole of despair that lurks within her gut. And what cringing consciousness remains to her hangs along the ledges of that gastric chasm, clutching tight, terrified, overcome as the vacuum surges, without relief when it recedes. But recede it does, and she's left pushing it down with these ridiculous blows to her body until finally, her tears nearly dry and one arm sore from punching, the other from being punched, she gets up and checks on Bobby.

He's not in bed either, but, like his mom was just a moment before, is sitting on the floor in the middle of his room. He's pinching himself on the wrist, and twisting what flesh he's pinched. His forearm is dark with bruises. When Penny opens the door, he looks up at her. His eyes are dry.

"Mommy," he says. "I want to go find Payne."

Ollie shows up late for dinner and most of the food is gone. Nearly everyone has left. Robert is still there at the end of the table, discoursing to Xavier and Carl about the number

36. A sparrow twitters in some high corner of the room. Elizabeth is nodding off in what's become a rats' nest of dirtied foam and feathers on the floor. Joseph regards her shyly from the table and picks at his dessert. Arthur sits catatonic on his own, his chair pushed back. He's slumped, his chin lolling on his chest, holding his drink on one knee, where it foams a beige stain on his trousers. Ollie takes the seat beside him and slaps him on the shoulder.

"You gonna eat any of that?" he asks, pointing to Arthur's neglected plate, piled high with the evening's meal—stewed chicken feet, each one clutching in its claws a single batter-fried chicken heart. Arthur grunts and shrugs. "Don't mind if I do, then," says Ollie, helping himself to a clawful of claws.

Popping a heart into his mouth, he nudges Arthur. "Art," he says, "you got some of that juice of yours dripping down your mustache. Better wipe that up or it'll eat through your chin."

Art again just grunts. His eyes blink closed.

"Zöe around?" Ollie asks. Arthur shakes his head.

"She okay?"

Arthur wipes his chin and speaks at last. "With Felix," he says. "She's taking care of Felix."

"Oh," says Ollie. "He's sick?"

Arthur nods.

"Hope he gets better," Ollie says.

Ollie gives Felix two days to do just that. But Zöe still does not return, so the next morning he splashes his hair and face with water and leaves it to run down his brow in drops. He wobbles outside and bangs on the door across the way. Hans answers, which is a surprise, because it's Sally's place. He's wearing black bikini briefs, black socks, and nothing else.

"Hans," Ollie grunts, "I'm sick. Go get Penny." He lurches forward and falls into Hans's arms. "Get Penny," he mumbles. "Or Zöe. Or both. I'm sick. Hurry."

Hans pushes him back outside and slams the door. He opens it again a minute later, dressed now in his usual getup and smelling of toothpaste, aftershave, and hair wax. Ollie's lying on the ground, moaning, so Hans grabs him by the ankle and drags him to his hut. He rolls him into bed and sprints off up the hill, over the moat, and through the rusting palace gates. He rings the bell, then rings it again. He's rung it fifteen times when Miss appears, his hair cropped short above his ears, but uncombed, and sprouting in a cowlick. "Get Penny," Hans tells him with a sneer.

Ten minutes pass before she comes down. Her face is pale and puffed with sleep, or with the lack thereof. She's wearing a threadbare terry-cloth robe and she pulls it tight around her chest, crushing her breasts with her forearms. Her legs are bare and unshaven and she's got white socks on her feet, little ankle-high tennis socks and no shoes.

"What is it?" she yawns.

Hans just stands there, gawking at her feet, so she pushes shut the door. Hans grabs the knob before she can shut it all the way.

"Wait," he says, recovering. "Good morning, Penny. Nice to see you."

"What do you want?"

"Ollie's sick." Hans smiles proudly.

"What's wrong with him?"

"I don't know. He's sick. He's sweaty. Falling down. Maybe it's cancer. I don't know. Maybe the flu. Maybe plague. Athlete's foot. Ebola. He didn't say. It's nice to see you, Penny."

"Is he dying?"

"Maybe. He didn't say. He's kind of sweaty."

"Why are you telling me this?"

"He said get you or Zöe. I'm just the messenger. Those are pretty socks, you know."

"Zöe's busy with Felix," Penny interrupts. "And I'm in bed. You take care of him. He'll be fine." And with that she shuts the door.

Carl and Xavier walk with Robert in the field behind the palace. They curve around a short, lumpy hill and the turrets of the palace walls fall out of sight. "Have you been counting?" Carl asks Xavier.

"I lost count," Xavier admits.

"What about you, Robert?" Carl asks.

"Yes," Robert says. "This is the thirty-fifth tree we've passed. That buzzard is the fourteenth bird I've seen. In the elm up there is the second squirrel. We've passed 4 old tires filled with lilacs, 19 shotgun shells, and 7 rats. Six plastic bags have drifted by on the wind."

"So that oak ahead," says Carl, "will be the thirty-sixth tree."

"A special number," observes Xavier.

"Indeed it is," Robert agrees.

When they arrive beneath the tree, Xavier pulls a rope from his backpack. Carl puts his arm around Robert's shoulders, and Robert smiles nervously. With his other arm, Carl grabs Robert's wrist and pulls it behind his back.

"Hey, guys," Robert says, "what are you doing?"

They tie Robert's hands together. Then his feet. "Hey, guys," he says again. Then they push him to the ground and make him crouch. They wrap the rope around him, tying it once with each turn until they've bound him into a ball, his head pushed so tightly to his chest he can't speak.

"Have you been counting?" Xavier asks Carl. He tosses what's left of the rope up around an overhanging branch.

"Thirty-six knots," Carl says. He pulls with Xavier, and they hoist the Robert ball precisely one yard, or 36 inches, above the ground. Carl produces a measuring tape and checks.

"A special number," they agree. Xavier tells Robert they'll be back to get him soon, in 36 hours or thereabouts. Carl tells him not to worry. They stroll back down the path to the palace hand in hand.

Later, julienning leeks in the kitchen, they start to feel a little bad, so they go back and cut him down and roll him home, not after 36 hours but after 9, which is nonetheless the sum of 3 and 6.

Miss and Penny are walking back to the palace, and a snake slithers across the path in front of them. Its scales are the color of pistachio pudding and its eyes are liquid black. Miss takes a breath. "What a beautiful creature," he whispers.

The snake stops in the middle of the path, rears its sleekened anvil head, bares its fangs, and hisses out its little cleft black tongue. Then, satisfied that it has made its point, it winds off into the bushes.

"Do you think it's poisonous?" Miss asks.

"Probably," nods Penny.

"Let's follow it," Miss says, and before Penny can protest, he grabs her hand and leads her off through the brush where the snake snaked away. They push through a snarl of weeds, scraping their shins and catching feathered barbs between their toes. They scare up a flock of doves, which settles in the scrub just fifteen yards away. Forgetting the snake, they follow the birds from bush to bush and before long they've lost the path that got them there.

"We should go back," Penny says, "before it gets too dark." But back is not a simple thing when you no longer know where front ran off to, so they agree to climb the nearest hill to see if they can spot something familiar. They scramble up on their knees, finding handholds in roots and chunks of poured concrete. But at the top all they can see is yet another hill beyond the one they've climbed. At its peak sits a billboard, huge and alone, its surface long since faded, a palimpsest of paper peeling like bark from a birch. They keep climbing.

Miss stops at the summit, hands on his bleeding knees. His chest heaves. Penny's panting too, but she keeps going, straight up the rungs that line the billboard's rusted frame. She stands on the narrow lip at the base of the old blank sign. "Can you see anything?" yells Miss from down below.

Penny clucks and shakes her head. "I think I see the snake," she says. "It's laughing."

Miss climbs up and sits beside her. They let their legs hang over the edge.

"We're lost," says Penny. "I haven't been lost in years. And it's all your fault." She kicks him.

"I'm sorry."

"Don't be. I'm very happy."

"What'll we do?" asks Miss.

"I don't know." She lays her head on his shoulder and listens to him breathe. She counts his breaths. When she gets to one hundred, she lifts her head and asks him. "Aren't you frightened?"

"Of being lost?"

"Yes. But I don't just mean now, I mean generally, by what you don't remember."

"Should I be?" Miss asks.

"I don't know. I think I would. I can't imagine. Maybe I'm jealous," Penny says, and bends to pick a burr from her calf. She bites her thumb and elbows Miss. "You didn't answer my question."

"No," he says. "It doesn't scare me. The only thing that frightens me is you."

"Me?" Penny says. She looks at Miss. She stands up. "We should go," she says.

Miss reaches for her hand. "Do you want to know why?"

Penny looks down at him, at his big, questioning eyes. She bends to kiss his upturned brow, then shakes her head. "No," she says. "I don't."

She climbs the rungs to the cement platform beneath and picks her way down the hill. Miss trails behind her silently, and they do their best to go back the way they came.

Hans troops back down the road from the palace, kicking a rock in front of him as he goes. A cat stalks along the side of the road, keeping pace with Hans. It's missing an ear and its ribs poke through its nearly hairless flesh. For some reason, it seems to feel an affinity for Hans, despite his relative health and strength and obvious noncatness. This sentiment is not returned. Hans picks up a rotting crab apple and whips it at the cat. The cat yelps, leaps in the air, and lands on its haunches, hissing. "Piss off," says Hans, and the cat does.

Hans pushes through Ollie's door without knocking. Ollie's lying in bed, reading a magazine, puffing on a joint. The room smells of hash smoke and sandalwood air freshener. A dozen candles burn around the bed. Ollie's changed his dirty sheets for silk ones that match his red pajamas. He takes one last hit and stubs out the roach in the crystal ashtray on the bedside table.

"All right, you fucker," Hans says. "Quit fooling."

"Is she coming?" Ollie croaks, letting the magazine fall to his chest.

"Zöe's busy and Penny can't be bothered, so I'm your nursemaid." Hans rolls up the sleeves of his black shirt.

Ollie pushes the sheets aside and stretches. He blows out half the candles. "Funny," he says, "I feel a little better."

"Get back in bed," Hans says. He cracks his knuckles. "You're sick."

Katerina and Sally lie side by side at Katerina's place, not in the hammock but on the futon. They're propped up on pillows, staring at their toes. "When I was a little girl," says Sally to the toes, "I remember thinking all my problems would be solved if I didn't have a memory. I didn't want any notion of time at all, just to live entirely right now, always now—now, now, now. I didn't want to know that anything had ever happened before, didn't want to know what before could even mean. I didn't want later either. There'd be no regret and there'd be no fear, and I'd be happy."

Katerina squeezes Sally's hand, and addresses the toes as well. "Sounds okay," she says.

Sally shakes her hand away. "I told my father this. I don't know why, but I went and told him. You know what he said?"

Katerina turns from the toes to Sally's face. She shakes her head.

"He said there's a name for people like that, who only know the present."

"What is it?"

"Sociopath."

"What an asshole."

Sally pulls her toes up beneath the sheet, curls them closer to her thighs. "Yeah," she says to the pillow, and takes Kate's hand, and squeezes back.

The second Zöe falters in her vigil and dozes off, Felix slips out of his hovel and makes for the shore. He fills his pocket with cigarette butts as he goes. At the beach, he sits on the edge of a jagged rock and squeezes the stale tobacco into a torn-off square of newspaper. He rolls it tight, licks and lights it up. A sand crab scurries over his foot. Maybe he's being stupid, Felix thinks. Maybe she doesn't love the new guy, just wanted to fix him up because she's like that. Maybe she does, though. Love him. And maybe he's being stupider still, imagining she ever might find something to love in this, his stunted frame, that she'd one day take solace from the gifts his stubby limbs could give her. Maybe she doesn't love anyone but Payne, and can't. Maybe she doesn't even love Payne.

What's to stop him, Felix takes another drag and wonders, from hitting the pipe again? All the world is sand and brine. You can't eat it or drink it and it won't hold you tight. The cold is inescapable, even on the balmiest of days. Why not chase it away with a flick of a lighter and a plume of blue smoke? Let it burn through his lungs 'til he's charred to ash and blown away. The sand crab pinches the tender flesh between his toes, but Felix doesn't notice. He's busy now with craving. His body remembers things his brain can only guess at.

You rebel at this dichotomy, this age-old mythic split, but have you ever fought your body? (The question is addressed to your mind.) Not just forgone a second pastry, but really had to battle with the fucking thing? If you have, you know it usually wins, meat though it may be. The itching cadaver likes to get its way. So the sector of Felix's brain that is in charge of *jonesing* sends its electrochemical mercenaries crashing through all the bulwarks flimsily erected by that more or less theological construct known as *will*. They chloroform the guards, dynamite the door to the vault of his remembrances, and make off with a single recollection, disregarding all the precious rest. This prize they expose to the klieg lights of his consciousness, and Felix no sooner recalls where he's hid a stash of rock than memos have been faxed to his feet to direct the whole corporeal package in that direction, posthaste. The feet obey.

Marching forward on this mission, glad to be charged with something, Felix at first does not feel the tugging at his belt. "Onward," the jonesing cells insist. But eventually the sensitive, patient receptor cells in his back and in his waist get their message through upstairs, and Felix wonders what that tugging is. He stops and turns around. It's Bobby.

"I need your boat," he says.

"Not now," Felix says.

"Now."

"Not now," Felix says again. "Maybe later. I don't know."

"Now," Bobby says, taking Felix's hand. "I need the boat right now." And Bobby, despite his size and age, being his father's son, and his mother's son, prevails over Felix's body and mind alike. Felix, spared for now another binge, takes him to the boat.

Penny looks for Miss in the kitchen, but Xavier hasn't seen him all day. She wants to get lost again. In fact, she needs to very badly. She misses Miss, is even almost willing to tell him that she does. She knocks on the door to his room and when he doesn't answer, she turns the knob. The room is empty. The bed has been stripped. The sheets are piled neatly at its foot. On top of them sits a piece of yellow construction paper, doubled over once, with Penny's name written in magenta crayon. She unfolds it, and reads:

Dear Penny,

I have to go. If you can know yourself, and do, love can take that from you. So I hear at least. If you have a past that you remember, that you can twist into a tale, if you have a name, a home with friends a pet and dinner obligations, love can make you lose it all without regret. But if you have none of those things, none of that knowledge and familiarity that make of you a self, where can love take root? Can you just be love and nothing else? Better said—can I? Who can I be if I am only your reflection? Understand: it is enough for me to mirror you, more than enough, so long as I can glance too, and sometimes catch sight of you. But I am afraid of this.

*There is enough of me now to be afraid, and so I'm leaving. I
don't have to tell you how grateful I am. Or how much I'll
miss you.*

Penny folds the paper in fourths and sticks it in the back
pocket of her jeans. She sits on the bed, takes the letter out
again but doesn't read it. She lets herself fall on her side,
her head in the piled linens. She sniffs them for the scent
of Miss, but they've been laundered, and only smell of soap.

Payne wakes from a dream of Penny, legless, her arms
reduced to stumps, writhing on her back as lines of men
take turns with her. They're faceless, but he somehow recognizes Izzy, and Yves, and thinks he knows the rest, the
same old crew of useless drag-ass faggots, dissolute enough
to take their perverse pleasures, too cowardly to wear a
face. When he wakes, his mouth is dry and his heart is
pounding. He wants to vomit, and when the bus crashes
through a pothole, nearly tossing him from his seat, he
thinks maybe he will. Payne hears a bang, and then a heavy
flapping, and he knows a tire's blown. The bus shudders to
a stop. The door creaks open and the driver climbs out. The
old lady sitting next to Payne spills her bourbon in his lap.
   "Old bag," Payne says.
   She twists her lips into a scowl and hisses through toothless gums. "Say it again," she says.
   Payne does. "Old bag," he says. But she's fallen asleep.
Her wattled neck goes slack and her age-shrunk head lands

dead on his shoulder. A trail of spittle leaks out on his shirt. Payne shrugs hard and she falls the other way, into the aisle and onto the black, grooved rubber floor. He steps over her and gets off the bus. He leaves the driver cursing, struggling in the dark with the jack, and marches off down the road. The crickets are humming, but all Payne hears is the falling of his feet.

12½

An Interlude

THIRTEEN (13) HYPOTHESES REGARDING MISS, harvested in the banquet hall over kidneys and cauliflower, claret and cocaine. All sources requesting anonymity. And more cocaine.

1. Miss is Payne's archenemy from a parallel universe. Everything on the right in our universe was on the left over there. Otherwise it was pretty much the same. They were born at the exact same moment to mirror-perfect mothers and were raised in perfect synchrony, licking at ice-cream cones and riding bicycles and jerking off in unison to identical porno rags, but each a universe away, and inexplicably burdened by their hatred for some great unknown: each other. Then something went wrong with the wiring, parallel lines intersected, the worlds combined. That's why this one is so fucked up. Left is right and right is left. Up down and down up. Payne and Miss met like matter and antimatter mixed. So explosive was it that Payne got blown to who knows where, and look at Miss, scarred and stupid, fat as a house and ruined through and through.

2. Miss is a rock star kidnapped by pirates. He was the greatest rock star ever, so beloved it would be an insult to say he was worshipped like a god. No god could command such love. Not just churches but whole cities were built to house and honor his every dropped guitar pick, sweaty towel, cigarette butt, condom. Mothers begged him to deflower their daughters and pleaded that he let them watch. Fathers did the same with sons. All across the world, girls and boys, the aged, the middle-aged, took their lives for want of him. What was life worth if they could not have him, had to settle for the radio version like all the other schmucks? The population dwindled. Album sales declined. Miss took it all in stride. Then a band of pirates disguised themselves as valets and hijacked his limo from in front of his hotel. He was presumed dead, and the world just died of sadness. People sat in their bedrooms, their stereos on, crying 'til the tears puddled and swamped and rose above their heads. Only his captors and a few oblivious fuckups here and there survived the flood. The pirates tore off their little valet tuxedos, revealing velvet capes, great plumed hats, eyepatches, and sabers. They chained him to the mast of their ship, passed a jug of rum around, and commanded that he sing. They cackled as they plugged his ears with wadded toilet tissue to deprive him of the pleasure of his own voice. They refused to give him rum. But his singing was so crushingly beautiful that the pirates wept and were blinded by their weeping, and in their blindness crashed the boat into a rock. Lashed to the mast, Miss kept afloat, but all the pirates perished. The chains rusted off, the mast rotted

and sank, Miss was battered by the waves until he washed up on our beach.

3. Miss is Payne's long-lost brother. They were separated at birth, joined opposing armies, and went away to War. Only after he had cut Payne down, when Payne lay dying in his arms, did Miss realize what he'd done. He cast himself into the sea and his guilt wiped his mind clean of memories, but the fates in all their cruelty directed him here, to Payne's old home. Don't tell him who he is!

4. Miss is a tumor that Penny grew. Look how small he was when he first got here, how he was always with her, how big he is now. Look at what he's done to her. What else could he be but cancer?

5. Miss is the pirate. He kidnapped Payne. After his victory at War, Payne set off for Home to return to Penny and lead us once more to glory, but he was waylaid by Miss and his dastardly crew of brigands. So heavy was Payne's ship with treasure that he could not escape Miss's lighter vessel, though Payne valiantly encouraged his crew to row until their chains ate through the flesh of their wrists and they expired of blood loss and fatigue. Miss was the first to board, and was nearly sliced to pieces by Payne, who slaughtered every last penny-ante privateer in Miss's crew and was defeated only when Miss snuck up behind him and beaned him with a gold bar. Miss lashed Payne to the mast and spent the next three

months transferring Payne's gathered booty from one ship to the other. But Miss's galleon was not made for such a load, and just as he brought the last chest of jewels aboard, pegs began to burst from boards, the sea rushed in, the rats out, and with them Miss, who swam straight here, to Payne's old turf, intent on making up his loss.

6. Miss is a serial killer prowling from island to island in search of prey. He eats what he kills and doesn't leave a trace. If we haven't already been killed, we will be soon. The scary thing is, we'll never even know.

7. Miss is Payne with makeup on. There was no War. He went away to test us. He learned to alter his appearance like a pro. They have schools for that out there. In malls. You can pay tuition with a debit card. It's him, come back to make us pay. He'll wash his face and you'll all see the truth.

8. Miss is nothing. He's disgusting. He's nothing at all. Not a man, not a woman, just a nasty old blob. Shaped like the letter O, like a zero, inside and out. Does nothing, is nothing. How could anyone ever want him?

9. Miss is a big fat faggot.

10. Miss is a spy sent by Payne to check us out. Payne is waiting just offshore with an armada, with countless riches he doesn't want to share. Miss in fact remembers every-

thing, every fart and belch, every word we speak, every hair in everybody's nose. He sends off memos tied to eagles' talons. Payne knows everything we've done and do, and soon he'll come for us. Worry about Miss, but Miss is just the beginning. Worry about what comes after. Soon he'll come for us.

11. Miss is a golem. He's all of us and also Payne. Penny made him out of our dead skin, snot from our snot rags, the hairs we leave behind, our fingernail clippings and piss and spittle, the dust in the pockets of Payne's old clothes. She mixed it all with sea water and glue and she squirted her own blood into his veins. She breathed him to life with a kiss. No need to worry, really—everything that's his is ours. Partly ours. Not enough.

12. Miss is a ballerina, the most beautiful ballerina of all. He dances up the world. The cosmos is created and refreshed with the slightest movement of his arched foot, his thigh, his wrist and slender throat. The world is born in beauty, that's why it's here, his dance. And if he should ever stop dancing, there would be nothing left, creation uncreated. And he stopped dancing long ago. Look at him. Even the sea could beat him. He's fat and broken and stumbles on the rocks. Look at us now. Look at everything.

13. Miss is nobody. He's just some hapless bum. He's a former middle-school librarian, laid off due to budget cuts.

He's a small-town wino. He refills ice machines. He's a mailroom clerk at a provincial polytechnic academy. He's a security guard at a chicken stand way out in the suburbs. He fell off a whale watch and washed up here. Doesn't matter what he is, he's nobody from nowhere. What matters is he's fucking Penny.

13

Couplings

or

More Vignettes

or

Something for Everyone,
Why Not Me?

THE TUBES OF THE MOTEL'S neon sign are cracked. Part of the O is missing, and one leg of the E, so now it reads **MCTFL**, but Miss knows what it is. The asphalt of the parking lot is cracked, the pool filled with creeping vines. A rusted washer-dryer rests in the jacuzzi. The windows of the office are broken, but the coffee maker's still there, a fern growing from the fertile caffeinated soil of the filter basket. The cash-register drawer hangs open like a lolling tongue.

Miss sits on the dusty office sofa. He's just a half-hour's walk from the palace, but the only shoes he's got are flip-flops and the rocks and glass that line the valley floors have been tough on his feet. He's thirsty and his back aches. He leaves the office and tries the doors to the rooms. They're all unlocked. The first room has been trashed— door dangling from one hinge, TV and windows shattered, plush chairs and mattress razor-slashed, feces of provenance ancient and unknown crusted on the walls, everything heavy with the sharp and musty scent of self-disgust. The other rooms, though, are nearly untouched. A window's cracked here and there, some rugs are breeding mildew, words now indecipherable have been scratched into the piling coffee-table dust, but otherwise they're fine.

Miss shakes out the bedspread in room 116 (Where is Robert when we need him? 16 + 1 + 25 + 14 + 5 + 12 + 5 + 19 + 19). He kicks off his flip-flops and tries the sink in the bathroom. To his surprise, the water runs. It's cold and a little rusty, but it's water nonetheless. He rinses the dirt from the floor of the tub, takes off his gown, and steps under the shower. The towels on the rack are caked with ocher dust, so Miss slaps one against the wall before drying himself. He stands in front of the bathroom mirror and regards the curve of his gut. It's still new to him, this body. He tries to see himself through Penny's eyes. The scars on his chest are obscured now among all the swelling flesh, but he can see three pink stripes rise twisting up his shoulders. His stomach droops over a grove of wired hair, beneath which his prick dangles like some cartoonish stranger. His nearly hairless thighs look heavier than they did the week before and the scars there too seem to have faded some as his flesh grew tight around all this new meat. His face is young still, his eyes bright and his brow unlined by age. Could Penny have been pleased by his expanded frame? Comforted? Repulsed? He doesn't know. His ankles hurt.

Miss lies down naked on the bed. The springs creak. The bedspread is rough against his calves. He lies on his back until the room darkens and the sun sets, and he doesn't move until it rises up again.

Joseph sits beside Penny in the Great Hall, and she takes his hand in hers. All through the fuss and blather of the evening meal, Penny holds his hand beneath the table, giving it the occasional squeeze, caressing his palm with her thumb. Joseph is dreaming, you see, and in his dream that's all that happens, nothing too steamy, they just hold hands. She doesn't even glance his way. But when Joseph wakes, he's hard. It's a comfort, this firm length swelling warm against his belly, anchoring him. He remembers Zöe's legs clenched around Ollie in the palace bathroom and imagines himself in Ollie's place: Zöe's thighs squeezing him, the Formica cold against his knees, her back stiffening as he enters her, her closed eyes and quick intakes of breath. He strokes himself off until he comes.

Wiping his navel with a Kleenex, Joseph can't help but feel ashamed. Though it was Zöe who took the leading role in his fantasy, it feels like it's Penny's body, not his own, that he's just filthed and stickied. But it is undeniably his own chest from which he mops his gobs of goo, his own hand that does the mopping, and that's a lonely business.

He tosses the tissues beside the bed and hugs a pillow to his face. This can't go on, he thinks. He remembers hearing Ollie and Arthur talking after dinner. Zöe is taking care of Felix, Art said. Felix is sick, or was. But Joseph's sick too. Maybe his nose isn't running and his throat isn't sore, but there are other kinds of illness. There's a sporadic tightness in his chest and a concurrent emptiness in the gut, regardless of hunger or lack thereof. Sometimes his heart beats too fast and his hands shake and he wants things he knows he can't have and isn't sure he can survive the privation. Sometimes all desire flees him, and the world's so thick he can barely move.

What picture of health is this? The more Joseph considers it, the more he's sure he's ill. And that he'd better send for someone soon.

Izzy brews a second cup of poppy tea and passes it to Nellie.

"Is it too hot?" he asks, unplugging the hotplate.

"No," she says, and blows on it.

"It is too hot," he says. "I'm sorry."

"It's fine."

"Is it sweet enough?"

"It's fine," she says. "Just drink."

They sit on the couch and sip. Nellie reclines, resting her head in Izzy's lap, her teacup on her stomach. Izzy runs his fingers through her hair until she falls asleep. He takes the teacup from her hand, swallows the sugary dregs, and puts the cup on the table in front of him. Through the open window, Izzy can smell diesel exhaust from the generator colliding with the scent of jasmine. A bird flies in and perches on the rim of the cup inches from Izzy's feet. A sparrow or a starling or maybe a finch, its feathers are brown and herringboned in black and white along its wing. Its head twitches from side to side as its beady black eyes inspect the room. They pause on sleeping Nellie, and move along.

"Hello there, birdie," Izzy says. "Make yourself at home." But his voice startles the skittish fellow, which imagined itself alone. It takes flight in a panic. Nellie wakes. They watch in silence as the bird leaps and dives through the green fluorescent light, unable to find an exit. At last, poor bird, it spies a window and hurries toward salvation. But little birdies don't know about such things as glass, and it crashes through the pane, leaving a small birdie-shaped hole in its wake. Izzy jumps to his feet, his robe flapping open in his haste. He pushes up the window and leans out. On the ground lies the still body of the little bird, broken but unbloodied. Izzy turns to Nellie. His face, in contrast to the erection swelling out from between the plaid flannel folds of his robe, is ashen, as if all the blood has drained from his head and into that bobbing protuberance.

"Please," he gasps, "don't touch me." And with that he rushes to the couch and tugs her sweatpants to her knees.

———

Felix taps his foot on the splintering floorboard of his shack and pumps one long, fluttering note out of his accordion. His hands are shaking, so there's even more vibrato than usual. He sucks in a breath and sings in a ragged, lingering falsetto: *I don't got you I won't got her I ain't got even me.* From the rag pile in the corner of the room, a mouse anxiously looks on. Felix slowly fingers forth a melody. It bellows out through his instrument and bounces around the tarpaper walls. Felix sways a little as he sings:

> *Shining up a quarter, shining up a dime*
> *Ain't got nuthin shiny, nuthin left but*
>   *time.*
> *Tie me up so tightly, tie me up so loose,*
> *I kick my feet I'm dancing, hanging from*
>   *a noose.*
> *Spoon another spoonful, shovel full of*
>   *dirt,*
> *I want another helping, nuthin never hurt.*
> *Penny, you're not with me, Penny, you*
>   *ain't here . . .*

He begins to croon the next line, but gets stuck on the first word: *Penny.* He sings it again: *Penny Penny*

Penny Penny . . . the same two notes. And as he chants, the tempo builds. He sings faster and faster, taps his feet and kicks his heels. The mouse disappears among the rags. Before you know it Felix is smiling, singing as fast as he can play, dancing as fast as his feet allow: *Penny Penny* until the smile breaks and turns to laughter and Felix can't help but fall to his knees and topple backwards, the accordion belching and moaning, pinning him like a beetle on its back, rolling on the floor, gasping and laughing and singing Penny's name.

When his fit at last abates, Felix sits up. He straightens his shirt and adjusts the shoulder strap on his instrument. He squeezes shut his eyes, lets a sigh rattle forth from somewhere high in his throat, then pumps out that same first note and trills again: *I don't got you I won't got her I ain't got even me.*

Sally's back at Katerina's and it's not nearly morning yet when Kate nudges her awake. Sally tries to roll over away from all the nudging, but they're wrapped up in the hammock and there's nowhere to roll. Katerina's face is swollen. Her eyes are rimmed with red. She takes Sally's hands in hers. Her voice is hoarse. "Would you leave me for Penny?"

Sally rubs her nose, snorts, sighs. "No."

Katerina brightens. She asks again, "Really?"

"Really," Sally says.

Katerina kisses her, beaming, and her whole body is transformed by relief. Her muscles soften, the tension leaves her neck, and she at last is able to drift off with her arms around Sally, her head between her breasts. But Sally's awake now, and she lies there watching the shadows circumnavigate the carpet as the hammock gently sways. She stares at her lover, now so placidly asleep. She pinches her neck. "Kat," she says, "wake up."

Katerina lifts herself up on an elbow, worry in her eyes.

"Would you?" Sally asks.

Katerina lays her head back down on Sally's chest. It's her turn now to sigh. "Of course."

"Oh."

"Are you angry?" Katerina asks.

"No," says Sally. "But I take it back. I would leave you. For her."

Katerina pushes herself from Sally's side, swings her feet over the edge, and stands in the middle of the room, arms akimbo and hands balled into fists.

"Are you angry?" asks Sally, the hammock swaying faster now.

"No!" yells Kate, and she runs out into the night.

Penny's tennis shoes are splitting at the toe, sole from upper, upper from sole. It's not irreparable at this point, and she'd hardly notice if pebbles didn't keep worming their way into the gap. But they do, so she sits on a log and pries them out with a twig. She had needed some air, and asked Yves to go find Bobby and give him lunch while she went out to stretch her legs. She walked two laps around the palace walls and would have lingered there longer, skipping stones into the moat, but Theo spotted her and Nellie too and she didn't wish to talk to any of them, so she wandered farther afield, up the hill behind the palace and down into the valley beyond until she could no longer ignore the pebbles collecting just beneath her toe and had to stop and pick them out. At least that's what she tells herself.

Someone with a more objective view of the situation would tell the story differently, if such a someone could be found. But while otherwise engaged in sneaker maintenance, Penny is silently sparring with just such an objective observer. Better put, Penny is arguing with herself, or with a disobedient fragment thereof that refuses to succumb to the prevailing narrative proffered by another part: the Tale of the Innocent Stroll. No, this competing voice in Penny's cranium insists she's up to something. It's more of a nagging whisper, and it nags and whispers that Penny is in fact searching for signs of a certain missing Miss, that it was only her hesitancy to own up to the truth that kept her so close at first to the palace walls. Now she's here and the palace is out of sight. The pebbles weren't really bothering her at all, but she has to decide which way to go.

But why would she look for him? What a ridiculous idea. He was always free to go. And all his talk of love was surely nonsense, just flirtatious banter, talk and nothing more. If he had meant it, he'd have stayed. You don't leave the one you love, do you? You don't just wander off. But if he had meant it and he had stayed, what good could have come from any of it? Just heartache for him and an extra burden for her, someone else to attend to. So it's good that he left, best for everyone. Why would she be such a fool as to search for him?

Penny unlodges the last pebble and flicks it off into the dirt. She stands, bored with this stroll already, resolved to head immediately home. Only her feet don't take her there. They head straight out through the valley and up the far hill behind it.

She rubs a bug from her eye and kicks her way over a mound of rusted cans. Her heart beats fast from climbing. But it's not just the hill. A crow caws somewhere behind her, and Penny realizes that she's angry. Or perhaps it's fear she's feeling, Penny doesn't know. She doesn't want to follow it too far, lest she force herself to ask: fear of what, and angry why? She pushes aside a branch and trudges onward. Lizards scatter in the rocks beneath her feet. A humming-bird hums twice about her head, its wings a blur, its breast a shimmer of gold and green and violet. She thinks of Miss and for a second can't help but smile. The world is bright, and beautiful. She reaches the top of the hill and gazes down at the landscape beneath her.

It's been so long she'd forgotten it was here. Her lungs

forget to breathe. The sign is still standing, if worse for wear. In which room did she and Payne sleep? She can't remember, except that it was on the second floor. She's almost running, curving down the hill and into the flats beneath. How can she not remember? It's been a while, and they all look alike. She slows her pace. The shadow of the motel's sign stretches almost to her feet. She's really frightened now, not of finding Miss or failing to—all thought of him has fled her mind. She's scared by time itself, by all she carries with her, by the worn edges of the past, its colors faded, its surface shiny and smooth from overhandling. What if it all is worthless? If the present is but the past decayed, like this motel thick with dust, returning slowly to the earth, what weight has anything? How old she feels! How shabby and long-winded is the world! The pool is empty of water and tangled with vines. The parking lot's a field of drying weeds.

The door to one of the rooms is open. Penny sniffs at the musty air within, and walks into the dim. She sits at the foot of the unmade bed. She lights a cigarette and stares at the face of the dead gray television that's sitting on the dresser. She tries to make out her reflection in its screen, but there's too much dust and all she can see is the dancing orange blur of the cigarette shaking in her hand.

The sea has calmed considerably, but still it's just wave after wave after wave, little variation in color, shape, sound. How it does go on! Waves rolling in from here to tomorrow and farther still to yesterday beyond. Wave bumps wave, bobbing young Bobby up and down and all about. The water moves. It swishes here and everywhere, but still it's just water—what's the point? This thirsty spectacle of infinitude has been enough to shake some men's hold on sanity, to mirror for their pissant conscious minds the unending nothingness in which they inevitably swim, and that to deleterious effect. But not Bobby. He sits in his sailor suit at the stern of Felix's boat, guiding the rudder with both hands. Except the rudder snapped off when he ran up onto that sandbar, so really he's just holding a stick. The mast too is gone, cracked in the squall just after the gale that shredded the canvas sails. There are no oars because Felix had them stashed up in his shack and Bobby wouldn't wait for him to fetch them. He's not sorry. Bobby rises and falls with the tides. The sea turns him whichever way it likes, shooting him to the fountaining peaks of its waterspouts, twirling him in the centrifugal depths of its eddies. It sucks him into its speediest currents, then spits him out to list in its calms. Bobby's gaze never flinches from the horizon. His grasp on the rudderless rudder does not falter once. His course is straight and true.

Arthur's in bad shape when Zöe finally returns. He hasn't shaved for days, and his beard is crusted with grayish-white scum. His skin is pale and beaded with sweat. Brown sacs abut his eyes. Stains dot his shirt and slacks.

He has no idea how long he's been drinking, only that no matter how much he pours down his throat, nothing seems to get him drunk.

He heaves himself off the couch when she comes in. His drink foams in his glass. Zöe forces a dram of optimism across her face. It forms something like a smile. "I'm home," she says.

Arthur doesn't look at her. He takes a sip.

"How's Felix?" he asks, and sits again.

"Better, I guess. I fell asleep and when I woke he'd gone out, so he must've been feeling better. I guess."

Arthur nods. "Must've been," he says, and then, almost as an afterthought, asks, "Did you get a chance to fuck Oliver on your way home?"

Zöe is genuinely surprised. She sits on the sofa beside him and regards him, wide-eyed, still smiling. Her shoulders are goosebumped, her skirt bunched between her thighs. She strokes his bearded cheek. Art only flinches slightly.

"So you noticed?" she says.

"I noticed."

She takes the drink from his hand and places it on the table. She crosses her hands in her lap. Her jaw sets.

"No," she says. "I did not have a chance to fuck Oliver on my way home. I was tired, and I came straight back home to you. I was too tired to fuck anyone, so I came straight home to you."

Arthur takes his drink back and lifts it to his mouth. "Good thinking," he says.

They sit like that in silence, side by side on the couch, conscious mainly of the perfectly transparent Plexiglas wall that, despite their proximity, inexorably divides them. It's invisible but infinitely tall and infinitely wide, so how can they even begin to go about knocking it down? Arthur smushes his face against it, but the grease on his nose and brow doesn't even leave a smudge. He runs his tongue over it, hoping to ink a message with his spit—any message, let her know I'm here and trying, trying to get through. But his saliva evaporates faster than he can lick. Zöe searches for a way over the wall or around it, but she can't even see where it starts, much less discern its limits. At last she notices one thing. Even as impregnable a barrier as this cannot block out Arthur's smell. Like a wedge of Roquefort marinated in gin and left too long in the sun, his scent could seep through lead.

"Arthur," Zöe says, "I need a shower. Come with me."

In the bathroom, she lets the water run until it's hot and the mirror's fully fogged. She pulls off her pants and steps out of her panties. She unbuttons her shirt and unhooks her bra. The water beats against her eyelids and uncoils the muscles in her back. Obscured in the steam-filled room, Arthur pulls back the curtain and steps naked into the tub. Zöe lets him step past her under the streaming water. The crust dissolves from his face. Streaks of murk flow down his belly and circle the drain.

Zöe soaps his back. She reaches around and lathers his chest and bloated stomach. She soaps beneath his arms, between his legs, his soft and hanging genitals, his thighs, the crease of his buttocks. She turns him around and washes the grease from his beard and brow. It's hard to tell if those are tears or if it's just the water running. She gives the soap to him and he rubs it into her shoulders, her slippery breasts, her navel. But holding his hand between her legs and washing her there, where other men have been, this is too much for Arthur. He drops the soap to the floor of the tub, then slips on it, stumbles, and falls to his knees. She catches his head, and pulls it to her belly. She massages shampoo into his scalp, rinses, then washes it again. Arthur stretches his hands to her shoulders and pulls her down to him, just a little, just enough that kneeling there, he can reach her nipple with his mouth. He takes it between his lips, his arms clutched around her back, and gently sucks. They are tears, she sees, and sheds her own.

Revulsion and relief battle hard for Zöe's favor. Neither prevails. She looks to the ceiling, searches for comfort in the billowing steam, gives up and does her best to pretend she's someone else.

When he hears the knock, Joseph rushes over to his bed. It's just an old mattress on the floor, springs poking through to rend the greasy sheets. He pulls a pillow over his face. "Come in," he says.

Someone opens the door and, despite the pillow, out of the corner of his eye, Joseph sees a pair of feet advance across the floor. The feet are bare, the right one bunioned, the ankles slightly fat but not immoderately so. It's not Penny, that much is clear, not Zöe either. But still Joseph asks, "Is that you, Penny?"

And whoever it is, in a voice that is as unlike Penny's as Joseph's own, plays along. "Yep," she says, "it's me."

Joseph feels the mattress sink beside him, and knows that she's sat down. He rolls over on his side. He can make out her legs and a cross section of her torso. She's wearing a gray woolen skirt. Tiny golden hairs shine on her thighs. A soft swell of flesh bulges above her waistline. His face still hidden beneath the pillow, Joseph grins.

"How are you feeling?" she asks, and gently removes the pillow from his face.

It's Sally.

"Not so bad," Joseph says. "A little better now."

Sally smiles and puts her hand to his forehead as if to feel for a temperature. "Is there anything I can do?" she asks.

Joseph takes her hand from his brow and kisses her palm. "Just stay with me a little while."

She curls up beside him, her hand flat on his chest, and rests her head in the crook of his arm. They rest.

Payne prefers the poop deck to the forecastle. He can loiter there and stare off into the ferry's churning wake, feed the birds, spit in the water if he wants to without it coming back to hit him in the face. But the smokestack exhaust gets sucked back here too, pooped out if you will, and Payne isn't sure how many more lungfuls of diesel he can take. He sips his beer and tosses another crust of bread to the gulls coasting along behind the boat. No sooner does one bird catch the bread in its beak than two others dive in squawking and crying to steal it from the first. The biggest of the bunch wrestles the crumb away, but it doesn't get a firm enough grip. The crust falls. All three dive headlong after it, and the wake spits up a claw of foam and pulls them under. Payne waits for them to bob to the surface a couple meters down, but they don't.

The sun is setting off to starboard, which means it'll be cold soon, and Payne will have to find a berth. The credit card is maxed out, so he couldn't book a private cabin. He coldcocked a porter and sneaked aboard two nights ago. Last night there were kids skipping and hollering through the aisles in the common sleeping cabin, and the air was too stale to swallow. The decks were wet with sea mist, so Payne climbed into a lifeboat, lifted the canvas, and spent the night in there, grinding his teeth and dreaming of home. He dreamed he made it back and no one remembered him. Penny was there, dancing and dazzling the rabble with her charms. He recognized each one of the sorry fuckers, but none remembered him. Even Penny said, "Payne who?" He woke up shivering in the dark, the canvas tarp obscuring the swift clouds above him, unsure where he was or if his past was his.

Payne coughs a mouthful of soot into the spray. Off to starboard he can make out what looks to be a boat, mastless and drifting, a little boy in a sailor suit sitting astern, gripping hard the rudder. But the dirty sun emerges from behind a cloud and blinds him, and he writes off this vision as a trick of the sea. There are still more birds hanging aloft in the air before him, so Payne sips his beer and tears off another crust.

In the morning Miss gets up to piss. He directs the stream to spray off the dirt clinging to the sides of the bowl. The sun's only been up an hour, but it's hot already. Miss splashes his face with water. He stands again before the bathroom mirror, wondering what now. He had meant to leave this morning, to throw himself into the world. But then yesterday he had meant to travel farther than this motel, to abandon all his longing in the palace, back there with its object. It hasn't worked so far. His gut hurts, and he's tired already. He turns from the mirror, decides to rest some more.

When Miss opens the bathroom door (yes, alone in a room in an empty motel—*all* vacancies—Miss is modest enough to close the bathroom door), he smells cigarette smoke. Penny is sitting on the edge of the bed. She's wearing navy corduroys, a faded yellow tee-shirt. Her legs are crossed and she's biting her nails and smoking. Maybe she's shivering a little too. She struggles to smile.

"You're here," she says.

Miss makes no attempt to cover himself. He nods. "You're here," he says. His smile comes easily. He walks over and sits beside her. The bed squeaks beneath his weight. Penny grips Miss's knee, her fingers cold. She can't look up at first, can't lift her gaze from the dust resettling on the rug, but she gets her courage up, squeezes his leg for support, and searches his black eyes. In them she finds an answer to a question left unasked. She poses another question, weighs his response, and, to continue this preverbal dialogue, lets her head fall to his lap. She curls her legs up on the bed behind her and lies like that, resting her head on his thighs, sucking at her cigarette and staring at the peeling veneer of the chest of drawers, at the smoke and dust dancing about together in one narrow ray of the sun. His penis twitches beneath her ear, but Penny ignores it, and so does Miss. He strokes her temples and her hair and with quavering fingertips wipes away the tear that's rolling down her nose.

Penny bites her lip. She whispers a word Miss can't quite make out. He thinks it's *stay*. His heart flips and swells beneath his ribs, and, sitting naked in that anonymous abandoned room, for once Miss feels at home.

14

Waiting

or

Time on My Hands

or

That Mad Sifter, at It Again

MAYBE YOU'D BE A DIFFERENT PERSON entirely if you could just forget one thing: forget you love her, forget he died or that she lives, forget the curve of her lips, the wrinkles round his eyes. Or if you could regain a memory now gone: how you got here, maybe—that would surely help. Are our skulls too small for that? It seems they are. What skull could hold a life?

There are things to remember and things to forget. There are tricks you can play to help seal in one thing or another, a fact, a date, a name, a formula. There are numerical concordances, anagrams, rhyming couplets, clever little songs you can make up. These may help. Rote repetition works too. But really it's not up to you, try as you might to hold on.

And if it were, how could you possibly know what you'd end up needing? What flash cards could you study to help you retain the crucial facts of a repressed eight-year-old summer afternoon, the collapse of a love long past, or one of many nights ill spent in blackout?

My point remains. Maybe it's not a point, but another question: Who made you what you are? Not you. I won't speculate as to the names of gods or goddesses, environmental factors, fates. It's not you. That's what matters. That's what's sure, perhaps that alone. And maybe I know this better than anyone, arriving here as I did, unclothed and empty-headed, born a second time (was there even a first?) on Penny's spare bed. I could pretend it tortures me, this loss, my enigmatic past, but that would be a lie. I don't want it. I don't wonder at it. I'm fascinated. Just let me give in to the wind and tide, see where they take me, what creature I become. How can I complain? What's to lose? If I had no hand in this project—me—what could there be to cry over? Let me drift.

These are lies. Let me drift, I should say, just so long as I don't float too far from Penny. I've found an anchor, and I'm unmoored. I am found and all is lost.

I don't remember winter, but my flesh remembers cold. It remembers Penny's hands, cold that night and stiff with fear, pulling at my chest, all their hesitance and need. She had come once before to the motel. Three days before that night, she came for the first time, in the morning. She laid her head in my lap, and lay there until she fell asleep. I slept too, and when I woke it was past noon and

I was alone, lying in sheets soaked with sweat. How much of it was mine and how much hers I don't know, but I had the sense that she'd just left, that the balance of the room had been recently disturbed by movement. I didn't leave that bed all day. Because of the heat, I told myself. And because only there had my sweat mingled with hers. I wanted to leave, I did, to go anywhere, to simply move. But I could not.

When night came and the air chilled, the sheets dried and I could no longer find a trace of her. I remembered where she'd sat, how she'd lain, precisely which parts of her body had rested on which of mine. I searched for footprints in the dusty carpet in the spots where I knew she'd stood, but there was nothing. I sniffed at the sheets like a hog out rooting, but all I could smell was the heavy must of the unused room. I stared at my thighs where her head had rested, at my hands which had brushed tears from her face, but I could detect no change. What horror! Just the smallest alteration, a discoloration or a dent, a grease spot or a wrinkled fingertip—even a wound, best of all a wound!— would have been enough to justify it all. And by all I mean *all*, everything, the whole naked cosmos twitching with loss. But there was nothing. What is memory worth if the world goes on unmarked?

In the morning, at the foot of the bed I found a hair too long to have come from my head. She had been here! It had happened—all of it! I wrapped it around my finger and let it uncurl. But in the light I saw that it was blonder than any hair of Penny's. I blew it from my fingertip. The whole room suddenly seemed heavy, thick with memory, too much mine for me to breathe its air, not mine enough for me to stay.

I did not make it very far. I moved to a room upstairs, precisely the same as the last room but with a different color scheme. Gray instead of beige. And the framed paintings on the walls depicted birds in flight, not seascapes. And someone had scratched initials into the glass of the TV screen. "BB + LB," it said, "4EVR." Otherwise it was the same. I pulled the drapes shut, unleashing an avalanche of dust, and slept in the hot, still room until after the sun had set.

That night I dragged a chair out to the pool, to think and get my courage up before heading on my way. There was a tiny slice of moon, and in its light I watched as mosquitoes sucked the blood from my wrists and the vines in the pool shook with the wind. When a gust blew, they barely whispered. Star after star fell from the sky until I was amazed that there were any left to shine. I sucked in my breath and did my best to listen to my hair grow and to the regeneration of my flesh, but I heard nothing, just my heart, the whine of insects and the wind.

The stars began to dim, the sky to brighten, and the sun finally rose above the hill. Within an hour my hair was wet with sweat and it was too hot to go anywhere at all, so I returned to the room in which I'd slept the day before. I went to the bathroom to piss, and saw that the tub was still wet from my last bath. My hairs curled on the rim of the toilet, and I remembered getting up yesterday three times over the course of the day to piss. The air was stifling. I couldn't stay.

I dried the tub and cleaned the toilet with the same cloth, washed it out and hung it to dry on the hook behind the door. I pulled the sheets from the bed, shook them out, and tucked them in again. When I left, more dust filled the air, but otherwise the room was as I'd found it. I took a room two doors down, this one beige again, with abstract geometric prints instead of paintings, and a Styrofoam cup on the floor. I kicked the cup into the closet, where I wouldn't have to see it, took off my robe, and slept until the sun set and the heat at last dropped off.

There was no wind that night, and no stars either. The sky was overcast. Sometimes I thought I could see the glow of the moon behind the clouds, but it would disappear almost immediately. I had been sitting by the pool for two or three hours with no real thought of getting up or going anywhere or doing anything at all when I saw the beam of a flashlight bouncing down the canyon, and heard feet crunching through the rocks. The light got closer, but it didn't fall on me. Instead it turned to the left, straight to the room in which I'd stayed that first night. I yelled to her, and the light bobbed bigger and bigger until she was right there standing beside me. She turned it off. "How long do you plan to stay out here?" she asked. Her lips were thin and white, and there was anger in her voice.

I gave her my chair, and dragged another over from the office. She sat, and so did I.

"You're just going to stay out here," she said, "in this motel?"

It wouldn't do to tell her how happy I was that my absence made her mad, how glad that this hurt her too, so I said nothing. She pushed her hair from her eyes. We sat there for I don't know how long. I made her wait, and when I could wait no longer, I reached out and took her hand. The hard-set muscles in her jaw began to slacken. She whispered: "Bobby left."

"Where'd he go?" I asked.

"I don't know." She shook her head and laughed, but it came out wrong, not a laugh at all, a sound a small animal might make when threatened. Then the clouds broke, and a light rain began to fall. She really did laugh then, and I tried to join her, but I wasn't sure what to laugh at, what was funny. I squeezed her hand and the rain got heavier until her hair began to stick to her head, and I knew she was wearing makeup because it began to run from her eyes down her face. That was funny, so I laughed, and she laughed with me. "Let's go inside," she said, and we did.

I took her upstairs. I got her a towel and stepped into the bathroom to dry myself. But she said, "Wait."

I stood there in the bathroom, the tiles cold beneath my feet. I do remember that, that pause, waiting there. Her voice was hoarse, unsure. A question opened up inside of me. I waited. I didn't shut the door. "Come back," she said.

I went back. She put her arms around me. Her hair was dark and wet, and I could see where it swirled on the top of her head, and the white of her scalp beneath. Her shirt clung to her shoulders. Half a smile fell across her lips, then broke. She reached out and unbuttoned the top button of my gown. Her hands were shaking. She undid it down to my waist and pushed it down off of me until it fell with a slap to my feet.

My hands shook too, so I steadied them on her hips. I unbuttoned her shirt. It had eight buttons. I remember eight white buttons on a dark-blue shirt. Fake mother-of-pearl and rayon. Her bra was black, and lace, and frayed. She reached behind her back, her shoulders arching towards me, and unhooked the clasp. She put my left hand on her right breast, underneath the loosened cup of her brassiere, and guided my right hand back to her hip, to where her skirt zipped closed. I felt her fingers on my back. I felt them on my chest, cold and stiff with fear, pulling at me and pushing me away all at once.

She left while I was still asleep, before morning, and when I awoke her pillow was still warm.

Do you understand that love is not only amnesia, but that love is suicide, that all love that falls short of suicide is sham?

I didn't see her for another three days after that, and in those days I changed rooms three times. I thought of going to the palace, but something kept me back. Maybe pride, maybe fear. I couldn't leave, couldn't stay, couldn't sleep, afraid that she might come and look in the wrong room. I waited and she didn't come. I don't know how many hours I paced, how many steps I took, how many times I stood in the bathroom to piss, door wide open and ears alert. I don't know how many times my heart beat, though I was aware of every time.

But she left hairs behind, and we left stains. I could smell her on the sheets. I could taste her. It got to be too much, to know she had been there and not have her there to touch, so I tore the sheets from the bed and dragged them to the bathroom. I left them to soak in the tub and scrubbed out every trace of her. I hung the sheets on the second-floor railing to dry, and all day they snapped in the wind, tearing little pieces out of me, pieces I didn't know I had to lose.

She was almost skipping when she came, the flashlight dancing down the path. She came straight to the pool, a basket in her arm. She brought cheese and bread and sausages and fruit, cigarettes, two chilled bottles of champagne, two varieties of white powder in tiny zip-locked plastic bags, one imprinted with an arrow pointing up (like this ⬆), the other with an arrow pointing down (⬇). She sat in my lap and threw both arms around my neck. She kissed me and, with a smile bigger than the sky, said, "I missed you."

"I've been here," I said.

"Don't sulk," she said. "I'm here now."

She crawled off my lap to pull a bottle of champagne from the basket. She tore off the foil and twisted out the cork, hopping with a laugh when the wine foamed on her foot, licking it from the side of the bottle as it fountained out, bubbling in her mouth, frothing white around her pink tongue and crooked teeth. "Take it," she said, handing it to me. "Quick."

I upended the bottle and drank from its neck, and as I did she dropped to her knees in front of me. Her fingers scurried up under my dress, and with her mouth she sketched a line of fluttering kisses all along my inner thigh. I tried to pull her up to kiss her, but she resisted, and took me in her mouth. When she at last looked up there was something very far away in her eyes that I'd never seen before. I pulled her to me then, and sat her on my lap. She swung her leg around and straddled me on the chair, and as she pushed forward the chair fell back, and I didn't notice that we'd smashed the champagne bottle until I tasted my own blood on her breast.

In a room in which I hadn't yet slept, she pulled shards of glass from my hand and forearm, and washed me with a moistened cloth. We drank from the other bottle as she worked. When she had cleaned me up she sliced wedges of cheese and fruit and sausage. I tore the bread into hunks. We fed each other. I placed a piece of cheese on her tongue, a slice of pear between her lips. She licked bread crumbs from my belly and I sucked the salty sausage grease from her fingertips. We filled our mouths with lukewarm wine and giggled as we kissed, sloshing it from mouth to mouth. She lit a cigarette, and passed it to me between drags. My hands were on her all through that meal, and hers on me, more hungry for each other's touch than for any other food.

These things I do remember: the smooth, hard ball of her knee, the dampness underneath it. Her pink nipples, sticky with champagne. The little triangular hollow where her throat meets her ribs. The harsh line of her cheekbones and the softness of her cheeks. Her smoke-scented fingers, cuticles rough. Her hip bone jutting in my palm. The down beneath her arms, wet and sharp with sweat. The syrupy warmth between her thighs. Her green eyes, aglow with present joys. The taut flesh of her bent elbow. A birthmark on her breast, the pale skin around it almost blue. Champagne rivulets begging to be dammed with a tongue as they run past her navel and through the brush of hair below. Her knotted spine. Her mouth.

She wiped the dust off the bureau and emptied one of the plastic bags onto its surface. With the blade of a knife she cut the powder into four lines of equal length. She did the same with the other bag a few inches away, then pulled a short plastic straw from the basket and handed it to me. I didn't know what to do with it, or what either powder was, so she showed me.

We didn't sleep that night. We barely left the bed, getting up only for a sip of water, another snort of this or that. We made love all night. We had everything anyone could ever want. All pleasures, right there and right away. There was nothing to wait for, nothing to hope for, nothing missing at all. We sculpted love out of each other's sweat and cum and cocaine shivers, with bites and probing tongues and humming fingers, with our lips and out of tears.

Because we did not sleep, I was awake when she left. She pulled her leg out from under me. She shimmied her panties up her thighs, stepped into her jeans, and slipped a tee-shirt over her head. She kissed me and whispered good-bye, but I caught her by the wrist.

"When are you coming back?" I said.

She twisted away. "When I can," she said. "I will come back." She said it again, her eyes sad, mad at me for making her repeat it. "I will."

I slept all through the day and part of the next night. I remember waking up with the sun shining blinding bright through a crack in the curtains, my throat dry and my temples pulsing with pain, but with the memory of her still on my tongue, however parched it was. A smile curled my lips, and I slept some more. When I finally woke my whole head hurt. My senses were dulled, as if a length of gauze had been stretched between the world and me. My stomach felt tight, a small hard stone, and from its darkest center I felt spiraling out an ancient fear, so deep and familiar that it was almost comforting, a fear born long before this waking, before any waking I was able to recall, a fear that knew me well. The night came back in fragments, little tickles and whispers of this or of that, of being rooted inside her, of the sweat sliding between our bellies, of her laughter as she came. It made me dizzy. If she could laugh like that with me, what could I possibly be afraid of?

I got up, steadied myself, and stretched. I found my way across the room to the bathroom and ran the rusty water. I washed the sweat and the stickiness from my body without regret. When fear welled up in my gut I tried to let the water wash it too away, as if I could be so easily cleansed. I told myself that she would be back, that nothing else mattered, but that, I know, is what I feared—that *nothing else,* and her embrace my shaky bridge above it, all rotted planks, frayed rope, and rusting joints, the vast and swirling nothingness roaring silently beneath, the plunge. But then the fear subsided and I grew hard again at the mere thought of her touch.

I dried myself and trudged on out to the pool. It was clear that night, and windy. The waxing moon was bright enough to cast thin shadows behind the rocks. I found a chair and watched plastic bags scamper in the wind, chasing each other up the hill, dancing in little crinkled eddies. One flew into my face. It wrapped itself around my head, blinding me. It smelled of motor oil, rot. At last it shook itself away and blew off into the hills.

I wandered into the office and then one by one through all the rooms. Except for the one that had been trashed and the one in which Penny and I had just spent the night, with its unmade bed and all the gathered refuse of the hours, every room was the same. Some were beige and some were gray. The prints on the walls varied. Some bedside tables contained Bibles, others phone books or TV guides, but these are not essential differences. The rooms were gloriously identical, anonymous, empty, free. The present cubed and carpeted, unhinged from past and future. Every day could be like this one, every night like the night before. What more could I want? What less would I settle for? What could I find to fear?

I wandered around to the back of the hotel and found an overturned dumpster, one side buried with silt from the collapsing hillside. Beside it was a bicycle wheel, a car battery melting in a pool of fluid, a child's patent-leather shoe, the skull of what must once have been a dog. Up at the top of the hill I could see a jagged rock. I hoisted myself up by a corner of the dumpster and commenced to climb.

The dirt fell away in miniature avalanches beneath my feet. Sharp rocks sliced into my ankles. My head began at last to clear, but halfway up the hill I was gasping for breath and had to stop to rest. The wind howled and another plastic bag blew into me. This one smelled like meat. When it flew off and my heart slowed to near its usual pace, I began to climb again. I slipped twice before the top, bruised my knees, cut the heel of my hand, and almost tumbled down the hill. At the top I found that the rock was not as craggy as it had looked from down below. Its peak was flat and smooth. I dragged myself up and sat.

I was higher than any of the hills around me. The sky brightened, and the sun was glowing pink just below the ridge to the east. When it rose I could see the ocean beyond it, just behind the sun, though I knew the sea to be to the west of where I sat. The waters were calm, unmarred by a single roll of white. On them I could make out a boat, barely bigger than a rowboat. Its mast was broken, and it had no sail. At its stern sat a little boy in a sailor suit. He was asleep at the rudder, drifting, barely a mile from shore. It was Bobby. I yelled his name, but he didn't hear and didn't wake. Then the sun rose higher. My head began to ache again, and I couldn't see anything for all the light.

Penny came back just two nights later. She carried no basket this time, just a flashlight and a bottle of Scotch. She didn't skip down the path, but walked, and slowly. When I rose to embrace her she grew tense in my arms. I asked her what was wrong. She didn't answer. I asked her if she was worried for Bobby. She pulled away from me, and in that motion I couldn't tell if she was shaking her head in answer to my question or just shrugging herself free of my grasp. I told her I had seen him from the top of the hill, that he was fine, and not far from land. She didn't reply. I promised to take her up at dawn so she could see for herself. She shrugged again, and smiled a wan half-smile.

I led her inside and into a room on the ground floor. Beige, with prints of bald eagles, some soaring, others perched on high branches and cliffs. As soon as we walked through the door, she pushed me down on the bed and knelt before me. I didn't have a chance to even kiss her, but she came when I did, with long, shuddering sighs. She wouldn't let me touch her for an hour after that, and lay curled in the bed, her eyes open, unblinking. And like I feared it would, that *nothing else* blew icy gusts into my lungs.

At last I roused her and coaxed her into a drink. We had no glasses, so we drank from the bottle. By dawn it was empty and we reeled out into the cool morning and struggled up the hill. Penny scampered right up without any trouble, as if it were paved and she hadn't had a drop, but I lost my footing about halfway up and rolled all the way down again. My gown was torn when I got to the top, and I was bleeding from a half-dozen gashes on my arms and legs. She didn't even look at me, but stared to the east, past the point where the sun was rising over the next line of hills. I followed her gaze, but this time I didn't see Bobby, and didn't see the sea at all. I saw Oliver's place, and through the window I could see Hans, smacking Ollie's raised red ass with a wooden paddle. "Hah!" I burst out laughing.

"Look," I said, "do you see them?"

She shook her head. Tears stuttered down her cheeks. She stared into that vague distance, and said, "All I see is Payne."

(Payne paddles just enough to keep afloat and let this latest wave lift him above the ranks of waves aligned in front of it. But he cannot see the coast. Not yet. Just leagues of spitting sea. So he squints up and cranes his neck to check the sun's position. His watch reads 0900 hours. He recalculates his course and angles his arms back into the ocean.

Payne's been swimming now for days. The ferry only took him so far. It dropped him on a boardwalk packed with touts and hawkers, underfed men painting names on grains of rice. The planks were sticky with soda pop. Payne shouldered his way through the crowd, stole a bicycle someone had left leaning against a palm tree. He rode down the shore to the next marina, but he couldn't afford to rent even a rowboat and every unleaking skiff he found was locked or oar- and sail- and engineless, so in the end he tied his clothes in a ball, tied the ball to his ankle, and dove from the end of the dock.

Now he doesn't sleep, just swims. He's slept enough in life, he thinks. And his dreams have been unpleasant lately. While the sun shines, he alternates, breaststroke and freestyle, maybe a half-hour's rest if the current allows, then a few minutes of butterfly to wake himself up. At night he swings his body over. He faces the sky, lines his fingers and toes against the paths of the stars, and backstrokes to his goal.

The nights are lonely, though. In the daytime at least he's facing the deep. Through the green blur below him Payne can sometimes make out flocks of rays and passing herds of sea horses. Once he saw a submarine. He watches guppies gum at his nipples and squids suction at his ribs. He shakes them off and swims. When he turns his head to breathe, he sees the sun shoving its way across the sky through vapor trails and clouds. He glimpses terns diving, frigate birds stealing anchovies from gulls, the low puffs of smoke coughed by freighters far away. And then the dry world disappears and there's the blue again, green and salty and bottomless for all he knows.

But the night is dark and there's nothing to see. The water stretches on, opaque and unforgiving, licking at his back and head and calves. The sloshing of the sea is something worse than silence. The moon sets early. The stars hurry to their spots. Their light is almost blinding. And it doesn't matter that Payne knows their patterns well, can tell Musca from Mensa and Corvus from Crux and name every star in Capricorn. His knowledge of celestial order doesn't help him now. It only makes things worse—this vast clockwork display, its dizzying precision, and Payne alone at sea beneath it forced to choose his path.

What if he's being stupid? What's past is past. You can't go home again. The clichés bounce in his skull. And what if Home was less than homey? Payne remembers, in the nighttime at least, that not all was well when he last saw Penny. He recalls that final morning, her body turned from his in bed, her eyes open but not seeing. Her shoulders stiffened at his touch. He sat beside her and pulled up his socks. He laced his boots. She wouldn't speak to him, wouldn't get up, wouldn't kiss him good-bye or even turn her face from the wall to look at him. He tied double knots and left without a word.

The stars scream down at him. The rushing of the sea echoes in his ears. He's alone and should get used to it. She didn't write a single letter. What kind of welcome will he get? The water's cold. His arms swing out like a windmill's as he swims. Surely she's filled his bed by now. If she hasn't left the palace long ago, run off with some bright-eyed, smooth-skinned cad. Or cads. But the stars twinkle and sometimes tumble from the sky and he remembers also her touch and the warmth of her eyes and what they had before they lost it. He knows for sure she's all he wants and that he'd let the sea pull him down before giving up on that.

The sky turns slowly violet. The starlight bleaches out. Payne rejoices at the night's demise, and when the sun has asserted itself sufficiently that he can distinguish what is east from what is not, he flips himself over and shows the stars his back. As the daylight gathers, Payne's doubt inverts itself. It becomes determination.

He'll reclaim all he's lost.

They'll start anew.

His nighttime fear remakes itself as wrath. His fingers twitch. He'll let no one stand between them. Payne pushes his arms up and onward and chases the sun homeward across the creased surface of the sea.)

15

Smoke Signals

or

One Last Letter

or

Another Tall Tale About Birds

*After a sleepless week of Sundays or maybe just
a weekend locked up in her room—and locked more securely
still inside a certain anguish, a dark spot somewhere between
guilt and dread (whose suites always adjoin)—Penny on tippy-
toes retrieved the typewriter from a high shelf in the closet to
which it had long ago retired, up there with the photo albums,
her wedding dress, and Payne's second-favorite handgun. She
dusted off the keys, replaced the ribbon, spooled in a sheet of
paper, and commenced to write.*

```
Dear Payne,
  It's been a while. Do you know how long?
I stopped keeping track long ago. It
```

doesn't matter. You're still gone. The only
way you will read these words is if, when
I burn this page, you, wherever you may
be, can decipher the smoke as it dissolves
in the sky. Perhaps you are already smoke,
and know its language well. No matter.
Nothing I say to you is for you anymore.
You've ceased to be outside of me. I don't
know how or when it happened, but you've
become my audience. I question you, lecture
you, explain to you. You have no choice—no
role at all, really—but to listen. In your
absence, you've been transmogrified into
something you would never have consented to
be, my silent listener. Sometimes, when I
speak to you, I reach out to touch you as
if you were here in front of me. I stroke
your face, brush my thumb over your lips.
If you were really here, in weight and
warmth and flesh, could I do these things?
Could I bear to touch you? Could I
convince my tongue to speak to you at all?

   A lot has happened since you left. Your
son has run away, and your wife's betrayed
you! Hear that. Read that. We did not wait
for you! Bobby sailed off to find you, and
I in my way did the same. Except that it
was not you I wanted to find, but me. Not

even—I wasn't trying at all, had given up
long ago.

I wrapped myself in you once, long ago,
wove you from what meager yarn I had.

Do you remember? A woman's arts, these
wrappings, no? To weave, to spin, to
nourish? To clothe and care for wounded,
helpless men? Isn't that how it's supposed
to go? There was so little material, so
little to work with, that I wove you too
tight, couldn't breathe for the
constriction. And when you left, Payne, I
do believe I would have been relieved had
I been the one to cast you off, to unfurl
you from my body. But it was you who did
it. You left me naked, and I was cold, so
I wove myself something to wear. That's
what girls do. We adapt. You marched
onward and I made do.

I wove a motherly housedress to wear for
Bobby, embroidered with chicks and ducks,
with big pockets for his bottles and toys,
Band-Aids for his boo-boos, wipes for
his silky bum. And out of silk I wove
a slinky, lacy little getup to keep the
other boys and girls guessing, to play
to their fantasies, to be their distant,
seductive mistress, and keep them all in

line. But mainly I wove myself a widow's shawl for you, Payne, for mourning you. I wore that one under all my other garments, and because I did, none of them fit. They lumped and bunched.

Bobby saw what clothes I really wore, the primal layer. He rejected my mothering, all mothering, almost from the start. All that cooing for naught. Billing and cooing, cold stares in return. Fair enough, I guess. We created a joyless child, Payne, to match my joyless life. Is that my fault, my failure? My great gift to the world: a robotic minimourner, deaf to laughter, blind to joy. Could I have maybe hidden my grief from him, donned a better mask for him, woven a more convincingly gleeful world? Would I have kept him then? Ask yourself as well—what could you have done? But then what would have become of him had you stayed? What variety of brat might he have been, well trained in wrestling, shooting, issuing commands, dismembering frogs and rodents? Perhaps sometimes even smiling.

My other costume was not such a failure. They were easily fooled. They want solely to be fooled. Teased and played with. Your

minions were never yours, you know. They
have always been mine, only ever obeyed
you to be nearer to me. You knew that,
didn't you? That's why you hated them. Not
out of jealousy, just because you knew
they weren't yours. Because you hate
everything that's not yours, and once it's
yours you hate it all the more for giving
in to you.

I hate them too, but they're just
children, more children than Bobby ever
was. Maybe that's not saying much. They're
loyal, jealous, fickle, cruel. Worse than
children. Simpler, crueler, less cunning.
They hate you, but they're no better. And
of course they love me, they live only for
the sight of me. But they don't know what
to do with it, this love of theirs, or
with me. I'm just another thing they want,
like booze or dope or food. If I give in
to one, even just a smile, the most
innocent caress, I have the rest of them
hanging foaming from my calves like dogs.
They'd tear me to pieces. That's their
love.

Maybe I'm too harsh. I do love them. All
of them. And I'm to blame, I'm sure. I
tease them. I give them just enough and no

more. Two words of kindness, then days of
silence, impenetrability. Let them suffer.
Let them work for it. Let them want me
more and more, because their desire feeds
me. Without it I would have starved long
ago, but it also sucks me dry. I'm their
want reflected, that's all. Everything they
are not, they push onto me. Even Felix,
darling Felix. There's nothing left for me.
They exhaust what I might be.

And then he came. I thought he was *you!*
He arrived the way I dreamed you would, a
wreck thrown up on the beach, needing me
to bring you back. I could have killed
myself I wanted so badly for him to be
you. God do I hate you. But something
snagged. I let myself want and something
snagged. Desire. Like a loose thread. I
played with it, rolled it back and forth
between my fingers, tugged at it a little
just to see what would happen. And when I
tugged I began to unravel everything, all
that I had so carefully woven. I felt the
breeze on my bare flesh for the first time
in I don't know how long. It startled me.
I stopped.

Then he went away. He left, just like you
left. He didn't go far, but he left. I

didn't understand. Maybe I do know why and just don't care to ask myself or still can't let myself care. Or maybe I was almost glad he left, maybe it was convenient. It doesn't matter.

Because then Bobby left. Our son. *My* son. He left me for you. Take him, Payne, he's yours. He never wanted me.

Of course it hurt, you know. More than you know. He tore from me that maternal gown, threw it at my feet, all those stupid duckies and rattles bouncing at my ankles, a reproach. Humiliation. That *little boy* did that! And standing there alone, hugging my rags around me, shivering, I noticed it again, that loose thread, hanging there. I went and found him, the other one, the one who wasn't you. I crawled into the hills and pulled that thread. With his help I unraveled it all the way. I shed all my clothes, my mourning shawl, all of it. I undressed myself. I had never been so naked. Every stain and every blemish, inside and out, I bared. No one had ever let me be so naked, had ever wanted me that way. He did. He bared himself as much for me.

Call it what you like. Use the L-word

even. Names don't suffice. For anything. Is
any feeling ever simple? Can any love exist
that doesn't contain already its own
betrayal? I want to give myself to him,
everything, and I want to shun him. I want
to punish him. I dress myself and run from
his bed. I stay away for days. I weave
myself another shawl. I tear it off and
run to him. In front of him I suture your
name with black thread into my breast. He
just watches. I know it tortures him; it's
meant to. But he won't fight back. He
washes away my blood with his tears. He
tries to kiss me clean. I try to let him.
We try, sometimes we just try, and
sometimes we succeed, and sometimes we
succeed too well. We touch each other
gently, because there is no skin between
us. It's too much to bear. I drug and
deaden myself. I hide beneath a gauze
of intoxication, but he joins me there
beneath it, he rips his way right through.
I convince myself that this nakedness too
is something I have woven, that there is
no undressing ever, no flesh but only
endless cloaks, layer upon layer, that
all I can do is sew and spin. For a while
I convince myself.

But I did something, I don't know how.
I let everything drop. In undressing myself
for him, in rushing back and forth, I
forgot what dress the others needed to see
me wear. I didn't even think of them, they
were so far from my mind. Like in a bad
dream, I went down to dinner naked. Again
and again I did it, and like in a dream,
I didn't notice I was naked until everyone
began to stare. Not really naked, of
course—I wore pants, shirt, socks,
whatever—but without guile. I had no more
strength for guile, and if I didn't notice
that anything was missing, they certainly
did. I didn't dole out the winks and
smiles, not even the stern words they
crave more than sweet ones. I ceded
control. They took it.

It happened after I don't know how many
weeks of my appearing before them like
that, déshabillé. (Are the accents in the
right places? Not that you'd notice.) They
waited 'til the meal was served and
cleared—some perverse Xavierian concoction,
dormice dipped in honey and sesame seeds,
better than it sounds—and they acted. The
wretches made Joseph speak for them, sweet,
bumbling Joseph. He needed Sally to hold

his hand throughout, and she needed Kate
to hold hers, and all the meantime that
awful Oliver stood behind them doing his
best to look serious and not show how
excited he was. Izzy stood beside him,
twitching with self-importance. But they
were all there. Theo and Lily, pillars
that they are, flinched each time Joseph
departed from his script. Nellie hung back
in the shadows, but it was all of them,
I know. No matter how crippled they seem,
they're still more than capable of
calculated malice. Robert's back went
straight with righteousness, all his
shivers ironed out. Even Felix didn't look
ashamed. Ruined, perhaps, but not ashamed.

I'm embarrassed to say they took me by
surprise. Joseph rambled on about a cloud
he saw, his fear of ice, the problem with
bananas. Then he gave me a garland of
flowers he grew himself. Ollie pinched him.
"Oh, yeah," he said. "You have to choose."
Ollie pinched him again. "Among us," he
added. "You have to choose among us."
Again the pinching. "You have a week," he
said. He blushed, grabbed Sally by the
wrist, and scurried out. She curtsied at
the door, and winked, the tart. The rest

of them grinned, puffed out their chests
like pigeons or flashed a little thigh,
and pranced on out as well. Hans, the
turd, saluted me.

What a fool I felt, Payne. How simply
stupid. I said nothing. Somehow I didn't
have the presence of mind to rise from
that ridiculous throne of yours and rage,
turn a good, bright royal purple and *shame*
them. To exclaim, *Choose? Among you?* and
laugh, with good vicious, shriveling
hilarity. That's all it would have taken.
They would have shrunk right down, arrayed
themselves again at my feet, wide-eyed and
waiting for scraps. The next day I could
have smiled selectively, rested my fingers
on an elbow here, a shoulder there, and
cemented their obedience once again. But
I just sat there, conscious only of my
nakedness, paralyzed, and yes, humiliated,
because I know you never would have let
yourself get caught unprepared like that.
Curse you and bless you, husband, you were
always ready.

Since then, the dinners have been
unbearable. They sit around that table like
dogs at a dog show, groomed and tidied and
miserably well behaved, shoving each other

oh-so-politely for a chance to pass me the
potatoes. And as much as I want to, I
cannot say a word. Can't raise my voice at
them, can't do a thing. It's not the drugs
and it's not the drink because there was a
time when I stayed sharp despite all that,
but now I sit there catatonic while they
frolic and fawn disgustingly.

I climb up to the motel and I can't even
speak to him, can't hear what he says, can
find no refuge even there. Is it guilt?
Fear? Of you? I hope I'm not so stupid. I
know I'm not afraid of them. What can they
do to me? Make me *choose?* It's not even
worth laughing at. It's him I worry for,
alone up there and god knows why he won't
come back, why he insists on staying by
himself in those dismal rooms, because
they could do something to him and they
would. I wouldn't put it past a single
one of them. And all of them together,
scheming, a ridiculous cabal. They're
foolish but they're dangerous too and he
doesn't know, can't seem to be made to
care. So I told him.

I told him a story to warn him, lying in
bed where he might listen, might really
listen, his hands in my hair, as naked as

I, I told him maybe this happened when I was a child, or maybe I dreamed it or read it somewhere so long ago I don't know the difference between what happened and what did not. But it was in a park, I know that. I was alone. There were trees everywhere, all in bloom, and great green fields to play in, hillsides to roll down, soft with moss. And at the center of the park was a pond. Lilies floated at one end. There were frogs and fish and turtles. Carp. The water was clear enough that you could see them swim. There were geese, ducks and grebes, a swan or two, a heron choking down a fish. And as I walked along the bank, I came across a duck. Its head was caught between two rocks. The duck's feathers were matted, more gray than white, and on its throat was a spot where the down had been worn off from rubbing against the rocks. I could see its chafed pink skin, and the feathers around the spot were red with blood. It was so fragile, that throat. I could barely stand to look at it.

This is the story I told him, and it's true, as stories go. This duck was thinner than the other ducks. Its little black

eyes seemed too big for its head. It was
too weak to fly, too weak even to push
itself up on the rocks and out of the
pond, but still it tried. In sad and
sudden bursts, its wings outstretched, it
struggled to propel itself up through the
rocks, pushing desperately but always
slipping back, succeeding only at scraping
more deeply at its wound. I went to get a
loaf of bread. I tore it in pieces and fed
it to the duck, to give it strength. With
each crumb it swallowed I could see life
coursing through its little body, and I
felt so proud—proud of it for wanting so
badly to live, for letting me help it, and
proud of myself for wanting to. For being
able to care, and be kind. But then the
other birds somehow sniffed out my
kindness. Like it was blood instead of
bread. They came flocking over, hundreds
of them, mobbing me. They pecked at my
feet and at my legs, desperate. I tried
to shove them and kick them away, to feed
just the one sick bird, the one that
needed to be fed, but the others were so
ravenous. Healthier and faster. They took
the bread before the sick one could get

anything. The more I tried to feed it, the
more they pecked at it. They pushed it
into deeper water and as I tried to feed
it still they bit at its face and neck.
Its feathers spread and floated off on
the surface of the pond. They piled on
its back and on its neck and pushed it
under water until it drowned. And when it
lay there floating, its neck limp, its
eyes dead, they came back to me to beg
for more.

I told him that story. He said he
understood. But what does that mean, that
he understood? Does he understand that
I can't lose him? Could I even admit to
that? And if he did understand, what would
he do? He's not like you, Payne. It's as
if something was taken from him, something
he can't find, can't remember what it was,
and all he can do is wait. He wanders
those shitty rooms and waits.

He won't do anything. He'll know they're
coming and let them come. He'll smile and
bare his throat if they ask him to. He'd
bare it if I asked, if anybody asked.
That's his revenge, and he doesn't even
know it's that.

Oh, Payne, don't ever come home, and
don't you dare forgive me.
    Your loving wife,
    Penny

*When the time came for Penny to write again, not to Payne
but to Miss—and it would come sooner than she would've
thought, sooner than even you might guess—she could not
then commit to ink and paper, could compose her missives
only silently, without the clatter of keys, without the scratch of
nib on paper, without moving her lips or even any help from
words, with only the cruel and silent syntax of regret, writ in
black strands afloat within her breast.*

16

Visits

or

The Missing

or

Things Come to a Head

WITH VARIOUS MOTIVES—curiosity, rage, affection, envy, sometimes just one of these demons, sometimes all at once and more frolicking within their busy breasts—like ants from an ant hole, one by one they stream and straggle forth out their doors beneath the mud-filthed walls and crumbling gun turrets, past the florid fires in the moat, on up the hill and down through the trash-strewn valley and up that other hill again to where the old neon motel sign fails to anymore blink, there where a single portly perpetrator is rumored to reside, room to room, one Miss gone missing, a Miss amiss. Take just a moment to appreciate the indolence of our assembled cast and realize the import of anything that might for them justify such expenditure of energy with no food, booze, drugs, or sex at the end of a full thirty-minute hike, nothing but a fat man in a nightgown.

Appreciate still more the depths of their almost saintly inertia—none makes it all the way to actually *see* Miss, though they try. With best intentions, some of them, others with intentions considerably less than best, but all with some variety of intention tucked away, they do try. Some fast, some slow, by varied and variegated paths, they make their way at least partway.

Robert is the first to go. Oh, he's foaming for it! In baggy black turtleneck and baggier black sweats, a turquoise pom-pommed balaclava concealing his face—for once Robert's hands do not shake. With one uncharacteristically stable mitt, he grips the black plastic handle of an eighteen-inch machete, fresh from the grindstone, so sharp that sparks fly unsolicited from its blade. At a quick colloquium at Oliver's last night, Robert's plan was unanimously granted approval of at least the tacit sort. Today he's eager to do the job, to avenge Payne, to divorce Miss's head from Miss's shoulders in one swift, heroic arc, to rid the land for once and all of this usurping parasitic freak. And so he marches, the palace wall and the shaky securities it offers shrinking behind him with each step.

As he walks, his brain trisects itself—one section enumerating his own determined footsteps, also counting trees, twigs, beer bottles, and birds, while another segment computes, calculates, and deciphers, unraveling the world's sleek mysteries one digit at a time, and a third third of

Robert readies him for this executionary act, rehearses the pulse of energy from his back leg up through his shoulder as he swings the blade on down. This final fraction imagines the spray of blood, a fateful *thwhisk*-ing sound, the spectacle of bone revealed, trachea still sucking at the air, the head hanging heavy from his fingers, gripped by a handle of hair. This third imagines the surprise in Miss's eyes as the machete whistles toward them, a surprise that continues to blink therein after the unexpected—but not, Robert would insist, uninvited—division of noodle from neck. And this third third, itself surprised, asks the other Robertian fragments to pause, to file their findings, to back up, recalculate, double-check—because what if he's wrong and 118 is just three dumb digits and doesn't mean *Paynekiller* and Miss is only Miss, an innocent fatty unburdened by blood?

Robert's feet slow down on him until he finds he's standing still. There's an old Toyota rotting here, and Robert sits on its russet engine block, lays the blade of the machete against his knee. Thus at rest, he allows the image of Miss's severed head to roll straight through the rounded folds of his own cerebrum, recalibrating as it turns each corner, here making delicate adjustments, fine-tuning the works, there smashing through passageways clogged with decades of detritus, and it occurs with sudden force to Robert, as it may already have occurred to the reader, that this arithmetic system of his, of which he has for so long been so peevishly proud, may in fact be groundless and entirely absurd. This thought has leaked into Robert before, and he has always managed to patch around it and push forth nonetheless. But until now his calculations had never bent his will towards grisly murder and Miss's head rolls onward through obscure encephalitic corridors, breaking up bottlenecks, tearing off duct-taped and jerry-rigged joints, preventing any such resuscitation of belief. A terrible shiver tears through Robert's body, beginning at the extremities and shaking its way inward until all Robert can do is grab at his gut. His face grows cold. He can't stand up. He lies curled up in the path, hugging his knees to still his tremors. His abandoned blade sparks silently beside him.

And Arthur, poor Arthur, doesn't make it far. For all his enthusiasm (call it desperation if you will, call it loneliness denser than the planet's core, call it self-revulsion just as deep, call it amiability, call it tender fellow feeling) to catch up with his old friend Miss, his old buddy whom he had, after all, so christened (and to whose murder by *machetazo* he too had mumbled his consent), Arthur barely makes it over the moat. Bending to reach for his plastic hip flask, he catches his foot on a crag of loose concrete. He awakes an hour later laid out flat on his back. Aching and confused, he elects to stay put until the sun rises, which that orb refuses to do for another six hours of frigid damp, following which Art staggers home to Zöe and pretends he never left. He does not have to try too hard, for Zöe never asks.

Sally also makes a brave attempt. She doesn't want to harm Miss or to be his friend, only to caution him that others will come if they haven't already. She wants to find a way to tell him that he is something less than popular, that his best interests, could they be discerned, are far from the minds of anyone around—save perhaps Penny's, but she can't be everywhere at once and lately, in fact, has been nowhere, not even at dinner, not even answering her locked door despite three hours' gentle knocking. Sally has always liked his eyes, and trusts Miss, and if she does not actively wish him well, neither does she wish him any evil, at least not in any immediate sense, so long as he consents to go away and not return. So, out of the goodness of her heart, she goes to warn him. But on the way, along the path on the slopes of the first hill, the one before the valley and the other hill, she comes across a most intriguing sight. A slug lies in the soil. It's eight inches long and yellow as a lemon, and it's slowly masticating a leaf. It's not even a whole leaf, really, just a fragment of a leaf, and to watch its slooowwww devouring is to enter another world, in which blood runs thick as syrup and we all live a billion years. Sally crouches, elbows on her knees, and by the time the slug swallows the last shred of green, her shadow has lengthened by a yard, and all thought of warning Miss has long since vanished from her head.

Others set out from their well-appointed hovels for the motel with more nebulous ambitions, hoping to encounter or at least observe its sole inhabitant. Carl and Xavier make it halfway there before they remember they've left geese roasting in the oven and there's no one in the kitchen to baste and turn the birds. Nellie walks until the motel sign is in sight, but she is overcome suddenly by uncertainty, doubting not only her intentions and the wisdom of this trip but the very possibility of return. Though she doubts in equal part the desirability of going home, still she runs. Izzy heads out independently and is almost through the valley before he realizes, if you'll believe it, that he has nothing at all to say. This is a first, and he's so startled that he races all the way home in a frantic attempt to flee himself, to jettison himself from the sticky inner silences above which he is usually able to keep himself aloft. Lily actually laces and ties her boots and makes it past the palace walls, out of sight even, around the bend, farther than she's been in years, but she tires fast and decides it's hardly worth the effort. Hans wants to go, to bring this pacific chapter to a prematurely gory close. Able-bodied, for the moment sober, filled with motivating vitriol, he is fully capable of carrying out his plan, but he can't get out of bed because Sally's tied him to the bedposts and forgotten all about him. Oliver finds himself in the same frustrating situation, except it's Hans who bound his wrists. They try, you see. They try.

The walk is nothing for Felix, intrepid wanderer that he is, even on a dark night, without even the light of the moon to guide him. He knows every rock and twig, every rusted nail and shard of glass for miles, and can skip with steps sure as a goat's to the motel. Tonight instead he slumps.

Here, alas, he can scavenge only pain. As he plods across the parking lot, the sky is just beginning to turn color in the east, and Felix lifts his palm to shield his eyes from even that meager early light. He passes in front of each closed door, but afraid of what he might find—what if Penny's there?—he is too afraid to turn the knobs. Miss, sitting outside just yards away, takes Felix's footsteps for those of a raccoon.

As for Felix, it doesn't occur to him to look out by the pool, and he slouches around behind the building, climbs the hill back there to get, he thinks, a little perspective. For Felix always likes a vista, a high point from which to gaze, or better yet, from which to shut his eyes (hence his fondness for the pipe). He sits at the flat peak of the hill, where Miss has sat almost every day but this one. At this very spot, on recent dawns, Miss has been puzzled and saddened and sometimes amused by visions of Arthur passed out on a couch alone, of an inflatable goose exploding in a swimming pool, of Robert sharpening a machete on a stone, of Theo and Lily making love, little Theo climbing her like a mountain, gripping handholds of flesh where he can, of Sally waking, hungover, and shrugging off Katherine's caresses, of the lot of them gathered in Ollie's hut, snorting drugs and rolling dice, of seabirds sucked beneath the waves, even visions of this selfsame Felix pacing on the beach, muttering, tossing bottle caps into the waves.

But this grand trick of the light is one trick that Felix doesn't know, and instead of gazing eastward at the sun as

Miss does, and at the gallery of sights behind the sun, he stares down at the motel roof below him and torments himself with images of his own conjuring. He sees Penny curled in the arms of the stranger. He lets rage bubble forth behind his eyes, lets it fall black and viscous as petroleum until he cannot even see the motel beneath him, or the stranger in question pacing by the pool, or the dirt and the rocks and all the piled rubbish, only the outlines and shadows of his own hurt. Blinded thus, he doesn't see the sun rise behind him. He doesn't see, as he scampers off in search of smoke and solace, what you would see if you were there and stayed, what Miss would see if he had bothered to climb the hill this morning— Felix does not see, there behind the sun, a man washed up on the beach, an old familiar figure, much transformed. With some combination of trepidation, zeal, and relief, this most recent castaway arrival lifts himself on his knees, shakes sand and strands of seaweed from his scarred and muscled body, plucks oysters from his armpits, sea slugs from his hair, periwinkles from his nostrils and from the folds behind his ears.

Rather than concern ourselves overmuch with such intangibles, with dawns unwitnessed and anthropomorphic flotsam unobserved, let us turn our attention to the plump personage who has been the cause of such concern. Miss is engaged in what have become his customary activities: fretting, waiting, waiting, fretting, and waiting more. It was a hyperintensity of fretting this morning that prevented him from climbing the hill behind the motel as he customarily does. For days have passed since he last saw Penny. Months perhaps. How long has it been since she last came? How long between that time and the first time? Maybe two months? Ten years? Time is not the issue. Days, surely, of waiting. Days of bitter longing. Enough that passion might rise and rise. Not so many that it could transmute, ossify into routine despair, the penumbral comforts of surrender. Days pass. Kingdoms rise and fall. The earth collides with the sun, is born again, the same. How long has it been?

It doesn't matter. Miss still waits. At dawn he rises from his chair and, to the unheard rhythm of Felix's retreating footfalls just yards away, he finds himself a room and in it finds the bed. He pulls a pillow over his head to block what light the curtains don't. Hours pass, and when enough have passed wakefulness at last releases Miss, handing him over to cruel, capricious sleep. Miss dreams only of Penny and Payne. He dreams an eagle perches on Penny's wrist, and he recognizes the bird as Payne. Its talons draw blood from the flesh of her arm. Miss is a sparrow circling her head, and at Penny's command the eagle tears him from the sky. He dreams Payne is the daylight, and Penny's flesh grows paler, brighter, until she's nothing but light herself, and when Miss leans in to kiss her, all he feels is his own warm breath.

He isn't sure if he's awake or sleeping still when the pillow is yanked from his grasp. He squints open his eyes, peeks out at this bright new dream world. Above him stands a man, not a bird and not the dawn, but a man of flesh like him. And not like him. He's holding the pillow tight in both fists, this man, and staring down at him. His clothes are torn, his hair is white with salt. He searches Miss's face, but finds there nothing that he knows. He drops the pillow on the floor, and speaks.

"Have you heard of a man," this new man says at last, "named Payne?"

Miss nods.

"Where is he?"

Miss doesn't know. He shakes his head.

"And his wife?" asks the man, his voice curling on itself. "Where is she?"

Miss wishes he could say, but can't. He wishes for a lot of things. He shakes his head again.

"And you?" the man asks. "Who the fuck are you?"

Miss wants to laugh. He tries to, but his face won't obey. Instead he shrugs.

"Are you dumb? Can you even talk?"

Miss is tired of this dream. He covers his eyes with his forearm and rolls over on his side. He hears the man spit in disgust. He hears him stride away, and the sound of his footfalls hardens as he walks from the carpeted room out to the concrete landing. Miss pulls the sheet over his head.

Again the next day Penny does not come. The sun rises again and sets. The stars come out. Again. The moon. The wind babbles through the valleys. A dog complains somewhere far away. Stars fall from the sky. Miss waits by the pool for Penny. He hears her whisper in every windblown leaf, but again she does not come.

He stands naked before the mirror once more. He hasn't been eating out here, and his stomach has shrunk. His face hangs from his bones. His body disgusts him, hair and scar, baggy flesh and useless bone. He brings it outside, still undressed, and exposes the whole package to the air, the heat, the sun. None of them comment. He cuts the soles of his feet on the rocks, tracks blood up the cement stairs, finds another room.

Night falls and Miss arises. He waits out by the pool, but still she does not come. Mosquitoes come to bite Miss and bats come to swallow the mosquitoes and somewhere far away a dog complains, but Penny does not come. He hears her whisper in every windblown leaf, but again she does not come. Before dawn he makes his way around the back of the motel to climb the hill, to see what he can see. The sun, damn the sun, at last it rises, purple and gold, and thus arrayed in royal hues, he sees a royal sight.

From beneath eyelids heavy with unrest, Miss sees two figures standing in the palace bedroom. The so-called master bedroom. He had only been there once, long ago, when Penny cut his hair. Her hands lingered on his face. Now those hands are balled into fists and she beats them against the chest of the man before her. His clothes are torn. His hair is white with salt. Miss can see her yell at him, punch him again and again. The man does not flinch. He absorbs the blows. Miss can see the strength drain from Penny's legs, can almost see it leak out of her and puddle on the floor as she sinks to her knees before this man. She rests her head against his thighs. She hugs Payne's knees.

The sun climbs higher, and Miss's vision washes out with the light. He stands alone on the crest of the hill, the dull world arrayed beneath, emptied of all expectation. Plastic bags dance around him in the wind.

He sleeps. Maybe sleep is not the word. It doesn't feel like sleep—more like a sudden and unthinkable wound. But there is a dream, a single dream, and dreams are sleep's affliction, so call it what you will. Miss dreams of piles of pebbles, growing taller stone by stone. At times he opens his eyes, observes the creases in the bedsheets, his sallow skin, dusty light on dusty papered walls, but even then he hears the clatter of rock against rock, and he hears it still when his eyes are closed again, and the stones rise up before him.

At last Miss shakes himself awake. Only after an uneasy moment of rubbing his eyes, sitting on the edge of the bed, does he remember what he's seen. Payne returned. Penny on her knees before him. Miss feels a huge trap open up inside him and everything he might ever want to keep falls through it.

Somehow Miss finds the strength to stand. He wanders from room to room, but there's no escaping. By now he's stayed in all of them. Nothing is new anymore, not a centimeter is unburdened. His eyes fall on a cigarette burn in a bedspread, white polyester filling charred at the rim and bulging out, and he remembers her back unfolding when she stood to dress, the curled ridge of her spine. A chip of paint, a torn lampshade make him remember lying here beside her, her halting breath, tracing jigsaw patterns in the sweat on her thigh. He remembers kissing her fingers, the shock of his own face reflected in yellow miniature in her wedding band. He remembers that she asked him, "Why do you stay here?" and rolled over away from him before he could answer. In another room he remembers another time, weeks later or maybe months, not long ago, when she pulled him to her and whispered, "Don't blame me, please," and asked him to forgive her. Not knowing how she'd sinned, Miss agreed. "Anything," he said.

Outside, rain is falling, and on the hill the dirt falls beneath his feet. His dress sticks heavy to his thighs, its white fabric rendered translucent by the rain, stained red and brown by the earth. He sits at the top of the hill until the sky finally lightens, but the clouds hide the sun and there is nothing to see but that pink obscurity, broken trees, and mud.

Was it just the inclemency of the weather, or have Miss's oracular powers abandoned him? Surely he is abandoned, but still we can ask: Had the barometer read higher, the humidity been lower, the moon more full, had a volcano not erupted on the other side of the globe and a comet not somewhere pierced the upper atmosphere, had a faraway war not kicked up so much smoke and sand and fire and a whale not blown brine into the sky, had Payne not returned and Penny not accepted his return—might then Miss have seen more than just cloud? Might he have seen Penny's suitors preparing themselves for supper, drinking and snorting, wanking and weeping and preening themselves? Might he have seen the carnage already abloom behind Payne's eyes, or the desolation already wrought in Penny's? Might he have guessed at his fate, or had the mystic wherewithal to choose it, and if he had done so, might we then also know it?

I can only tell you that he leaves. He slides down that muddy hill, shuffles past the old motel and all its open doors without looking once to the right or to the left or up or down and especially not back. Does it come as a surprise, this quick descent? This precipice from which we're together falling? Were you insufficiently warned? I'll say it again: this is not a love story. Miss lumbers hurried through the sticking muck. Rainwater gleams red in the ditches like so many mirrored shards, reflecting nothing but the dirty sky above. Worms worm up from beneath the sodden earth. A crow alights on a rock with a laugh. Miss leaves. He puts feet straight to path, but which way does he turn? Does he exit stage right or stage left? Does he head down the hill and through the valley and down the other hill, over the stinking moat and through the pitted walls? Does he seek out abjection, and return to the palace to claim it? Is he there with the others, waiting to be fed, when Payne arrives in place of Penny? Does he join in their final banquet? Or does he head the other way, away, alone, unknown?

Look for yourself. I can't bear to follow.

17

One Loose Thread

LET ME PLEASE REDEEM MY COWARDICE. Let me try. Come, follow me and look. The sea is rough, the sky not very bright. Mottled by haze, the sun shines dumbly forth. The sand is black, the rocks huge and sharp and broken. Waves scrape each against the last. They bicker. They scratch and spit and shove. The sea is not fond of the shore. See how it rages and foams, booms and roars in sharp protest. Look how it flees the land. If you were the sea, would you not do the same—chafe and claw at these demeaning limitations, fight to escape, take flight from escape, boom and roar in sharp frustration?

Look how it struggles—wave upon wave upon wave, always tiring but never exhausted. The stars inflict their orbits on the sky, the sun dozes through its drab commute, and still the waves keep shrieking their dissent. Will no wave be the last? Will there be no final silence? Not final, even, let's ask for less, for just a moment's respite from this ceaseless hollow rumble, a place to lay our heads, some brief home, something like what love promises, and sleep promises, and death insists upon, a moment's pause from this monstrous screaming back and forth.

We can ask, and ask again, but the ocean's answer does not change. No, it says, there is no end and no respite, no home, no sleep, no love. There is not even any shore to wash up on. Ask Bobby, lying there, washed up on the shore.

This by now familiar image. A man washed up on the shore. Cast out by the sea. But this time it's a boy. This shriveled child, dried too long in the sun, his skin darkened, cheeks hollow, hair a mess of rags. And this time the sea is calm. The waves still come, but they beat soft against the sand. Sometimes the sea is calm. Bobby lifts himself to his knees. In his ears the ocean still roars, not calm at all, a slap and a rebuke. He picks an anemone from his groin, a parody of the hair he won't have yet for years. He shakes periwinkles from between his toes. There are mussels on his muscles and barnacles on those. A band of kelp blindfolds his brow, and when he peels it off, he can see again. He sees the sea, the sky, the line between them, more blur than line. The heavy sun stares down at him. Bobby coughs out a single sand crab that was grabbing at his tongue. He snorts out a couple of minnows, and his nostrils bloom with the seafunk smell of life.

Bobby's hungry and he's thirsty and the sea roars in his head. This sea that's cast him out. Small shriveled child. Dangling thread. He stands. He stares hard at the sun.

Pull this one loose thread.

Pull hard, and pull again.

Acknowledgments

Thank you:

To my agent, Gloria Loomis, for taking a chance and sticking with me, for taking care and looking out, for being tough and smart and generally terrific; to my editor, Megan Hustad, for caring so much and working so hard, for being so impossibly, infernally smart, and for being a friend; to everyone at the Djerassi Resident Artists Program and the Headlands Center for the Arts for the peace of mind without which this book would have taken five extra years to write; to all of my earliest readers of my earliest drafts—Diane Aranda, Heather Blurton, Jacob Forman, Adam Goldman, Joe Loya, Alanna Marks, Anton Piatigorsky, Ava Roth, Brian Siberell, and especially Jon Robin Baitz—for the encouragement (and criticism) that kept me going; to my brother, Alexander F. M. Ehrenreich, for believing in me so completely that I had no choice but to believe a little bit myself; and to Laurialan Reitzammer, for more than I can say.

DATE DUE
